NIGHT SECRETS

NIGHT SECRETS

Thomas H. Cook

G. P. Putnam's Sons   New York

G. P. Putnam's Sons
Publishers Since 1838
200 Madison Avenue
New York, NY 10016

Library of Congress Cataloging-in-Publication Data

Cook, Thomas H.
    Night secrets / Thomas H. Cook.
    p. cm.
    I. Title.
PS3553.055465N54   1990   89-24268 CIP
813'.54—dc20
ISBN   0-399-13527-8

Printed in the United States of America

1 2 3 4 5 6 7 8 9 10

This book has been printed on acid-free paper.
                    ∞

For Neil Nyren

"Long is the night to him who is awake."
—**DHAMMAPALA,** *The Commentaries*

1

Frank stared at the photograph the man had just handed him. The woman was posed against a high stone wall, and just over it, Frank could make out the gray-white tumble of a windswept sea.

"I took it at our house on Cape Cod," the man said. He smiled quietly. "We've always had such good times up there. We'd just gotten back from sailing when I took that picture."

Frank nodded silently, his eyes still on the photograph. Just behind it, he could see the camera he'd used on his last job, its parts spilled out over the desk. He would have to get another one when he took another case. "How old's the picture?" he asked.

"Just a few weeks. It's the most recent photograph I have."

Frank fingered the edges of the photograph. "I'll need to keep it," he said.

The man nodded. "Yes, I know."

Frank glanced back down at the picture, noted the way the woman's eyes looked somewhat distant, as if, at the moment the picture had been taken, she'd been thinking of another world. It was the sort of look he'd seen in other women: It always meant there was about to be a change.

"You won't have any trouble recognizing her from that picture," the man assured him. His eyes darted toward the photograph, then shot back up to Frank. "She's a very beautiful woman, don't you think?"

Frank concentrated on the face, the long blond hair, the light-blue eyes. It was a beautiful face, but not the kind that looked unreal, unlived-in. The blushing innocence was gone, and the eyes looked as if they'd seen a few things along the way.

"What you have to understand," the man went on, "is how very concerned I am about her. That's why I would like for you to get on it right away."

The man's name was Phillips, and he'd come into Frank's office only a few minutes earlier. He looked to be in his late forties, but well preserved, with sleek grayish hair and just enough lines around his eyes to give him an air of indisputable dignity. He was dressed with the typical Wall Street reserve, even down to the acceptable flair of paisley suspenders, but when he talked about the woman, his manner seemed less secure. His hands fidgeted, and there was a line of perspiration just above his upper lip.

"Her name is Virginia," he said, almost wistfully, as if something about her had already been lost. "She's from the South, actually, like you. I mean, I assume that . . . from the accent."

Frank nodded slowly as his eyes drifted over to the window. In his mind, he saw granite canyons, winding creeks and lonely strands of pine, the raw South of his raw youth. Then the South dissolved like powder in a dense gray liquid, leaving only the cement stairs that led up to Forty-ninth Street.

"The thing is, I think she's going through some sort of personal crisis," Phillips said emphatically. Then he shrugged. "It happened to my first wife," he added reluctantly.

"What happened to your first wife?"

"She had a nervous breakdown," Phillips said. "It came on slowly, then it just got worse. She ended up in a sanitarium. I don't want that to happen to Virginia."

"How long have you been married, Mr. Phillips?" Frank asked.

"Nearly a year."

Frank noted the silvery hair that lay perfectly in place on Phillips's head and compared it to the shimmering blond of his wife's. "How old is your wife?"

"Twenty-four."

"Where did you meet?" he asked.

"At a party," Phillips said. He looked at Frank sheepishly. "I never expected to marry again, not after what I went through with Clarissa. And, of course, Virginia's young enough to be my daughter."

Frank thought of his own daughter, Sarah. She seemed to be dissolving slowly, like his pictures of the South. He never saw her face anymore. Only what the animals had done to her hands after she'd walked into the woods, stretched out by the river and taken a handful of pills she'd brought with her from his house.

"I'm sure that Clarissa . . . her condition," Phillips went on, "I'm sure that's why I'm so worried about Virginia."

Frank drew his eyes over to him. "When did you get worried about her?"

Phillips looked slightly unnerved. "Well, there are really two things. The first is just the way she seems, distant, preoccupied. That's the way it's been the last few months. As if all the time she's with me, she's really someplace else entirely. She won't talk about it. I'll ask her if there's something wrong, and she'll say no, she's fine. But it's like she's a million miles away."

"Has anyone else noticed that? Her friends?"

"She doesn't really have any friends," Phillips said. "She'd just come to New York when I met her, and I'm not much of a social person."

"How about relatives?"

"There are no relatives," Phillips said. "Virginia was an only child, and her parents were killed in a car accident only a year or so before she came to the city." He smiled softly. "I think that's part of what made her so attractive to me. That she was all alone, vulnerable. That she needed to be protected. That's how she seemed when we met."

Frank took a deep breath and pulled out one of his little green notebooks. "And you said that this was about a year ago?"

Phillips nodded. "Just over a year."

Frank wrote it down, giving in reluctantly to the idea that he would take the case. It didn't sound that exciting, but he did need the job.

"As I said," Phillips added, "we've been married for almost a year now."

Frank sat back slightly. "You said there were two things. What's the second one?"

Phillips glanced away, his face somewhat stricken. "I've noticed that a few things are missing. Things that she should have cared about."

Frank leaned into the pencil, pressing its lead point against the plain white paper. "What things?"

Phillips returned his eyes to Frank. "Jewelry. Brooches and pendants. Pieces that I've given her over the last year or so."

"How much are they worth?" Frank asked.

"Several thousand dollars, I'd say," Phillips answered. "I haven't really kept track of what's disappeared."

"When did you first notice it?"

"Probably last October was the first time."

"Tell me about it."

Phillips ticked off the vanishing items one by one, and as Frank listened, his eyes wandered back toward the window. The old woman who slept at the bottom of the steps had left an empty bottle of Wild Rose behind. Its metal cap rested beside it, faintly blue in the half-light of late afternoon. A few feet away, a crumpled potato-chip bag fluttered briefly, then came to rest. Barbecue-flavored, the old woman's favorite.

"So, it comes to almost a dozen pieces," Phillips concluded. Then he leaned back in his chair, and the sound of its squeaking hinges drew Frank's attention back to him.

"Worth several thousand dollars," Frank said. "And you have no idea what she's done with them?"

Phillips shook his head.

"Do you have a safe in the house?"

"Yes," Phillips said. "That's the first place I looked. But none of it was there."

"How about a safety deposit box? Does she have access to one of those?"

"She has access to several," Phillips told him. "I checked them all." He shook his head. "But it's not the jewelry," he said worriedly. "It's Virginia, the way she seems to have gone offtrack."

Frank glanced at the picture again, this time noting the intensity in her light-blue eyes, the way her lips formed a thin, red line across her mouth, the radiance of her hair in the light. Then there was the way one gloved hand squeezed determinedly at the other. She didn't look like the sort of person who went offtrack very easily.

"What about drugs?" Frank asked. "Could she be feeding a habit?"

Phillips looked offended. "Absolutely not."

"Gambling," Frank suggested. "People can get squeezed."

Phillips shook his head.

Frank let the most ominous possibility drop last. "When people have suddenly come into money, there's always the chance of blackmail."

Phillips looked astonished. "Blackmail? For what?"

"Well, that would be the whole point," Frank said. "That you would never find out."

Phillips shook his head determinedly. "That would be absurd."

"Maybe not," Frank said. "Did you ever have a background search done on her?"

"No," Phillips blurted. "And I don't want you to do one, either. I'm not hiring you to dig into my wife's past. I want to know what's happening to her now."

"Well, they're often related. It has to be something," Frank said bluntly. "And you're ruling the most likely things out."

Phillips started to speak, then hesitated.

Frank looked at him sternly. "I need to know what you're thinking."

"Well, my worst thought is that she wants to . . . run away or something," Phillips told him.

"Do you know of any reason she might want to do that?"

"No."

"Before you," Frank asked cautiously, "was there someone else?"

"No one she's ever mentioned."

"And as far as you and her, it's . . ."

"A happy marriage," Phillips said firmly.

Frank looked at him doubtfully. Sheila, his ex-wife, had always claimed that happy marriages existed, and he still thought that it was possible. It was just that he'd never seen one. "I have to ask these questions," he said.

"I know," Phillips said. "I don't mean to take offense, but it's just that I know things are fine—*were* fine—between us, and that's why I think that she just wants to get some point across, and, perhaps because she's young, she doesn't know how to do it."

"What point?"

"That she's unhappy," Phillips said, "that she wants to leave New York."

"Where does she want to go?"

"Back to the South," Phillips said. "She's mentioned that several times, about moving away from New York. But I can't do that. All my work is here." His voice tightened. He fought to control himself. "And then, there are times when I think she might just want to get away from life in general." He looked at Frank intently. "People get like that, too, don't they?"

Frank nodded. "Yeah, they do." Instantly, he did an inventory of all the things he'd gotten tired of during the last few years. He remembered the times he'd wanted to get away from Karen, from remembering her sister's murder in Atlanta, from the whole story of how he'd finally fallen in love with her while he'd worked on the case, then followed her to New York and fallen out of love as quickly and decisively as he'd fallen into it in the first place. After that, it was only a matter of time before he'd moved out of her Park Avenue apartment, and into the dank little office where Phillips sat now, eerily backlit by the grayish light which shone through its single dusty window, and where the inventory now abruptly ended.

Phillips's face suddenly grew hard and tense. "I need a solution," he said emphatically. "I need to find out what's happening to my wife." His eyes glistened slightly. "If she wants something, I'll try to provide it. But first I have to know what it is she wants."

"Why not ask her directly?"

Phillips shook his head. "I'm afraid . . . that it might precipitate a crisis. Push her over the edge, into whatever she's thinking of doing. I—I just don't want to confront her yet."

Frank glanced down at the small stack of mail which rested on his desk. "What do you want me to do, exactly?" he asked.

"Find out what she's up to," Phillips said. "But, of course, discreetly."

"Nothing else?"

"I wouldn't want you to confront her yourself, if that's what you mean," Phillips said. "Just find out what you can, and let me know. I can handle the rest."

Frank looked back up at him. "It's two hundred dollars a day, plus expenses. Five hundred in advance."

Phillips watched him expressionlessly. "Money is not a problem," he said. He immediately took a wallet from his jacket pocket and placed ten crisp hundred-dollar bills on Frank's desk. "I'd like to up the advance a little, if you don't mind. It's just to encourage you. And I'd also like to make it nonrefundable."

Frank didn't reach for the money. Instead, he pressed the tip of the pen down on the paper. "What's her address?"

"Thirty-two East Sixty-fourth Street."

"Is she there most of the time?"

"As far as I know. I'm at my office a great deal. I travel."

"What about a job?"

"She has a few charity connections, that's all," Phillips said. "It's social clubbing, nothing more. The committee to do this, the women's auxiliary to do that. You know the kind of thing I mean."

"So, she doesn't work?" Frank asked, a little impatiently.

"Not at an actual job, no."

"How does she spend her day?"

"I really don't know," Phillips admitted. "As I said, I'm very busy. I'm not home all that much."

Frank drew in a deep breath, wondering at this man who knew so little about his wife of one year. "I'll need a few numbers," he said.

Phillips didn't seem to understand. "Numbers?"

"Bank account numbers," Frank explained. "Commercial and telephone credit card numbers. Things like that."

Phillips looked at him suspiciously. "Why would you need all that?"

"To find out if there's anything suspicious going on with her private accounts," Frank explained. "Money going in or out in strange amounts."

"And the phone credit card?"

"It wouldn't hurt to know who she's been talking to."

"You really need all that?"

"If you want it done right."

"Very well," Phillips said reluctantly. "I have everything here."

He drew his wallet from his jacket pocket and ticked them off methodically.

Frank recorded them in his notebook, then shoved it back into his pocket. "Okay, I guess I have enough to work with for now," he said. Then he stood up and offered Phillips his hand. "I'll be in touch."

Phillips looked slightly offended, as if he'd been peremptorily dismissed. "So you'll be able to get to work right away then?" he asked as he got slowly to his feet.

"Yeah," Frank said. He offered a quick, reassuring nod. "I'll report to you as soon as I find something."

Phillips looked at him pointedly. "Just keep in mind that time is very important in this situation," he said. "For Virginia, I mean."

Frank smiled quietly. "It may not be that serious," he said, trying to ease him slightly. "It usually isn't."

"No, it is very serious," Phillips said emphatically. "Virginia would not be stealing from me if it weren't very serious."

"If she's stealing at all," Frank reminded him, "she's stealing from herself."

"It's the same thing when you're married," Phillips told him, his face almost brutally severe. "That's why I really believe something very serious is wrong. It could be a matter of life and death, Mr. Clemons."

Frank smiled again, though his eyes didn't. *Isn't everything,* he thought.

Once Phillips had gone, Frank returned to his desk, pocketed the money, then began going through the afternoon mail. He could tell that one of the letters was from Sheila, his ex-wife. The rose-colored paper alerted him. She wrote him only once or twice a year now, always when she was thinking about their daughter's suicide, picking at the wound. Still, a letter was better than the melancholy phone calls, the low moan of her voice as she went through it all again, how good Sarah was, how kind, smart, full of possibility. She never failed to recite the entire litany, all the "hows" but one: how lost.

He slid the letter from under the rest, swept it over the edge of his desk, into the open drawer, then went on to the next one, hoping that it might be something interesting, perhaps something that would move him onto a different path because it had that "something extra" which most cases didn't. But it was only a thank-you note from a client, along with a check for six hundred dollars, full payment for the time he'd spent trailing a retired security guard whom an armored car firm had come to suspect of plotting an inside job. He read the note quickly, then threw it in the garbage. The check went into his jacket pocket.

The rest were bills, except for a single letter in a light-blue envelope. He was beginning to open it when he glanced up and saw Farouk's enormous legs move ponderously down the cement stairs, then heard him lumber along the littered corridor and open the office door.

"Hello, my friend," Farouk said.

Frank nodded.

"Forgive me for the intrusion," Farouk added as he walked to the chair opposite Frank's desk and eased himself down into it. He glanced at the letter. "You are in the middle of something?"

"Nothing important," Frank told him, the last letter still unopened in his hand. "Why, you feeling lonesome?"

"No," Farouk said lightly. "I am my own companion." There was no pride in the way he said it, only the brief acknowledgment that such was the way things had turned out for him.

"Well, I noticed that Toby wasn't at the bar last night," Frank said.

Farouk scratched the side of his face absently. "And because of that, I am supposed to be lost?"

"No," Frank said. "It's just that I didn't see her, that's all."

Farouk's face screwed up slightly. "That is because she is gathered with the saints."

"With the what?"

"Back in her village," Farouk said. "In Colombia. It is her village that has the Jesus Tortilla."

Frank looked at him quizzically.

Farouk smiled, but with a strange, aching darkness. "Some years in the past, an old woman was frying tortillas," he explained. "She turned one over, and there it was, a miracle." His eyes widened in mock amazement. "The face of Jesus." The smile disappeared. His eyes closed worshipfully. "The face of Jesus," he repeated.

"On the tortilla?"

"As if burned onto it by the hand of God," Farouk said reverently, his large hand over his heart, still feigning astonishment. "It has since then become a shrine for the local people. Once every five years or so—when the urge comes upon her—Toby returns to it." He drew in a deep breath. "But she comes back as she was before," he added wearily. "Only the tortilla was transformed." He stood up and stretched, groaning slightly as his arms hung motionless in the dimly lighted air.

Frank smiled, but said nothing.

Farouk's arms sank down again, held rigidly, as if bolted to his sides. Dust swirled around him like tiny flakes of dirty snow. "The rites of spring," he said, as if to himself, "they are not so kind to a man my age."

"They're not that great for anybody," Frank told him dryly. He returned his attention to the letter, opening it hurriedly as if it might actually contain something important.

When he'd finished reading, he passed it over to Farouk. "It's from Imalia Covallo," he said. "Trying to explain herself."

Farouk's eyes narrowed menacingly. "Covallo," he whispered as he reached for the letter. "Some things cannot be explained."

She'd once been a leading fashion designer, but in a long, winding investigation, Frank had uncovered a lost history, which, in the end, had resulted first in one murder, then another. For this, she was now in prison.

It was during the ordeal of this investigation that Farouk had come into Frank's life, an immense, nearly motionless figure in an after-hours bar, one who earned his living simply by "lending assistance in difficult matters," as he himself had put it at their first meeting. After that they'd moved forward together, as if sewn to each other by a weird, invisible thread, the two of them mismatched in size, Farouk so large against Frank's lean and hunted look; by color, Farouk's desert brown, Frank's Appalachian white; and even by the most basic habits of mind, Farouk cautious and meticulous, Frank hurled forward by a sudden passionate surge.

In the end, it was a union that had saved Frank's life, and as he watched Farouk reach for his glasses, he remembered the flash of the pistol that had suddenly materialized in Farouk's enormous hand, saw Riviera tumble forward, then Farouk again, standing massively behind him, his eyes as calm as his voice when he finally spoke: *Come now, my friend. It is not time to die.*

Farouk finished the letter, folded it again, then handed it back to Frank. "Do as you wish," he said. "But I do not forgive." Then he smiled brightly as he slapped his great thighs with his hands. "Perhaps we should take in the evening air," he said.

Frank shook his head. "I don't know," he said reluctantly.

Farouk smiled. "Are you waiting for a better offer?"

"No."

"Then take what is handed to you," Farouk said as he got to his feet. He walked to the door and waved Frank through it. "Come."

Within a few minutes they were in Hell's Kitchen Park, enjoying the unusually warm breeze that filtered through the empty swings and seesaws. Frank sat on one of the cement benches, his eyes concentrating on two men who leaned against the black metal bars at the other end of the playground.

Farouk sat beside him, watching them too. He craned his neck, then scratched beneath his chin. "It is the pettiness that kills you," he said, as if it had just occurred to him. "One should not be eaten in small bites."

"Good cases are hard to find," Frank said. He thought of Phillips, the blond woman in the photograph. "The dull ones pay the bills."

"And a man has to eat, yes?"

"That's right," Frank said. He could tell that something had suddenly gone bad between the two men. They faced each other edgily, their voices growing louder and more strained. In an instant, faster than anyone could imagine, it might all be over, with one body sprawled across the cement, another hanging limply from the fence.

He looked away, toward the only other people in the park. It was a family of four. The man and woman bounced up and down on the seesaw, one small child cradled in each lap. The woman said something, and all of them laughed. Watching them, Frank wondered what contentment felt like, whether it was real, or just a dream you hadn't questioned yet.

"Do you know the tarot?" Farouk asked, in a question that seemed to come from nowhere.

Frank shook his head.

"It is an ancient way of learning the future," Farouk explained. "Like palm reading. Only with cards." He glanced over at the two men, who were still arguing loudly beside the fence. "One of them should do a reading, to see if he has stepped too near the snake."

Frank nodded as he watched. One of the men moved up close to the other, pushed him hard with the flat of his hand, then rotated on his heels and slowly began to walk away, his back turned arrogantly to the other man.

"To insult and then turn your back," Farouk said. "One should never be that sure of the weakness of another man."

Frank dragged his eyes away from them, let them settle on the gray metal steps of the slide. He started to think of his daughter, as he always did in playgrounds. He blinked quickly, batting her away, then stood up, suddenly tense, agitated.

"Where are you going?" Farouk asked.

"I don't know," Frank said. "Just moving."

Farouk groaned as he rose beside him. "Then I will go as well."

They headed back down the avenue. The traffic was moving rapidly alongside them, cars, trucks, Chinese delivery boys on rusting bicycles, and as he walked along, watching it speed by, Frank felt his own unease like thousands of tiny arrows whizzing down the blue corridors of his veins. He didn't know where it came from, or where it would lead, but only that it was the most authentic part of his character, the part he couldn't direct, anticipate or control.

"Look, there, my friend," Farouk said after a moment. He pointed to a small storefront on the east side of Tenth Avenue. A plain neon sign hung between a dark blue curtain and the unwashed glass: FORTUNES READ.

Frank stared at the sign. "It's been there for a few weeks."

"Yes, I know," Farouk said. "I have been watching it."

"Watching it?" Frank asked, surprised. "Why?"

Farouk's face seemed to grow very thoughtful. "It is an odd thing, memory," he said. "To think that it might move in both directions, that it might be possible for one to *remember* the future."

Frank regarded him quizzically, but said nothing.

Farouk drew one side of his coat over his large belly, then pulled his tie up to his throat. "Do you wish to join me?"

"Join you what?"

"To discover the future."

Frank looked at him unbelievingly. "You don't believe in that stuff, Farouk," he said.

"But it is just an entertainment," Farouk told him. "A way of passing the time. Will you join me?"

Frank shook his head.

"Why not? It can do no harm," Farouk said insistently. "And besides, it is possible that one may sometimes find a truth stuck in something false."

Frank shook his head again, then started to move away.

Farouk grasped his arm. "Then at least come and observe," he said insistently. "The Gypsies are an ancient people." He smiled and tugged Frank forward. "Come."

Frank hesitated a moment as Farouk headed across the avenue, then he moved forward slowly, following him reluctantly until they reached the door.

Farouk knocked gently, and the door sprang open like a trap. A small, very slender woman stood in the hallway, her hand still on the knob. She wore a blue skirt, embroidered here and there with black horses, and a white blouse. Her face was very brown, and badly wrinkled, with deep webs around the nearly black eyes. Her hair was stone gray, but most of it was hidden beneath a large red scarf.

"You wish to have your fortune told?" she asked matter-of-factly.

"That is my wish, yes," Farouk said. He glanced down at her bare feet. Three of her toenails had been freshly painted a bright purple. "But, perhaps another time?"

"No, no," the woman said hastily. She pushed the door open instantly. "Now is good." She turned and led them through a red beaded curtain into the adjoining room. It was very small, the walls hung with paintings of Jesus, the small tables filled to overflowing with plaster statues of what looked like the Virgin Mary, except the eyes were without pupils and looked strangely blank.

"Please sit down," the woman said.

Farouk lowered himself into the plain metal chair that rested beside an equally small table. The table was covered with a very ornate cloth, bright green with red trim, that was embroidered with complicated scenes of jungle life, panthers peering out from behind thick clusters of green foliage, boas coiled around overhanging limbs.

The woman walked to the window which looked out onto the street and quickly drew a light-blue curtain over it. Then she sat down at the table, facing Farouk, her hands flat down on the cloth, the elbows locked rigidly in place. "I can tell you of yourself," she said to him, "or I can tell you of your destiny."

"They are not the same?" Farouk asked, in a tone that struck Frank as surprisingly serious.

"They are never the same," the woman replied crisply. She smiled quietly, with one eye closed, the other one focused intently on Farouk. "You must choose."

Farouk nodded. "And one costs more than the other, yes?"

The closed eye shot open. "Destiny is always more."

Farouk glanced over toward Frank. "What should I ask for, my friend?"

Frank shook his head, then leaned more heavily into the doorjamb at the entrance of the room. Strings of red beads hung over his shoulders like the shredded remnants of a shawl. He raked them away. "Up to you," he said.

Farouk looked back at the woman. "Destiny."

The woman nodded quickly. "Give me your hands."

Farouk stretched his hands toward her.

The woman took them in hers, turned them palms up, stared at the deep lines. The light in her eyes seemed to dim slowly, then go out. "Ah, yes," she said, her voice suddenly flat, trancelike. Then she released his hands and drew a deck of cards from beneath the table. "The tarot," she said, as she began to arrange them on the table. "The cards of divination."

A shadow darted across the blue curtain, and Frank leaned forward slightly and glanced to the left, toward the rear of the house. The interior room was separated from the front by another curtain of red beads. It was entirely empty except for several strange musical instruments which hung from one of the walls, a white wicker chair, and a small table, upon which a large red candle burned almost motionlessly, casting netlike shadows over his face as its light passed through the beaded curtain.

"The Ace of Coins," the woman told Farouk, "the light of the world." But Frank could hear her voice only as a faint monotone. It was followed by Farouk's.

"Better than the Ace of Scepters," he said, "the eye of the serpent."

Frank continued to watch the place where the figure must have passed in order to throw its shadow on the curtain, but nothing moved. He cocked his head for an instant, tried to hear something other than the fortune-teller, but everything was silent except for her flat, drowsy voice.

"Another ace," she said as if suprised, "The Ace of Cups." She bent down farther, her eyes now concentrating on Farouk. "You must know the truth."

Frank glanced back at the fortune-teller, let his eyes linger on her for a time, then drew them back toward the rear of the house. He leaned forward again, inching closer to the thin silvery slits of light that passed through the slender red tentacles of the curtain.

The candle had been put out, throwing most of the room in deep shadow and leaving only an eerie tunnel of light, which fell directly upon the chair and the woman who now sat silently in it, her face lifted high, her eyes staring boldly into his. She wore a long black dress embroidered in bright designs. A profusion of swirling colors gathered at her waist, and there were two embroidered scorpions curled at her breasts. Her skin was very brown, and her long black hair fell in curls and ringlets to her bare shoulders.

For an instant, he pulled away, then drew back, watching her more closely, taking everything in, the white sandals that clung to her feet, the long swirling hoops of her earrings. He could tell that she saw him, but she gave no hint of it, not the slightest gesture, but only stared directly toward him, her black eyes burning wildly through the screen of dripping red.

He nodded toward her gently, awkwardly, and for a moment felt the strange sensation that they were already locked together in a primitive collusion, as if they'd exchanged in whispers some searing line of vital information: *I know what you know.*

Suddenly she stood up, stared at him a last smoldering instant, then vanished from the room.

Frank felt his breath release in a sudden burst, saw the glittering beads again, then heard the fortune-teller's voice, and pulled his eyes back to her and away from the now empty room.

She had turned the last of the tarot cards and was staring at it intently, her eyes fixed on the swirling colors of its intricate design. "The Ace of Swords," she said suddenly. Then she shivered slightly and let her hands drop helplessly to her sides. "No more," she said quietly.

Farouk stared at her penetratingly. "You see danger?"

The fortune-teller shivered again. "Please, you must go now."

Farouk leaned forward. "Death? You see death?"

The fortune-teller stood up. "Go now. I can say no more."

Farouk slowly got to his feet. "Please, tell me more," he insisted. "You must have seen something." He reached for his wallet. "If it is a matter of money . . ."

"No. No money," the woman replied coldly. "Nothing. Nothing." She bolted toward the door, opened it instantly. "Please, you must go."

Farouk dropped his head forward tragically and moved ponderously out of the room, pausing at the open door. "Madam, are you sure that you . . . ?"

"No," the woman snapped. "No. Nothing." She stepped back and closed the door tightly behind her.

Farouk snapped his head up immediately after the door had closed, leaving him alone with Frank again. A mocking smile played on his lips. "It is always the same," he said. "For a thousand years, it has not changed."

Frank looked at him questioningly.

"To see something fearful, then order you to leave," Farouk explained. "To pretend that money means nothing to you. That is how they deceive." He shook his head. "It is what they call the *Hokkano Baro*, the Great Trick, the heart of the sting."

"Then why do you go to them?" Frank asked.

Farouk's eyes darted away. "For the experience," Farouk said crisply, his eyes not looking back at the door. "And because they are Gypsies," he added, "the last of the vagabonds." His dark eyes swept over to Frank. "Have you ever heard the Gypsy prayer, my friend?"

"No," Frank said, thinking of the woman again, the strange, invisible net she seemed to have cast over him for an instant, the way his breath had leaped from him when she vanished, as if a lethal grip had been suddenly relaxed.

Farouk grinned mysteriously. "The Gypsy prayer," he repeated, crossing himself as he quoted it. " 'Thank God I got away.' "

— 2 —

It was past midnight before Farouk finally roused himself from the sofa in Frank's office and lumbered to the door, hesitated for a moment, then looked back. "I must go to Toby's now," he said. "Are you coming later?"

Frank nodded. "Maybe."

Farouk opened the door. "Well, good night then, my friend," he said as he stepped out into the brick corridor.

"Good night," Frank said, then watched out the front window until he saw Farouk mount the short flight of cement stairs, carefully pulling his large frame over the woman who now slept at the bottom of them.

For a long time after Farouk had disappeared, Frank watched the sleeping woman, how she drew her legs up to her enormous drooping breasts. Even in the shadowy light that covered her, he could still make out the details of her clothing, the tattered shoes and mismatched socks, the long orange coat she used to protect herself from the evening chill.

He pulled open the bottom drawer of his desk, took out the bottle and poured himself a round. It went down warm, as it always did. He poured a second round, brought it nearly to his lips before he stopped, his eyes fixed on the blue paper that lay crumpled up in the wastebasket beside his desk. He drew it out again, spread it faceup on his desk, and stared at it. It seemed far away, an artifact from a distant time. Then he thought of the woman behind the beaded curtain, and he suddenly returned the whiskey to the bottle, and the bottle to the desk drawer. He didn't know why, except that if he took another shot, he would take another and another until tomorrow would seem entirely irrelevant.

He sat back in his chair, closed his eyes and waited. Sleep came upon him slowly, as it always did, like water rising in the room, cutting him off from the dusty light and the sounds of the street that banged against his window. At first it was a kind of slow muffling, then a vague, uneasy darkness, and finally an oblivion so dense and dreamless that, each time he awoke, he sensed that it was not so much from a suspended consciousness as from a dream of death.

It was a sound that jerked him up a few hours later and made him pull forward in the chair, his eyes searching the room like a hunted child. He listened for it again, the slight screech that had awakened him, and as he listened, he thought of all the things that it might be, a crackhead lurking in the shadows, a prostitute looking for a dingy corner to turn a five-buck trick, an old tosspot, sucking the last pink drops from his bottle of Thunderbird. In the silence, the fog of sleep lifting steadily, he opened the top drawer of his desk and felt for the .45 which nestled among the papers there. It was in his hand when he heard footsteps in the corridor, and as he moved toward the door, he felt his hand caress the pistol grip more firmly, his finger pull down with a hard impulsive longing upon the steel lip of the trigger.

He threw open the door in a single, quick motion, hesitated an instant, then stepped out into the corridor. He could see two feet as they bounded up the stairs then disappeared over the top of the landing, but he felt no need to pursue them. Instead, he walked out to the stairs and checked on the old woman.

For a time, he remained with her, leaning against the jagged brick wall, just to make sure that no one returned to do her harm. As he kept watch, he thought of his mother, the one who'd left them all so many years before.

The old woman shifted fitfully, then drifted back to stillness, and not long after that, Frank returned to his office and tried to do the same. But it was no use, and so after a time he sat up at his desk and began going over what he would need to do tomorrow.

He thought of the address Phillips had given him. He would begin there, with the wife. He would follow her trail wherever it led, while all the time hoping it led to that "something extra," the sort of case that called to him, that involved a truly deep detection.

The sun had not yet risen when Frank made his way over the old woman and up the stairs. The air was faintly pink with the approaching light by then, but the retreating darkness clung to it insistently, as if fighting for a position it could no longer hold.

He headed west, toward the river, moving slowly down the nearly deserted street until he could see the massive pillars of the West Side Highway. Just beyond them, the Hudson swept out in a long black strip, a single tugboat chugging northward, its rugged hull framed against the twinkling shoreline of New Jersey. For an instant, Frank felt the impulse to raise his hand and wave to the pilot, then realized that from the distant vantage point of the wheelhouse, he could only appear as a ragged shadow, his waving hand a vague, barely perceivable movement against the city's wall of sprinkled light.

He dropped his hands into his jacket pockets, then turned back east. He thought of going to Toby's after-hours place, perhaps sitting down across the table from Farouk. But the thought didn't really appeal to him, and so he decided to walk the streets instead, until he was ready to begin work.

At the corner of Tenth Avenue, he glanced to the south. Several police cars were parked on either side of the avenue between Forty-sixth and Forty-seventh Streets. The orange stripes of an EMS ambulance were clearly visible in the revolving flash of their lights, and just to the right of it, Frank could see the blinking pale-blue neon of the fortune-teller's window.

He turned and headed down the avenue, moving more quickly as he crossed Forty-eighth Street, and faster still by the time he came to Forty-seventh. From there, he could see several men gathered in small clusters on the sidewalk. Several of them were uniformed patrolmen. Some were stringing yellow strips of CRIME SCENE tape. Only one detective was on the street, but even from nearly a block away, Frank could tell that it was Leo Tannenbaum from Manhattan North.

Tannenbaum turned toward him as one of the uniformed patrolmen stopped him with a quick "Who are you, pal?"

"Let him through," Tannenbaum said. "It's a local PI."

The uniform stepped aside grudgingly and let Frank pass.

"Out for a little stroll, Frank?" Tannenbaum asked as he offered his hand.

Frank shook it absently, but didn't reply.

"Strange time of day for it," Tannenbaum added.

"I don't sleep much," Frank said. He glanced toward the window just as a flash from the Crime Scene Unit camera exploded behind the blue curtain.

Tannenbaum smiled. "Haven't seen much of you since Farouk iced that Riviera bastard."

"I've been around."

"Crawling the night," Tannenbaum said matter-of-factly. "You must give a few people the creeps."

Frank said nothing.

"Covallo got twenty-five years," Tannenbaum told him. "I guess you heard that."

"Yeah."

"My guess is, she'll do about a dime, then she'll be released. Powerful friends, Frank. It's the way of the world."

"Maybe," Frank said indifferently. He nodded toward the line of police cars, the EMS ambulance. "What happened?"

"Nothing you'd be interested in," Tannenbaum said. "We got the smoking gun." He smiled. "Only it was a razor."

Frank glanced back at him. "Man, woman, what?"

"Woman," Tannenbaum said. "Early fifties, I'd say."

Frank thought a moment. "Gray hair?" he asked finally. "Toenails painted purple?"

Tannenbaum's face tensed. "Right on the button. How'd you know?"

"I saw her this afternoon. Farouk had his fortune told."

Tannenbaum laughed unbelievingly. "I'd didn't know Farouk was into that kind of stuff."

"It was just for the experience, he said."

Tannenbaum took out his notebook. "When was this?"

"Around four in the afternoon."

"See anybody else?"

"Another woman."

"What'd she look like?"

Frank thought a moment. "She was very . . . very . . ."

"Beautiful?"

It wasn't the word he'd been looking for, but he let it go. "Yeah, I guess," he said.

Tannenbaum nodded. "Well, it won't do anybody any good now," he said. "She's the smoking gun. We got her cold. Everything but the blade in her hand. We're going to book her, then take her downtown for arraignment. My guess is, she'll break somewhere on the way."

Frank's eyes shifted to the right slightly, peering just over Tannenbaum's shoulder, so that he saw her clearly when suddenly she came out of the door, very erect, with a single lumbering detective at her arm, his faded-green suit pressed against the radiant embroidery of her dress. At first she moved forward very deliberately, her face held high, her eyes staring straight ahead. Then she stopped, and Frank watched with amazement as her eyes shot over to him, then clung briefly like two dark hooks before they abruptly let go.

"That the woman you saw, Frank?" Tannenbaum asked immediately.

She moved forward again, and Frank's eyes followed her as she made her way to the car, the detective still walking closely at her sides. At the door she paused a moment, as if gathering herself together, then bowed her head slowly and got in.

"That the same woman, Frank?" Tannenbaum repeated. "The one you saw?"

Frank continued to peer over Tannenbaum's shoulder, staring intently as the detective pulled himself in beside her, groaning softly as he did so. He could still see her face in vivid profile behind the glass, and for a moment he concentrated on her once again, taking in the proud line of her nose, the fullness of her lips, the way her hair fell in wild ringlets across her brow.

"Yes," he whispered, "that's her."

Tannenbaum leaned toward him quickly. "What?"

Frank turned his attention back to Tannenbaum. "The woman I saw."

"You're sure?" Tannenbaum asked insistently. "This afternoon, you said?"

Frank nodded.

"Well, you know the next question as well as I do, Frank. Did anything look suspicious?"

"No."

"Nothing at all, even just a mood?"

"I didn't notice anything."

"Where was she?"

"Sitting in a chair."

"Alone?"

"Yes."

"Did she say anything to you?"

"No."

"And the old woman was there, too, right?"

"She was there."

"Telling Farouk's fortune," Tannenbaum added with a short dry laugh.

"Yes."

"Did you see anybody else?"

"No."

"Did you hear her say anything to the old lady?"

"No."

"Did she say anything to you?"

"She was in another room."

"How about Farouk? She say anything to him?"

Frank shook his head.

"So, as far as you know, she . . ." Tannenbaum began.

"What's her name?" Frank asked, interrupting him.

Tannenbaum smiled. "Well, that's the funny thing, Frank. We don't know yet."

Frank glanced toward her again. "No name?"

"Oh, she's got a name all right. She just won't give it to us, that's all."

"She won't talk?"

"She wouldn't even acknowledge that we'd read her the Miranda warnings," Tannenbaum said. "My guess is, she's doing what she figures is a great imitation of a fruitcake. You know, working up an insanity defense."

Frank nodded.

"But it's not going to do her any goddamn good," Tannenbaum

said confidently. "Because we got blood all over her blouse, and good solid fingerprints on the razor, and a guy who saw her with it in her hand." He shook his head. "No doubt about it, she killed the old lady."

"Who was she, the fortune-teller?" Frank asked.

"As far as we can figure out, her name was Maria Salome," Tannenbaum answered. "And there was another old woman who lived here, too." He pulled out his notebook and flipped to the appropriate page. "Her name was Maria, too. Maria Jacobe. We're talking to her now. She claims she was somewhere else when it happened." He closed the notebook. "The three of them all lived here, running this fortune-telling scam." He looked at Frank strangely. "Three women," he said. "One's dead, one says she didn't see a thing, and one won't talk to us at all, not a goddamn word."

Frank looked back toward the car as it pulled from the curb, then moved slowly away from him, the taillights burning through the dense gray air like two infuriated eyes.

The old woman was pulling herself to her feet as Frank came down the stairs. She stepped quickly out of his way, grunting softly as he continued past her and headed down the dark narrow corridor that led to his office.

He stopped at the door, pulled out his keys, glancing idly at the rusty metal letter box that hung precariously from the brick wall. Someone had dropped something into it. The slight screech of the small rusty hinges sounded softly as he opened it, reminding him of what had woken him earlier in the night.

He took out the envelope, brought it to his desk and turned on the light. The paper inside was blank, but as he opened it, a small red bead dropped softly onto his desk. He recognized it immediately, saw the woman again through the curtain that had separated them.

He placed the paper on his desk, picked up the bead and held it gently beneath the light of his desk lamp. It was very delicate, and the hard white light from the lamp seemed almost to melt it into a single moist drop of blood, one which his flesh immediately absorbed.

— 3 —

Tannenbaum had said that she'd be booked, then arraigned, and as the nearly empty subway rattled toward Foley Square, Frank glanced at his watch and calculated that he might already have missed the arraignment, that she might be locked up in one of the tiny cells of the Women's House of Detention by now, standing in the corner, as he saw her in his mind, her face staring silently from behind the bars. Mrs. Phillips wouldn't be up and about yet anyway. He had time.

The halls of the criminal court building in lower Manhattan were already crowded despite the early-morning hour, and Frank found it necessary to elbow his way through scores of milling people as he moved from courtroom to courtroom until he reached Municipal Courtroom 7, where, according to the docket posted outside the door, an unnamed defendant was soon to be arraigned.

Inside the courtroom, a smudgy haze of cigarette smoke engulfed the long wooden benches where people sat silently or muttered quietly to one another. Some were lawyers waiting for their turns at the bench. Others were the relatives of those who'd been arrested during the night. They were the ones he'd always felt sorry for each time he'd seen them trudge wearily into the station house when he'd been a cop in Atlanta. No matter what the hour or the weather outside, they'd seemed always to be shivering with cold or wet with rain. He knew what had happened only a short time before. The phone had jangled, pulling them from the only peace they knew. Then a voice had broken over them, screeching or wailing, telling them that they were in trouble again, that they needed money.

Frank knew that in the end they nearly always brought it, that it was often all they had left after the weekly bills, and that even as they forked it over to the little shiny-headed bondsman, they knew that the voice was lying, had always lied, but that they would still have to spend their lives taking it for the truth.

"Yo, man, got a light?"

Frank turned and saw a wiry little man in a sleek blue suit as he leaned forward to talk to the large black man on the bench just in front of him.

"Yeah, I got one," the man said. He pulled out the book of matches and handed it to the other man. "You can keep it."

"Thanks," the man said. He lit the bowl of a brown Kaywoodie pipe, then waved out the match, his eyes still on the other man, studying him carefully. "So how you doing?" he asked lightly.

"Okay, I guess," the man replied wearily. He was wearing gray flannel work clothes and smelled faintly of motor oil.

"My name's Upjohn, brother, glad to meet you."

The man shrugged halfheartedly.

Upjohn smiled. "You need a lawyer, by any chance?"

The other man kept his eyes fixed on a young boy who stood near the bench while two attorneys huddled before the judge. "I don't know yet," he said.

" 'Cause I know a good one, if you do."

"Like I said, I don't know yet."

"Well, let me ask you this, brother, what we talking about here?"

The man glanced back at him. "You mean, who's in trouble?"

"That's right."

"My son done something to a girl. Cops say she's underage."

The other man's eyes flitted toward the bench. "He don't look that old, himself. What'd he do, knock her up?" He grinned. "My guess is, he didn't have much choice. You know how it is. Things happen, then somebody gets knocked up. You think that's what it is?"

"I don't know."

" 'Cause if that's the situation," Upjohn told him, "I got another guy could handle that for you." He smiled. "It's all a matter of money."

The man looked oddly encouraged. "It is?"

"Always," Upjohn told him. He plucked the pipe from his mouth and pointed the black, well-chewed stem at the other man. "You don't mind my saying so, brother, I think you could use a little advice."

The man nodded. He had an open, trusting face, an easy mark.

Upjohn smiled sweetly. "Well, lemme come up and talk to you." He stood up immediately, brushed quickly passed Frank's knees and joined the other man, huddling with him closely, his words now lost in a flurry of conspiratorial whispers.

Frank turned away from them and watched the bench. The lawyers were still standing shoulder-to-shoulder, talking earnestly with the judge, a slender red-haired woman who covered the microphone carefully with her thin white hand.

To the left of the bench, a large glass enclosure separated the men behind it from the rest of the people in the room. It was lighted a shade more brightly, and the mood behind the glass was a bit more defiant. In such places, the edge turned sharp, and the air seemed to grow hard and desolate around those particular people who had obviously offended the peace and good order of the City of New York more deeply than the minor-league felons who filled the benches behind the rail.

In Atlanta, Frank had spent long hours looking at the same sort of men who now slumped behind the glass. He had watched their lost, hunted eyes comb the walls around them, and of all the people he'd ever known, they'd seemed the least connected by the common ties of life. Even now, as he moved ceaselessly along the midnight streets, he would sometimes see a man smoking sullenly in a doorway or moving with a quick, nervous gait down a deserted back street, and he would know with certainty that within only a few hours—at most, a few days—the man would end up behind the glass, and that nothing could be done about it, absolutely nothing, either for him or for those he was doomed to harm. For everyone involved, it was already too late.

He thought of the bead again, then the woman who'd sent it to him, and he felt his body tense slightly as he began to search the room, trying to find her. He saw small knots of bleary-eyed lawyers, court stenographers and bailiffs, but the woman obviously had not been brought in for arraignment yet. He leaned back, lit a cigarette and waited, his eyes following the stream of people that shifted about the room in a way that seemed as random and directionless as the lives that had brought them there.

He was on his third cigarette when he saw her come through the large wooden door at the front of the room. Instantly, he felt a tremor move through him, a gentle quaking that he acted quickly to control. He sat up immediately and blinked the long night's tiredness from his faintly burning eyes.

She was escorted by a policewoman in full uniform, and as she moved to her place before the bench, the men behind the glass snapped to attention, laughed and muttered to each other, their eyes fastened hungrily on the sway of her body as it moved into position before the bench.

She stood very still and utterly silent while the judge took a moment to review her file. From where he sat in the smoky gallery, Frank could see only the blue prison dress they'd given her and the long black hair that fell across her shoulders. He already knew what had happened to her during the time that had passed since her arrest. They'd taken her to Manhattan North, stripped her of the black, blood-soaked dress, searched her body with a cool, methodical indignity, then tossed her the plain blue dress: *Put this on, sister, before you catch a cold.* The black dress was now the property of the district attorney's office, and unless she copped a plea, it would be pawed over a thousand times before the prosecuting attorney finally waved it dramatically before the jury's eyes, his voice rising in phony outrage: *Look at this, a woman's blood.*

The judge closed the file slowly, then stared directly at the woman's eyes. "Do you still refuse to give your name, miss?" she asked.

The woman did not move.

"You realize that your attitude will have no effect on our competence to proceed," the judge told her.

The woman said nothing.

The judge cast a final quick glance in her direction, then went on with the arraignment. "You will be listed as a Jane Doe Defendant until your true identity can be determined. You are charged with a violation of the New York Penal Law PL 125.40. That is, murder in the first degree. How do you plead?"

The woman did not answer, but Frank could see her shoulders lift slightly, her head rise as she looked squarely at the judge.

"You choose not to plead?" the judge asked.

The woman did not reply.

"Very well, then," the judge went on matter-of-factly. "Let a plea of 'Not Guilty' be entered on behalf of defendant number 778224, and I assign Mr. Andrew Deegan as her attorney of record." The judge looked out over the room. "Mr. Deegan, are you here?"

"I'm here, Your Honor."

Frank turned and saw a short, somewhat stocky black man surge forward to the bench and take a stack of papers from the judge.

"For the record," the judge said, writing it down as she spoke, "let's show that Defendant Number 778224 will have assigned to her as her court-appointed attorney of record Mr. Andrew Deegan of the firm of Canton, Harrison and Meyer, 260 Broadway, New York City."

Deegan began shuffling through the papers. "Should we discuss bail, Your Honor?" he asked absently.

The judge looked at him somewhat scoldingly. "I can't discuss bail until I have an identity, Mr. Deegan," she said. "How can I assess the likelihood of appearance if I have no idea who she is or her resources or anything else for that matter?"

Deegan nodded. "Yes, Your Honor."

"The amount of bail remains pending," the judge said loudly. She looked up, stared directly at the woman. "Do you have anything to say, miss?"

The woman didn't answer.

The judge turned to Deegan. "I suggest you have a long talk with your client, counselor. She has been charged with a very serious crime."

"May I have a word with her before she's remanded, Your Honor?" Deegan asked immediately.

"Yes, all right," the judge told him. "Use the conference room behind chambers."

"Thank you, Your Honor."

The judge banged the gavel. "Next case."

For a moment, the woman remained absolutely still. Then Deegan took her arm and tugged it slightly. She followed him immediately, moving silently to the right until the two of them finally disappeared behind two double doors at the rear corner of the room.

Frank got to his feet and walked out into the outer corridor. For a long time, he stood beneath its long fluorescent lights, watching silently as the dawn parade passed by. Across the way, he could see Upjohn making his final pitch to the man who'd sat on the bench in front of him. His fangs were sunk deep now, his nose already twitching with the scent of such a large, slow-moving prey.

They'd both moved down the corridor, Upjohn's arm draped protectively over the other man's shoulder, by the time Deegan came rushing through the doors of the courtroom. He wore a shiny blue suit, papers sprouting in all directions from its various pockets, and carried a battered briefcase, which he swang in a wide arc as he hustled forward.

He was already in the crowded elevator before Frank caught up to him.

"My name's Clemons," he said, flashing his official PI identification.

Deegan barely glanced at it as he punched the first-floor button. "Something on your mind?"

"I was wondering what you'd found out about the woman," Frank asked.

Deegan's eyes shifted over to him immediately, twitching left and right. "Woman?"

"The one they just assigned to you."

"I see," Deegan said, his voice very level. He looked either vaguely shaken or simply ill at ease. Frank couldn't tell which. "That woman," he said, then stopped, as if they were the first two words of a sentence he'd decided not to finish. He started to speak again, but the elevator doors opened and he walked out briskly, waving Frank alongside him as he headed toward the revolving doors at the other end of the building.

"I know you had a talk with her," Frank told him, "and I was just wondering . . ."

Deegan slammed through the doors, out into the crisp morning air. He drew in a long, deep breath. "That fucking smoke," he said. He glanced eastward, his eyes settling slowly on the slick pinkish flow of the East River. "That's better. Calms you down." He drew in a second deep breath, his large belly swelling out from under his jacket.

"I think the woman may have tried to hire me," Frank told him.

Deegan's eyes turned toward him. "To do what?"

"She didn't really say," Frank told him. "She just sent me a note. Well, not a note exactly, but . . . a bead."

"A what?"

"A bead," Frank repeated. "A red bead."

"How did you get this bead?"

"It came in an envelope," Frank said. "Nothing else. No letter, nothing."

Deegan shook his head and glanced back toward the river. A barge was moving slowly out to sea, trailed by a tumbling foamy wake. "How do you know this bead was from her?"

"I don't know for sure."

"Why did she pop into your mind, then?"

"Because I think the bead came from that fortune-telling operation they were running on Tenth Avenue."

"Tenth Avenue? That's where the murder occurred."

"I know."

Deegan looked surprised. "Really? How do you know that?"

"I came by the place just after it happened," Frank said. "I talked to one of the cops from Manhattan North."

"Which one?"

"Leo Tannenbaum."

Deegan eyed him doubtfully. "And you saw this woman and these red beads?"

"That's right."

"And you'd never heard of this woman before you met her at the fortune-teller's?"

"No."

A thin smile crossed Deegan's lips. "You wouldn't bullshit me, would you, Mister . . . Mister . . ."

"Clemons. Frank Clemons."

Deegan's eyes returned to the barge, drifting slowly southward along with it. "You wouldn't happen to have a card, would you? Something with your address and phone number?"

Frank gave him a card.

Deegan looked at it closely, as if trying to see through the scam he was sure it represented. "And you're licensed in New York State?"

"Yes."

Deegan pocketed the card, then looked at him very sternly. "What do you want in all this?"

Frank shrugged. "I don't know," Frank said weakly. "Just to help her, I guess."

Deegan laughed. "Come on, now, Mr. Clemons," he said, "why don't we be honest with each other. What's your angle on this? There's got to be a pot at the end of the rainbow, right?"

Frank shook his head.

"Money?" Deegan suggested.

"No."

Deegan smiled knowingly. "Maybe some kind of romantic thing? Maybe in a little payment in kind?"

Frank felt his eyes grow cold. "Nothing."

Deegan still wasn't buying it. "Well, I'll tell you what. You stay in touch, and if I think you could help me out on this thing, I'll let you know."

He started to turn, but Frank touched his arm.

"Did you find out anything when you talked to her?" he asked.

"No."

"Not even her name?"

"Oh yeah, I got a name," Deegan said.

"You did?" Frank asked, realizing suddenly that he was sorry she had given in, had finally revealed some part of herself that she had fought so desperately to hide.

"Yeah, I wrote it down," Deegan said. "It's some weird name." He patted himself down, searched one pocket then another, until he came up with a small slip of paper. "Puri Dai." He laughed. "What is that, some Gypsy name?"

"I don't know," Frank said as he wrote it down. When he'd finished, he glanced back up at Deegan. "I'd like to talk to her," he said.

Deegan's face turned grim. "I don't think that'll do you much good. She's not much of a talker."

"I'd like to try."

Deegan's eyes bore into Frank. "Are you telling me the truth, Clemons?" he asked. "You really didn't get a fee?"

Frank shook his head.

Deegan considered it a moment, his large brown eyes narrowing in concentration. "All right, I'll take you at face value for now," he said finally. Then he wagged his finger in Frank's face. "But only for now. Tomorrow morning, I'll see if your card checks out, your license, all that shit. If that's in line, I'll let you talk to her. But if it's not, pal, you're going to disappear from this case, you understand?"

"Yeah," Frank said. He returned the notebook to his pocket. "I just want to look into it a little," he added.

Deegan stared at him intently, like someone trying to decipher some arcane, ancient script. Then he nodded crisply, turned and walked away.

Frank watched him go until the round globe of his head had disappeared down the subway stairs a few yards away. Then he turned and walked to the river. He could feel his eyes burning with sleeplessness, and for a moment he yearned to lie down. But it was too late for that, and so he simply stood in the open air, breathing in the morning cool, a single figure, very small, against the city's gray enormity.

— 4 —

The glare of sunlight was very bright on the nearly blank page as Frank glanced down at his notebook, matched the address Phillips had given him with the one across the street, then eased himself back against the wall and waited. It was a four-story brownstone in a part of Sixty-fourth Street where such places could go for five or six million, depending upon the condition, and from the look of it, this one was in very good condition. The upper windows were done in stained glass, the lower ones covered by polished wooden shutters. It was easy to imagine what lay behind them—antique furniture, marble fireplaces, crystal chandeliers, all of it sealed off by the elegant facade.

The street was different, open to anyone, and as Frank slumped against the wall, he watched the various people who moved up and down it—delivery boys, museum workers bound for the vast halls that ran up and down Fifth Avenue, people out for a morning stroll, their small dogs trotting along beside them. But they seemed pale and far away compared to the vivid colors and tangible presence with which his mind continued to see and feel the woman in the blue prison dress. It was as if she'd managed to pass something of herself over to him, slip it secretly into his hand like a lock of hair pressed through the slender vines of the beaded curtain.

For a little while, his mind remained with her, as if, in the early-morning hour, he was still lingering in her arms. Then, because he had to, he forced himself to draw his attention back to the brown-stone across the way, and he stared determinedly at the black wrought-iron gate that separated it from the street, then at the doors

45

beyond the gate, the first one made of thick glass panels, the second a few feet behind it, dark, wooden, with a shiny brass knocker.

He took a deep breath, then let it out slowly. It was the worst time for any case, the time when you didn't know anything, and when only long periods of watching and waiting could get you what you needed to know in order to stop the waiting itself. He knew that he might be here for an hour, two, eight. Until he'd established Mrs. Phillips's routine, he simply couldn't know. She might be a woman who bustled about Manhattan more or less continually. Or she might be reclusive, a woman who rested for long hours in the upstairs bedroom, or stretched out in her private sauna.

He took out the picture Phillips had given him, stared at it closely, as if it might be able to reveal something of her character, an edginess that would mean she'd be on the move, or a tired, withdrawn exhaustion, which meant that she'd stay put. But the face told him nothing. It was a beautiful face, no doubt about it, with blue eyes set against smooth white skin. Her shoulders were raised assertively, like her chin, and she stared directly toward the lens, rather than edging away from it, like other people sometimes did. Only the hands said something, the way the long fingers of one of them wrapped around the slender wrist of the other, squeezing at it forcefully, as if it were a small pink throat.

She came out almost an hour later, and Frank quickly checked his watch, then noted the time in his notebook.

She was wearing a black leather coat with a high collar, and she kept the collar turned up against her throat despite the warm spring air. Her blond hair was pulled back tightly and bound in a silver clasp behind her head. Her skin was very white, almost glistening in the bright morning sunlight.

She seemed somewhat thinner than in the photograph, and in some sense more withdrawn, her blue eyes shielded behind a pair of gold-rimmed dark glasses. She moved slowly, with an oddly broken gait, until she reached Fifth Avenue. Then she straightened herself abruptly, in what appeared as a sudden, bold stiffening of the spine, and turned south, walking briskly until she reached the Pierre Hotel at the corner of Sixty-first Street.

Frank continued behind, waited a moment after she'd disappeared into the hotel, then walked in himself. For a moment, he didn't see her. Then a quick streak of blond passed through the remotest corner of his peripheral vision, and he saw her dart around a single marble column and disappear again, this time into an elevator with two other women. As the doors closed, he could see that one of the women had begun to talk to Mrs. Phillips casually, as if she knew her.

Frank watched the lighted numbers of the elevator, wrote in his notebook that it had stopped at the second floor, then walked over to one of the uniformed bellboys and smiled. "Lot of women going up to the second floor," he said amiably.

The bellboy nodded.

"What is it, some kind of conference?" Frank asked.

The bellboy nodded.

"On what?"

The bellboy shrugged. "Something about the rain forest," he said dully. "Friends of the Rain Forest."

"Rain forest?"

"They're raising money for it or something," the bellboy said. "They meet every Monday."

Frank nodded, then stepped away, took a seat in the lobby and waited. He'd only been in his seat for a few minutes when a shadow passed over him, and he looked up to see a large man in a dark-blue double-breasted suit.

"Excuse me, sir," the man said. "But are you a registered guest of the hotel?"

Frank shook his head.

"Here to visit someone?"

"No."

The man's eyes darkened. "My name's Mortimer," he said. He smiled thinly. "Ben Mortimer. Hotel security."

Frank stared at him coolly. "You rousting me?"

"Well, we can't let the lobby . . ."

"Start to look like a bus terminal?"

The smile disappeared. "Exactly."

Frank pulled himself up slightly, drew out his identification, then handed it to Mortimer.

Mortimer glanced at the ID, then returned it to Frank. "It's not the sort of thing we like here at the Pierre," he said.

"Part of the job," Frank told him.

"May I ask . . . ?"

Frank shook his head. "Sorry."

Mortimer nodded. "I understand client privilege and all that, but I hope you can understand my position, too."

"Sure," Frank said, "but the fact is, I have to keep an eye on somebody, and that person happens to be in the hotel. As long as that's the case, I have to be here, too."

"Yes, but . . ."

"And I can't afford a new suit everytime I step into a fancy hotel."

Mortimer's body remained tightly drawn. "I'm not looking for a disturbance," he said."

"I'm not either," Frank told him.

"So, what's the solution?" Mortimer asked stiffly.

Frank kept his voice a few degrees below freezing. "Maybe you should have a waiting area for private dicks."

"I don't think so," Mortimer said humorlessly. "And I don't want this to become a common practice. The people at the Pierre . . ."

"Don't always trust each other," Frank interrupted. "That's why some of them hire me."

Mortimer looked at Frank cautiously. "You mean you're working for one of our guests?"

Frank nodded.

Mortimer looked as if he'd been let off the hook. "I see," he said, obviously pondering the situation. Then he evidently came to a decision. "Well, I've done my job. I've checked you out." He smiled politely. "Now I'll leave you to do your work." As he eased himself away, his eyes drifted toward the floor. "Your job," he said, "it's rough on the shoes."

"Yeah," Frank said. And the feet, he thought, the legs, the eyes, whatever was still kicking in your soul.

But it was mainly his back that was giving him trouble by the time Mrs. Phillips finally walked out of the elevator again. He felt a dull ache near the base of his spine as he rose slowly and followed her out of the hotel. In his notebook, he noted the time: 12:15 P.M.

She stopped briefly under the hotel's elegant gold-and-white awning, nodded politely to the doorman, then headed south again, moving slowly, her shoulders hunched, as if against a cold wind that wasn't really there. At the corner of Fifty-ninth Street, she stepped off the curb and hailed a cab.

Frank waited a few seconds, then did the same. "There's a cab up ahead," he told the driver. "It has some kind of black bumper sticker. Stay close to it."

Mrs. Phillips's taxi didn't stop again until it reached the heart of Greenwich Village, a brownstone on West Twelfth Street that looked only slightly less elegant than the one on Sixty-fourth.

Frank remained in his cab, watching at a safe distance, while Mrs. Phillips paid the fare, then stepped into the building's vestibule.

Then he got out, walked to the building and copied the name on the buzzer into this notebook: Kevin A. Powers.

It was only an hour later when she came out again. From a shadowy corner almost a block away, Frank watched as she hailed a cab, then stepped out and hailed his own. She went directly home, marching up the street and through the black wrought-iron gate.

Frank took up his position once again, his eyes staring blearily at the ornate brass knocker on East Sixty-fourth Street. He opened his notebook and went over the brief details he'd recorded in it. As far as he could tell, she'd done nothing unusual, though he'd check out this Powers person.

Mr. Phillips arrived home at six in the evening, and by that time, Frank was feeling the long day's tedium like an angry man screaming in his face. Still, to do the job right, you had to wait and wait and wait. Farouk called the long hours his "meditation time," and seemed to withdraw into some remote corner of his mind, find things to engage him there and come out only when a sudden move drew him back into the broader world. But to Frank, it was just waiting.

Farouk laughed as he came through the door of Frank's office.

"You look as you did yesterday," he said. "Perhaps it is the wrong work. Perhaps you could sell shoes."

Frank flipped the next page of the magazine. A tall woman stood before a wild tropical setting, a fan of brightly colored birds spread out behind her like a peacock's tail. At first glance, the birds seemed merely part of the background, placed behind the woman like a wall of flowers, but their eyes were intense. As his eyes lingered on the picture, Frank realized that they were watching the woman with that sinister stillness that all birds of prey assume at the instant before they dive. "They're going to tear her apart," he said softly.

Farouk looked at him. "What?"

Frank shook his head, then turned the page.

Farouk eased himself back in the sofa, his body draped in a soft purple light that came through the window. "Toby," he said. "She returns soon."

"Good."

"Yes," Farouk said. "It is a good thing, a woman."

Frank instantly saw the other woman—not Mrs. Phillips, but the other woman—as he'd seen her the night before, moving unhesitantly toward the waiting police car, its blue lights pulsing over her as she walked.

"You know that fortune-teller you went to yesterday?" he asked.

Farouk nodded.

"She was murdered."

"Yes, I know," Farouk said. "From the street I hear it is, as they say, open and shut."

"Maybe," Frank said. "What do you know about the woman who was murdered?"

Farouk looked surprised by the question. "Know? Nothing."

"Had you ever seen her before?"

"I have observed her at various times."

"You mean, for pay?"

Farouk shook his head. "No. I have seen her here and there. She is not entirely new to the neighborhood." He looked at Frank piercingly. "What is your interest, Frank?"

"Well, I walked right into the middle of it early this morning," Frank told him. "They were still stringing the tape when I got to that little storefront she worked out of."

"You saw the body?"

"No, I didn't see the body. But the CSU car was there, and they were snapping pictures inside the place."

Farouk stroked his chin thoughtfully. "And the officer in charge, did you get his name?"

"It was Tannenbaum."

"Ah, yes. And what did he say?"

"That one of the women did it," Frank told him. "The younger one."

"And the woman herself," Farouk asked, "what does she say?"

"Nothing. She won't talk to anybody."

Farouk shrugged. "The Gitano, they are a curious race."

"Gitano?"

"The Gypsies," Farouk said. "How was the murder done?"

"She used a razor," Frank said. "Right across the throat."

Farouk looked doubtful. "That would not be usual," he said. "Of course, it could have happened. In a moment of great rage, we use whatever is at hand. But it is not usual. Especially for a woman. It is very ugly. And it is not so fast a way as people think."

"They were bringing the woman out while I was talking to Tannenbaum," Frank told him.

"Ah, so you saw her, as well?"

"Yes, I did," Frank said.

Farouk's hand crawled from his chin to the right corner of his mustache. He studied Frank's face carefully, as if the shadow of something new had just risen unexpectedly from its battered form, but he didn't speak.

"Tannenbaum said she wouldn't talk. I mean, not a word. She wouldn't even tell them her name."

"Perhaps she is mute?"

"Mute?"

"It is possible," Farouk said. "And the Gypsies sometimes do not bother with writing." He thought a moment longer, turning something over in his mind. "But Tannenbaum believes her to be the killer?" he asked finally.

"Yes."

"On what evidence?"

"Blood, prints, witnesses . . . quite a lot."

"Motive?"

"I don't know."

"Opportunity?"

"I don't know that either."

Farouk considered it all a moment longer, then shrugged. "It does not seem so interesting, Frank," he said disappointedly.

"Well, there's one other thing," Frank added hastily. He took the white paper from the envelope and handed it to him, the bead tucked securely inside.

Farouk held the bead up to the light. "From the curtain, yes?" he said.

"I think so."

"When did you get it?"

"I heard something out in the corridor last night. It must have been around two in the morning. I heard something, and then I saw somebody running up the stairs. The most I could get was a glimpse of feet."

Farouk lifted the small envelope and waved it slightly. "The bead came in this?"

"Yes."

Farouk looked at the bead again, this time more closely, turning it slowly in his fingers. "From the woman?"

Frank nodded.

"In place of her signature," Farouk said.

"More or less."

"Do you have a name?"

Frank reached for his notebook. "Yeah, I do."

Farouk looked quizzically at the notebook. "You are doing an investigation?"

"I talked to the woman's lawyer, that's all," Frank told him.

Farouk looked surprised. "When was this?"

"Early this morning," Frank said. He found the page he was looking for. "Here's the name," he said. Then he got up, walked over to Farouk and handed him the notebook.

Farouk looked at the name for a moment, then let his eyes drift slowly back up to Frank. He said nothing, but Frank could see a strange disturbance in his eyes.

"What is it?" he asked.

Farouk glanced back down at the notebook. "The Gitano are not all the same," he said.

"Meaning what?" Frank asked.

"For them there was also a diaspora," Farouk said. "They are scattered across the world."

"What does that have to do with the woman?"

Farouk smiled quietly. "My father used to say that a soul should be like a woman's veil, not lifted by too slight a wind."

Frank stared at him determinedly. "What are you talking about?"

"The woman is playing games," Farouk said. He handed the notebook back to him. "What she told her lawyer," he said. "It was not her name. Only a *gorgio*—one who is not a Gypsy—would think it was."

Frank looked down at the name: Puri Dai. "If it's not a name, what is it?"

"A place in the world," Farouk answered authoritatively. "A high function. It means 'Tribal Woman' in Romany, the Gypsy language." He smiled, but with an unmistakable darkness. "It means that this woman, she is the keeper of the *errate*," he added, "the pure blood of her race."

"Then how would I find out her name?" Frank asked.

"There is no name," Farouk answered. "The Tribal Woman is a thing." He shrugged. "That is the way it is with some of the Gitano."

Frank started to ask another question, but Farouk stood up abruptly.

"I must go now," he said.

"You don't want a drink?"

Farouk shook his head. "Not now," he said. "There is a problem with someone. I am being of assistance."

"Okay."

Farouk nodded, then walked to the door. "Believe me, my friend," he said as he opened it and stepped out into the darkened corridor, "when it comes to the Tribal Woman, there is nothing you can know."

Frank walked back to his desk and sat down. For a long time he thought that Farouk must be right. Then he saw her again, the black eyes and raven hair, and by some shift whose exact currents he could not fathom, he decided suddenly that no, Farouk was wrong, that whatever else she might be, she was still a woman, and her secrets could not be covered by the night.

He took out his notebook and looked up the name of Deegan's law firm. Then he picked up the phone and called it.

"Andrew Deegan, please," Frank said.

"I'm sorry, the offices are closed," the woman said. "This is only the answering service."

"It's very important that I talk to Mr. Deegan," Frank insisted.

"I can't give you his number, sir," the woman told him a little crisply.

"Then get in touch with him," Frank said, "and tell him that Frank Clemons called." He gave the woman his number. "Tell him to call me."

"I'll see what I can do, sir," the woman said, then hung up.

Frank waited by the phone, his urgency growing as the minutes passed. He wasn't sure where it came from, perhaps nothing more than the intensity of her look, the dark skin and black eyes, the long, loosely tangled hair. Often, momentous things could be reduced to such small elements, slight and trivial in themselves, but that produced an atmosphere of inescapable longing, a profound disturbance of the peace, an urge to test the limits once again.

The phone rang, and Frank snapped it up immediately. "Yes?"

"This better not be a habit, Clemons," Deegan said sharply. "I'm not on duty twenty-four hours a day, you know."

"It's just that I only have the nights to work this case," Frank explained.

"Well, what do you want?"

"I was wondering if you'd had time to check me out yet."

"Yes, I have."

"Any problems?"

"You aren't always nice to people," Deegan said bluntly.

"It depends on the people."

"Where does my client fit in?"

"I'd like to see her for a few minutes."

"Well," Deegan said after a short hesitation, "I guess that could be arranged."

"Tonight," Frank said firmly. "It's the only time I have."

"All right, I'm too fucking tired to argue the point," Deegan said. "I'll clear you. Be at the Women's House of Detention in half an hour."

"Okay," Frank said. He felt a sudden excitement lift him up like a wild wind, the kind he could still remember from his youth, that careened along the great stone face of the granite canyon, then suddenly shot upward violently, like a spirit from beneath the river's flat green surface, its cold invisible fingers tearing at his hair.

He hung up immediately and headed for the door. The old woman groaned as he stepped over her, then glanced up fearfully, her hand reaching for his leg.

He knelt toward her instinctively and briefly touched her hand. "It's all right," he said. "It's only me."

— 5 —

She was escorted by a female guard who held her arm very gently as she guided her into the room, then stepped in front of her and looked sternly at Frank.

"This the one you wanted to see?" she asked.

Frank stood up from the long wooden bench, which sat behind an equally long row of tables.

"Yes, it is," he said. "Thanks."

"The captain said you could only have ten minutes," the guard told him. "They're not supposed to have visitors after eight o'clock."

"I understand," Frank told her.

The guard nodded stiffly and left the room.

For a moment Frank simply stared at her, noted the small losses that were already visible, the sleek black hair now somewhat dulled, a slight pallor beneath the darkness of her skin. But she stood very erect, and her dark eyes stared directly at him, still immobile and unflinching.

"My name is Clemons," he told her quietly.

She said nothing.

"I'm a private investigator," he added. "I spoke to your lawyer right after you were arraigned."

The dark eyes glared hotly, but she didn't speak.

"He got me in to see you," Frank said. He stepped toward her, and she reacted to his movement instantly, her entire body growing very taut, as if preparing for an assault.

He stepped back immediately and sank his hands into his pocket. "I'm here to help you," he said softly.

Her eyes remained on him, sharp and glittering, like two small fires glowing out of the jungle thickness. Her long brown fingers curled into fists, the nails biting fiercely into the soft flesh of her palms.

"I'd like to ask you a few questions," Frank said. He waited for her to reply, then went on when she didn't. "Mostly about the day of the murder," he added. He took out his notebook and flipped to the first blank page. "A friend of mine had his fortune read by your . . ." He stopped, looked at her penetratingly. "By the woman who was killed."

The Puri Dai said nothing. One of her eyes glimmered slightly, but there was no other sign that she heard him.

"Who was she?" Frank asked.

Silence.

"The woman who was murdered," Frank continued, "whoever she was." He could feel himself being drawn toward her, almost physically, as if he were standing on a carpet which tiny, invisible legions were tugging gently toward her. "Was she a relative, a friend?" he asked.

The Puri Dai did not reply.

Frank walked behind one of the long benches a few feet away, sat down and tapped the opposite side of the table. "Why don't you sit down?"

She did not move.

"We only have ten minutes," Frank reminded her.

The Puri Dai remained in place.

"All right," Frank said, twisting around slightly so that he could watch her closely, "you can stand up if that's what you want."

Her eyes shot over to him, then darted back, staring straight ahead at the light-green wall of the room.

"Anyway," Frank began, "I think you sent me this." He pulled the bead from his jacket pocket and held it up. "Didn't you?"

She glared at the single red bead he lifted toward her. Her lips parted briefly, then closed together in a rigid line.

"Didn't you?" Frank repeated.

Her eyes narrowed quickly, then snapped back.

"It came from the curtain," Frank said. "The one in that storefront you lived in."

She didn't speak, but Frank could see a terrible woundedness in her eyes, along with a powerful, perhaps irresistible urge to escape one way or another.

He leaned toward her. "Do you want to die?" he asked very gently. "Is that what you want?"

Her face stiffened.

He looked at her, felt a stirring in himself, fought to keep it from his voice. "Because if you do," he said, his voice growing firm, "believe me, I understand it."

Her eyes softened, but she did not turn toward him.

"I understand it," Frank repeated, as if he were admitting it to himself as well.

Her eyes closed slowly, then opened. She said nothing.

Frank got to his feet, walked directly over to her, let his eyes bear down toward hers. "Live or die," he told her, "but don't accept this in-between." He turned and started toward the door, then glanced back as he opened it.

She was standing completely still, her arms flat against her sides, until, just as he started to leave, one of them rose very slowly upward, the wrist limp, the fingers dangling gracefully, delicately, like long brown strands of Spanish moss. Then one of her legs shot into the air, and she made first one rapid turn, then another and another, her legs flying higher and higher as she flung herself wildly into the air, spun and spun, her body thrashing madly as she whirled, her face lifted slightly toward the overhanging lights, but her eyes directly on him, steady and unflinching within the chaos of her dance.

It ended almost as abruptly as it had begun, and she stood rigidly near the center of the room, her long naked arms pressed tightly against her sides.

For the few seconds before the matron rushed forward, seized her and pulled her from the room, Frank simply stood, staring, transfixed, so much her prisoner that as the cell door clanged shut behind her, it seemed to open one for him.

"Night crawling again, Frank?" Tannenbaum asked, as Frank walked up to his desk.

Frank nodded as he glanced about the room. It was entirely deserted, nothing but plain green walls and empty desks. The clock at the far end of the room said that it was a quarter past midnight.

"As you can see," Tannenbaum said, "I'm working the graveyard shift these days."

Frank looked at him. "How come?"

"My choice," Tannenbaum said. He smiled quietly. "Maybe I'm getting a little like you in my old age." He pulled a chair over beside his desk. "Have a seat."

Frank sat down.

"So, what's on your mind?" Tannenbaum asked.

"The murder," Frank told him. "The fortune-teller."

Tannenbaum didn't look surprised. He nodded, then glanced toward the large windows at the front of the room. They were covered over with an opaque mixture of dust, soot, and urban grime, so that the panes looked dull and milky, like rows of square, pupil-less eyes which watched the room from behind a thin wire mesh. For a moment, Tannenbaum's eyes moved over them in a steady sweep like two nightsticks thumping down a corridor of steel bars. Then he snapped out of it suddenly, and looked back at Frank. "Did someone hire you?"

"No."

"But you're working it?" Tannenbaum asked. "I mean professionally?"

"Just at night."

A curious, uneven smile fluttered onto Tannenbaum's lips, then instantly disappeared. "Well that's the kind of thing it is," he said. "A night case."

Frank looked at him quizzically.

"You know the kind I mean, Frank," Tannenbaum said. "A beautiful woman, an untimely death." He smiled. "Add a little cigarette smoke, maybe a saxophone, and you got all you need to get you through the night."

"There may be more to it than that," Frank said.

Tannenbaum smiled his worldly smile. "Frank, there's never more to anything than that."

Frank didn't feel like arguing the point. He shrugged.

Tannenbaum leaned back in his chair and put his feet up on his desk. "Well, you know how it works, Frank, in this case just like any other one. You get anything, I'm the one you show it to." He pulled a cigar out of his jacket pocket and bit off the tip. "Have you got anything on it yet?"

"Maybe a little something that might save a few steps," Frank told him.

The end of the cigar twitched slightly. "I'm listening."

"You'll never find her name because she doesn't have one," Frank told him. "She goes by a title: Puri Dai. It means she's the Tribal Woman."

Tannenbaum looked at Frank unbelievingly, but said nothing.

"Farouk says that's the way it is."

"And he's some kind of expert on Gypsies?"

"He knows things," Frank said simply.

Another detective came into the room, shifting slowly through the maze of desks and file cabinets. He wore a faded green suit and moved very heavily toward the far end of the room. When he finally got to his own desk, he switched on the small plastic radio that rested on top of it, and a distant, scratchy wail of steel guitars swept the room.

"That's McBride," Tannenbaum said. "He's like you, another Rebel. Louisiana, I think." He laughed softly. "Talk about a fish out of water. They just shipped him over to Manhattan North from some place in the Bronx."

Frank's eyes shifted over toward him. He'd grown up with boys who looked much like him, pale faces, greenish, watery eyes—boys with slow, lumbering gaits who kept silent until the moment they exploded.

"Somebody raped his wife a few years ago," Tannenbaum said. "Then shot her. She's been paralyzed since then. From the neck down, I hear. He brought her up here for treatment. Never left." He drew his feet from the desk. "You should talk to him sometime. He was the first guy from Homicide on the scene."

Frank nodded. "Does he work the night shift, too?"

"Yeah," Tannenbaum said, "Always has." He took a deep breath. "You Rebels are like that, night crawlers. It makes me glad you're on our side."

"Not all of us," Frank said.

"At least the ones I know," Tannenbaum said. He shifted slightly in his chair. "But getting back to this Gypsy thing," he said, "what you gave me, it's not that much, Frank."

"It's all I've got right now."

"And now you want something from me, right?"

Frank took out his pen and notebook. "What do you know about the dead woman?"

"We've come up with a few new things," Tannenbaum said. "She had a driver's license from New Jersey, and she'd been living in that place for about three months." He looked back at Frank. "Her name turned out to be a little longer than the first one the other woman gave us."

"What was it?"

"Immaculata Maria Salome," Tannenbaum said. "And she was born in Hungary in 1924."

Frank took out his notebook and wrote it down. "What do you know about her?"

"That's about it," Tannenbaum said. "She'd been running that fortune-telling gig since she moved to Tenth Avenue. She had no criminal record. She'd never been married, as far as we could tell." He shrugged. "It's pretty much the same with the other old lady, too." He opened one of the drawers to his desk and pulled out a manilla folder. "I got her full name right here," he added. "You want it?"

Frank lowered the pen to the paper. "Go ahead."

"Immaculata Maria Jacobe."

"Where is she?" Frank asked as he wrote down her name.

"Still on Tenth Avenue, as far as I know," Tannenbaum said. "She claims she wasn't around when it happened."

"Where was she?"

"Over at some little storefront church on Forty-sixth Street, Saint Teresa's," Tannenbaum said with a shrug. "She claims it's her regular routine. She goes around three in the morning, lights a candle, stays about an hour, then comes back home."

"Do you believe that?"

"I don't have any reason not to," Tannenbaum said. "Who knows, maybe she's casing the place, planning to boost the poor box and a couple of candlesticks on the way out one of these nights."

"Do you think she could have had anything to do with the . . . ?"

Tannenbaum shook his head. "There's nothing to connect her to it. She went to Saint Teresa's, and that's it."

"And when she got back?"

"She found the body," Tannenbaum said. "But she didn't see the other woman. She just saw the body, that's all."

"So she called the police?"

Tannenbaum shook his head. "The Gypsies don't ever call the cops."

"Who did?"

"A kid who was delivering groceries."

Frank looked at Tannenbaum doubtfully. "At four o'clock in the morning?"

"That's right," Tannenbaum said. "There's an all-night grocery on Forty-third Street. They make deliveries twenty-four hours a day." He opened the drawer of his desk and pulled out his own notebook. "Here, I'll give you the kid's name. You can check it out yourself." He flipped through the notebook until the found the page he wanted. "Pedro Ortiz, that's the kid's name. He works at the Food Palace. On Forty-third Street, like I said."

Frank wrote it down, then glanced back up at Tannenbaum. "What'd the other woman say?"

Tannenbaum shrugged. "Not much, just what she saw."

"Which was?"

"She came home, opened the door, walked in, and there it was, the old lady on the floor." He glanced toward the window again, then looked at Frank sympathetically. "The young one did it, Frank," he said. "The woman, I mean. Your client, Puri Dai, or whatever she goes by. She killed that old lady, pure and simple."

Frank's pen stopped. "But why?"

Tannenbaum shrugged. "For now, I don't know," he admitted.

"The other woman, this Maria Jacobe, did she have any idea?"

"She was a basket case, Frank," Tannenbaum said. "She barely knew what country she was in."

"So you don't have a motive?"

"Not yet," Tannenbaum said. "But like we say in the trade, the body's still warm. We'll find one."

"Have you talked to any of the neighbors?"

Tannenbaum laughed derisively. "The neighbors. What a bag of Halloween candy they are."

"What do you mean?"

"You got a local drug dealer on one side with a yellow sheet as long as your arm," Tannenbaum said. "On the other side, you got a family of illegals, refugees who figure that in the end this is going to get them sent back to Haiti." He lit the cigar, took a quick puff. "But who knows, Frank, maybe you can get these people to cooperate."

Frank glanced back down toward his notebook. "How's the physical evidence standing up?"

"The Rock of Gibraltar," Tannenbaum said confidently. "We could nail her six ways from Sunday." He lifted his hand, shot one finger into the air. "The blood on her sleeves and under her fingernails came straight out of the old lady's throat." A second finger joined the first. "The prints on the razor couldn't be better. Clear as a goddamn bell. Textbook shots, I mean it. Unmistakable." The third finger rose. "The little guy who runs the bodega next door saw her go into the house only a couple minutes before the old lady died, so that's two people who can testify that she was present, like they say, at the scene of the crime."

"Are you sure the razor's the murder weapon?" Frank asked, as he continued to write in his notebook.

"According to the medical examiner, it is."

"What did the autopsy say?"

"That she died from a single cut to the throat," Tannenbaum said. He picked up one of the sheets of paper in the folder and read the exact words. "A deep cut which severed the major veins and arteries of the neck." He returned the paper to the folder. "It was very deep, and it was pretty much ear to ear."

"Must have been a sharp razor," Frank said. "What kind was it?"

"Kind? What do you mean, kind? It was a razor."

"A shaving razor?"

"That's right."

"In a house with no men?"

Tannenbaum smiled. "Not bad, Frank."

"Did you check it out?"

"First thing."

Frank waited.

"There were no traces of hair or hair follicles on the blade," Tannenbaum said.

Frank nodded.

"So what that tells us is that nobody had ever used it to shave with," Tannenbaum said. "It was clean as a whistle."

"Except for fingerprints," Frank reminded him.

"That's right."

"And they belong to the woman."

"Yeah."

Frank tried to put it all together. "So the razor had never been used."

"There was nothing but the old woman's blood on it," Tannenbaum said. "My guess is the woman bought it new, just for the occasion."

Frank wrote it down.

"I hear the woman has a lawyer now," Tannenbaum said.

"Yeah, she does."

"The lab report will be on his desk in the morning," Tannenbaum said. "By the way, who is he?"

"A guy named Andrew Deegan," Frank said. He closed his notebook. "I'd like to see where it happened," he said.

"Why?"

"Just to get a feel for it," Frank told him.

Tannenbaum drew in a weary breath. "Okay, I'll arrange for you to take a look."

Frank stood up immediately.

Tannenbaum looked at him incredulously. "You mean, now? At this hour?"

"It's the only time I can," Frank told him. "I'm working something else during the day."

Tannenbaum drew in a tired breath, then pulled himself out of the chair. "Okay, Frank, I'll give you the okay." He smiled. "Why don't you go over now? The old lady may be awake. From the look of things, the Gypsies don't sleep much either."

— 6 —

He arrived at the fortune-teller's storefront only a few minutes later. It was a two-story building and the upper floor was entirely dark. The fortune-teller's blue neon sign was dark as well, but he could see a faint light glowing through the light-blue curtain which still covered the front window.

He stepped up to the door, tapped lightly, then waited. He could hear footsteps as they neared the door, then stopped. The door did not open, and so he tapped at it again.

The door opened slowly, and through the small space between its edge and the jamb, he could see a single dark-brown eye.

"My name's Clemons," he said. He quickly took out his card and held it up the lone staring eye. "I'm a private investigator."

The woman stared at him expressionlessly.

"You got a call from Manhattan North, right?" Frank asked.

The woman nodded silently.

"Well, I'm the guy they told you about, the one who was coming over."

The old woman looked closely at the card, then turned toward him.

"I'm looking into the murder," Frank said. "Trying to find out a few things about it."

"You are not from the police?"

"No, just someone who's looking into the case," Frank said. "Are you Maria Jacobe?"

The woman said nothing.

"If you're not, I wonder if you could tell me where I could find her," Frank said.

"I thought it was the police," the woman said. "I open only for the police."

Frank smiled quietly. "If I could find her, I'd be happy to pay her for her time."

"I open only for the police," the woman repeated.

Frank took out one of the crisp hundred-dollar bills Mr. Phillips had given him the day before.

"I'd start with this," he said, as he held it up to her.

The woman's eyes widened. "I open only for the police," she said. "But also those who wish to know their fortunes."

Frank nodded. "All right," he said.

The door opened immediately, and Frank walked into the building.

The old woman was already in the other room, seated at the small table. "Please come in," she said.

Frank swept back the red-beaded curtain and walked into the front room. He sat down opposite the woman and glanced through the second curtain and into the interior room where he'd first seen the Puri Dai. The large wicker chair still rested at the center of the room, along with the small black table beside it. The red candle was still there, as well, and beside it, neatly coiled, a gold chain and large medallion.

The woman glanced at the money, and Frank immediately handed it to her.

"Thank you," the woman said. "Now, may I have your hands, please."

Frank stretched them out toward her, and she turned them palms up and peered deeply at their criss-crossed lines.

"You are going to be very successful," she said.

Frank's eyes drifted back toward the other room, concentrating on the medallion that hung over the table. It was very large, and even from a few feet away, he could follow its details, the flaming tongues which leaped out from its circular edges. It was made of brass, and at its slightly raised center there was an engraving of a scorpion.

"You will find much joy," the woman said. She turned his hands over. "Much joy and happiness."

Frank turned to her and drew his hands away. "I'm not really interested in my fortune," he said impatiently.

The woman stared at him solemnly, but didn't speak.

"I gave you a hundred dollars," Frank reminded her. "I have a few questions to ask, and I expect some answers."

The woman glared at him. "If you are not from the police, I do not have to answer."

Frank looked at her sternly. "You do if you want to keep that hundred-dollar bill I just gave you."

The woman hesitated for a moment, then spoke. "I do not know what you are looking for."

"I want to know what happened here yesterday," Frank told her.

"You know about the murder," the woman replied immediately. She shook her head mournfully. "I weep for Maria Salome. She was a good woman."

"How long had you known her?"

"For many years we live together."

"Alone?"

"But for the other woman," she said bitterly. "She who is no longer with us."

"The Puri Dai," Frank said.

The woman looked at him, astonished. "How do you know about this name?"

"She gave it to the police."

The old woman's face soured. She bent forward and spit on the floor. "Damn her soul," she cried. "Damn her soul to hell for this crime."

"Did you see her do it?"

She looked at him as if the question were absurd. "Her hands were full of blood," she said. "And Maria Salome, she was dead."

"Why did she do it?" Frank asked.

The woman shook her head. "She is strange, this woman."

"There must have been a reason."

"She did not know her place."

"What place?"

"In her blood, there was an evil thing."

"Her blood?"

"She did not do her task."

"What task?"

"She was born to know her place."

Frank stepped forward slightly. "But she didn't?"

The old woman didn't answer.

"Did she fight with the other woman?" Frank asked.

She didn't answer.

"Were they related at all?"

She hesitated an instant, then shook her head.

"So how did they meet?"

The woman's body stiffened. "I do not know," she said. "I know only that the Puri Dai, that she did not know her place in this house, and that when this happens, things can be lost, things can be ruined."

"What are you talking about? What things?"

The old woman looked at him determinedly. "There are things a *gorgio* cannot know." She held up the hundred-dollar bill and waved it defiantly in his face. "Things a *gorgio*'s money cannot buy."

"What things?" Frank demanded.

She sat back, her eyes suddenly very frightened. "You must go. Even if you remained, you would learn nothing."

Frank did not move. "I want to see where the body was," he said flatly.

She glared at him with eyes that looked half-enraged and half-terrified.

Frank stood up immediately. "And I want to see it now," he said very firmly. "A hundred bucks buys something, even here."

The old woman glanced longingly at the bill in her hand. "To see, that is all?"

"Yes."

"Very well," the old woman said wearily. She got to her feet slowly and led him through the second curtain and into the adjoining room.

Frank stopped at the small table and picked up the medallion. "What is this?" he asked.

She glared at it resentfully. "There are no questions," she said sharply.

"It's some sort of symbol, right?" Frank asked.

She walked in front of him, hunching her shoulders slightly as she passed him.

"Is it the symbol of the Puri Dai?" Frank asked coldly.

She wheeled around to face him. "You must not speak of her again," she said. "She is dead to us."

Frank picked up the medallion. "Why did she take this off?"

The old woman snatched the medallion from his hand. "She is dead to us."

"She was wearing it before the murder," Frank persisted. "Why did she take it off?"

The old woman shook her head. "You must go," she said.

Frank remained in place. "Where was the body?"

The old woman drew in a deep, resigned breath. Then she pointed to a door which opened onto another room. "There is where I found her," she said.

She walked over to the door immediately, but did not step through it. Instead, she stopped and pointed inside. "There," she said.

Frank walked over to the door and looked in.

It was a large room, and three beds were arranged head to end along its enclosing walls.

Frank walked to the center of the room, then turned slowly, surveying it from one angle to another.

"All of you slept in here?" he asked.

The woman nodded quickly, then crossed herself.

Frank turned away from her to look at the room again. To the right, he could see the chalk outline of the old woman's body as the police had drawn it across the unpainted wooden floor.

"Blessed among women," the old woman repeated, hugging herself gently now, as if against a sudden blast of cold.

Frank walked into the room and looked at the chalk outline. The body looked as if it had fallen forward, then lain face down across the floor.

"Go, now," the woman said.

Frank looked back at her. She was standing very stiffly in the doorway, her long hair flowing chaotically over her shoulders, her hands clenched in front of her, the long red nails scratching at her wrists.

"You have seen," she said. "Now you must go."

Frank didn't move. "Where were you when you first saw the body?"

"Here," the woman said, pointing to the right.

"What did you see?"

"The Puri Dai was over her," the woman answered, "standing over here."

Frank stepped toward her instantly. "You saw her? I thought you didn't see her. That's what you told the police."

The old woman shook her head brokenly. "It was a lie," she said softly. "I saw the Puri Dai." She shivered. "With my own eyes, I saw her." She drew in a long, trembling breath. "The razor was in her hand, like this." She lowered her arm to her side. "In her hand, like this."

"Did she see you?"

"She stared into my eyes."

"So she was facing you?"

"Face-to-face," the woman said.

"Standing where?"

"In the doorway."

Frank stepped over to the outline. From its configuration, he could tell that she had lain on her stomach, her arms stretched out over her head, her legs drawn up near her chest. He studied the outline a moment longer, then took out his notebook and drew it on a blank page.

"You must go now," the woman said to him.

Frank paid no attention to her. Instead he let his eyes move up the chalk outline, beginning at the feet, then sweeping upward, past the head then beyond it for a few feet to where there was a second closed door at the far end of the room. "What's in there?"

The woman didn't answer.

Frank pointed to the room. "What's in there?" he repeated.

The woman stood in place.

Frank walked over to the door and opened it. Inside there was a small table and on it a small painting of a woman, clothed in purple, her head covered with a dark hood. She wore a medallion identical to the one in the other room, and her feet were sunk deep in foamy green waves, as if she were wading in the sea. There was a small rectangle of uncovered foam rubber, which looked as if it had simply been shoved into the room for storage.

Frank stepped back out of the room, closing the door behind him, his eyes absently moving up the door until they settled on the hook-and-eye latch, which had been screwed loosely into the outer door-jamb at just about the height of his shoulder.

For a moment he stared at the latch, then turned to the woman. "What was that for?" he asked.

"To hold the spirit in," the woman answered, then smiled eerily as if the words themselves were part of a code which only she could comprehend.

Frank took a quick sip from the glass, his eyes roaming over the room, settling here and there on one lone figure after another. It was the usual crowd, and over the past few months he had become familiar with them. There was the thin young man who chain-smoked Chesterfields and never spoke at all, except to order the one drink he always ordered, a Jameson's, straight up. To his right, an older couple sat, one mask drinking with another, and just beyond them a woman who nearly always dressed like someone a good deal younger than she was.

Farouk was looking at her too when Frank returned his attention to him.

"I do not trust a woman who wears large ribbons," he said.

Frank took a long pull on his cigarette. "Why?"

"One must understand the stages of life," Farouk said, "that we are not now what we once were, and that we will not be later what we are now."

Frank smiled. Sometimes he wondered where Farouk got these sayings.

"What do ribbons have to do with that?"

"They lack the dignity of experience," Farouk said.

Frank smiled again and took another drag on the cigarette.

"You are very quiet tonight," Farouk said.

"I get that way sometimes."

Farouk leaned toward him. "Something troubles you, Frank."

Frank shook his head. "No, nothing."

"The day case, or the night?"

Frank crushed the cigarette into the small glass ashtray. "I spoke to Tannenbaum about it."

"Ah, so it is the murder."

"Yeah."

Farouk laughed quietly. "It does me good to know that you will never change."

Frank shook his head. "There's something about it, this case. It bothers me."

"Because you do not know, that is what bothers you," Farouk told him. "What did Tannenbaum say?"

"He thinks she did it."

"You do not think so?"

"Something doesn't fit," Frank said. "But I don't know what it is."

Farouk took a quick sip of whiskey, then put down his glass. "I do."

Frank looked at him questioningly.

"It's the woman," Farouk said. "You do not want her to be a murderess."

Frank nodded. "Maybe," he admitted.

"It has been a long time, yes?"

"Long time?"

"Since you have felt it?"

"Felt what?"

Farouk looked at him knowingly. "The great sorrow is that we make it a wall between us, when it should be a gate."

"What should be a gate?"

Farouk smiled quietly. "Desire," he said.

— 7 —

He was still thinking about what Farouk had said when he took up his position outside Mrs. Phillips's apartment the next morning. While he waited, he glanced through the notes he'd made the previous day, trying to gear himself up for another tedious round of working what he now thought of simply as his "day case." He went through the various times of arrivals and departures, the addresses of her destinations, noted the only name that had cropped up so far: Kevin A. Powers.

It was time to check him out.

The first place to look was a telephone directory, and after waiting a moment longer beside the wall, he quickly darted into the nearest shop and asked for one. The woman behind the counter produced it immediately, and Frank quickly flipped through the pages, ran his finger down the long line of names until he came to "Powers, Kevin A." There were seven men by that name, but only one of them listed his address on Twelfth Street. A second address was listed as well, this one for his office: 485 Fifth Avenue. Frank wrote it down quickly, along with what the directory said was his profession: gynecology.

It was noon before he saw Mrs. Phillips, and he quickly wrapped the square of wax paper back around the sandwich he'd just begun to eat and tucked it into his jacket pocket. All the while, he watched her, carefully noting her clothes so that he could keep track of her in a crowd, pick out her long red coat, feathery black hat and small matching purse from a sea of shifting colors, textures, fabrics.

She walked west again, just as she had the morning before, turned onto Fifth Avenue and immediately hailed a cab.

Frank waited on the curb for a few minutes then took one too, a yellow clunker that wheezed slightly as it pulled away.

"That cab ahead," Frank told the driver, "just to the right of the limo. Follow it."

The driver glanced back at him, a young woman with red hair and light-green eyes. "Are you kidding?"

"No," Frank said.

The woman smiled brightly. "You a foreign agent or something?" she asked mockingly.

"Just follow it," Frank told her.

"Yeah, right," the woman said. "Just like in the movies."

Frank leaned toward the seat and fixed his eyes on Mrs. Phillips's taxi. It took her first to Fifty-ninth Street, then turned right, headed to the western end of Central Park, made another right onto Central Park West and moved uptown, slowly at first, then more quickly as the traffic thinned.

At Seventy-second Street, the cab turned left, pulled over to the curb in front of the dark wrought-iron gate of the Dakota, and stopped.

"Pull over at the edge of the park," Frank told the driver quickly.

She did as she was told, then looked back at Frank. "I got it now," she said. "Your wife's cheating on you."

Frank gave her a withering look, then paid the fare and got out.

Across the traffic of Central Park West, he could see Mrs. Phillips as she stood at the passenger window of the cab. She drew several bills from a small black purse, paid the driver, then turned toward the entrance of the building. For a moment she stared about, as if looking for someone, then she turned quickly, stepped up to the building's small bronze guardhouse and said something to the uniformed guard who kept his place inside it. The guard nodded politely, picked up the phone in the guardhouse and made a quick call on the building's security system, while Mrs. Phillips waited beside the guardhouse.

Frank quickly took out his notebook and scribbled down what

he'd seen during the last few minutes. By the time he'd finished, Mrs. Phillips had passed beneath the large archway and disappeared into the building.

Frank glanced at his watch and noted the time: 12:45 P.M. Then he pocketed the notebook and walked across the street to the Dakota.

The guard was a middle-aged man who wore a dark-blue greatcoat with shiny brass buttons. Frank nodded to him politely as he approached the guardhouse.

"What can I do for you, sir?" the guard asked.

Frank smiled quietly and handed him his identification.

The guard returned it immediately. "If I don't talk to the cops, they start ticketing the delivery wagons, giving them a lot of shit. But you're not a cop, so I don't have to talk to you."

Frank shook his head. "No, you don't," he said. He pulled one of Mr. Phillips's crisp hundred-dollar bills from his pocket and slipped it into the guard's hand. "Unless you want to."

The guard sank the bill into his pocket without looking at it. "What are we talking here?"

"A C-note."

The guard looked pleased. "Just so it doesn't interfere with my job."

"It won't."

"Then shoot."

"It's about that woman, the one who just went in."

"Miss Driscoll," the guard said.

"Driscoll?"

"Yeah, Miss Driscoll," the guard repeated a little impatiently. "What about her?"

"She come here very much?"

"Maybe once or twice a month, something like that."

"Who does she see?"

The guard hesitated briefly.

Frank moved quickly to urge him along. "Now look," he said firmly. "You have a hundred-dollar bill in your pocket, you're not going to go soft on the first question."

The guard thrust his chin out slightly. "No," he said. "She comes to see Mr. Devine."

"What's his whole name?"

"Preston Devine. With an R in the middle. Preston R. Devine."

"And he lives here?"

"That's right?"

"Which apartment?"

"Four-C"

"What's he look like?"

"Short, a little on the stocky side, but he buys the kind of suits that cover up his belly, you know?"

"Is he bald?"

"Getting there."

"Gray hair?"

"Yeah, mostly. Gray-black."

"What do you know about him?"

The guard shrugged. "He's got a lot of money. But everybody in the Dakota has a lot of money."

"Where does Devine's money come from?"

"His business dealings, I guess."

"What are they?"

"You mean, what does he do?"

"That's right."

"I don't know for sure," the guard said. "Importing stuff, I think."

"Importing what?"

The guard laughed to himself. "Probably Jap TVs, something like that."

"You don't know?"

He looked at Frank mockingly. "I'm not the guy he discusses that shit with, know what I mean?"

Frank nodded. "Do you know the name of his business?"

"Allied something," the guard told him. He struggled to think of it. "Global-East," he said quickly when it came to him. "Allied Global-East. It's somewhere down on Forty-seventh Street, I think."

"West Forty-seventh Street?"

"That's right."

"The diamond district," Frank added.

The guard shrugged. "Maybe that's what he imports."

"Is he married?"

"Yeah. Two kids, I think. But they're both in college. We don't see them. We don't see the wife much, either. She lives in London."

"London?"

"Yeah, London," the guard said. He smiled. "These people, they got their own way of doing things. The whole world, it's their playground, you might say, their . . . what do you call it? . . . their oyster, you know?"

Frank nodded dryly. "When Miss Driscoll comes here, does she always see Devine?"

"Yes."

"Is she always alone?"

"I've never seen her with anybody."

"Does she always come by taxi?"

"Yeah."

"Does she ever bring anything with her, like a package, anything like that?"

"No, just whatever a woman carries, you know. A purse, something like that."

"Do they ever go out?"

"You mean out here, onto the street?"

"Yeah."

The guard shook his head.

"So they meet in Mr. Devine's apartment, and stay there?"

"They stay inside, yeah."

"You've never seen them together?"

The guard's face changed slightly, as if he were thinking about something. "No," he said. "Which means you've figured it out, right?"

"Figured out what?"

The guard laughed. "Well, come on, pal. It's got all the signs."

"Of what?"

"It's an affair, man," the guard said confidently. "He's married, away from the wife for months at a stretch. You got to develop quite an itch in all that time."

Frank nodded.

The guard looked at Frank quizzically. "She's married, too, am I right?"

Frank didn't answer.

"The husband's suspicious, so, whammo, he hires his own private dick to check things out."

Frank said nothing.

The guard smiled cunningly. "I hit the bull's-eye, didn't I?"

Frank pulled out one of his cards. "If you hear anything, I'd like to hear it, too."

The guard shook his head. "Our deal ends when you walk away," he said. "A hundred bucks don't buy a lifetime contract."

Frank smiled edgily. "The well's not dry."

"Then the next time we meet," the guard told him, "we'll send the bucket down again."

"Absolutely," Frank said. Over your shiny little head, he thought.

Two hours later, Mrs. Phillips walked out from beneath the archway, slung the small black purse over her shoulder and headed eastward, first crossing the street, then moving into Central Park. From his position across the street, Frank could see that she turned without hesitation, as if she knew exactly where she was going. He took out his notebook, recorded the time, then followed her at a distance.

She moved slowly into the park, her shoulders drawn in somewhat, but her head erect, staring straight ahead. Her hair was very bright in the afternoon sun, and had he simply been another stroller in the park, Frank realized that he would have sensed nothing at all about her.

The area of Central Park was known as Strawberry Fields, a small garden which had been set aside as a memorial to John Lennon. Near its center, there was a mosaic walkway inscribed with the word IMAGINE. For a time, Mrs. Phillips stood at the edge of the mosaic, her eyes staring at the word with an odd intensity, before she finally moved forward again, heading down the long winding walkway which led further into the park.

She turned left onto the broad circular sidewalk that went around the park, ambling slowly, glancing left and right, like a tourist. She never looked back, and because of that, Frank felt that he could stay somewhat closer to her without burning his cover. It was as if she had no idea, had never even entertained the notion, that someone might be following her, taking down her movements in a little green notebook which he would later use to report to her husband. From a distance, it was hard for him to know where such trust came from. It might be naivete, or arrogance, or some combination of the two. It might be that she simply didn't care, or that, in some complicated way, she wanted to be seen, caught, punished.

Near the eastern edge of the park, she headed north, moving around the boathouse pool to a large bronze statue of Alice in Wonderland which was surrounded by a circular cement bench. There were a large number of people around her, mostly women with their children, and the bench was littered with the things they'd brought with them. For a time she stood very stiffly among them, her head turned slowly left and right as if trying to find the best place to sit. Then she suddenly walked to the right of the statue and sat down among a crowd of other women.

Frank remained at the edge of the pool, his back to her, his eyes staring out across the glittering surface of the water. From time to time, he glanced back toward her, but only for an instant, barely long enough to notice how her blond hair shimmered in the bright afternoon light.

For a long time, she sat very straight and still, staring directly at the children before her. Then she rose, and Frank turned away from her quickly and walked several yards toward the opposite side of the pool. From there, he could see her clearly as she headed east again, along a winding path that led at last to the edge of the park.

He was still several yards behind her when she reached the street. She paused at the light on Fifth Avenue, then moved forward when it changed, heading nonchalantly across the wide avenue. It was only then, as he watched her from across the street, half-hidden by the stone wall which bordered the park, that something struck him, something that was missing. He edged himself forward slightly, still staring at her intently as she headed south, then made an quick turn onto Sixty-fourth Street and walked the short distance to her home. She was only a faint reddish blur when she passed through the little wrought-iron gate and disappeared into her house, but it was a blur from which something had already disappeared.

He turned away from the street, let his eyes study the park. In his mind, he went over everything he'd seen, concentrating on something that was missing. He retraced her movements after she'd left her house early in the morning, the ride in the cab, paying the driver.

He stopped.

Paying the driver.

She'd taken the money out of a small black purse that hung from her shoulder. She'd had the same purse a few hours later when she'd left the Dakota and headed into the park. She'd had it when she'd stood above the star-burst mosaic and as she'd walked along the circular path. She'd had it when she sat down amid the cluster of parents and children at the statue, amid all the paraphernalia of parenthood, bags, strollers, knapsacks . . . purses.

Then he knew instantly that that's where she'd left it, cleverly, like a letter hidden among other letters.

He headed back toward the statue, walking quickly but inconspicuously, until he reached it. Then he sat down on the cement bench and let his eyes move around it, searching through all the other scattered array of things for the single small black purse he knew she'd still had with her when she'd sat down to watch the children. He looked once, twice, three times, futilely looked again and again and again, his eyes spinning around the rough gray rim of the cement bench like two dark balls around the wheel of chance.

8

Mr. Phillips took a seat opposite Frank's desk, glancing at his watch as he did so. "I'm not early, am I?"

Frank shook his head.

"I'm rather obsessive about time," Phillips added. "I don't like to be either early or late. I'm a little extreme. I admit it."

Frank said nothing.

Phillips drew in a deep breath and folded his hands primly over the burnished leather briefcase which rested in his lap. "Well, what have you found out?"

"A few things," Frank told him. "Maybe you can help me put them together."

"Good," Phillips said eagerly. "I'd like to think that we're working together in a way. Perhaps something you say might trigger something in me that could help us both."

Frank nodded. "Okay," he said. He took out his notebook and flipped to the appropriate page. "This is what I have so far."

Phillips leaned forward expectantly. "Fine, fine. Anything might help."

"I've been trailing her for the last two days," Frank said. "On Monday morning, she left the house at 9:15 A.M. and walked to the Pierre Hotel. She went to the second floor, a meeting of a group called Friends of the Rain Forest."

"Yes, I know that group," Phillips said immediately. "It's one of Virginia's pet projects." He shrugged. "Should be harmless enough."

Frank nodded crisply and went on. "She left the meeting at 12:15 P.M., walked to the corner of Fifty-ninth Street and Fifth Avenue. From there, she took a taxi to the Village, 124 West Twelfth Street."

Phillips leaned forward slightly. "What's down there?"

"It was a brownstone," Frank told him. "The name on the door was Kevin A. Powers."

Phillips stared at Frank quizzically. "Powers?"

"You know him?"

"No."

"Think carefully. Have you ever heard of him?"

Phillips thought a moment longer, then shook his head decisively. "Not at all."

"Maybe in connection with some of her charity things?"

"The name doesn't sound familiar," Phillips said determinedly. "I've never heard the name. Who is he?"

"A doctor," Frank said. "A gynecologist."

"A gynecologist?" Phillips asked wonderingly. "Perhaps that's it then. Perhaps Virginia is ill, and doesn't want me to know."

"Maybe," Frank said. "But the thing is, she didn't go to his office, she went to his house."

Phillips did not look unnecessarily alarmed. "For a private consultation, that's possible."

"Yes, it is," Frank admitted.

"So perhaps all of this problem has been about Virginia's health."

"It's not quite that simple," Frank said cautiously.

Phillips eyed him coolly. "Go on."

Frank leaned back slightly. "Mr. Phillips, have you ever thought that your wife might be unhappy?"

"Unhappy?"

"Yes."

"You mean with me?"

Frank took a deep breath, trying to choose his words carefully. "Well, you know how it is. There's always the possibility that Mrs. Phillips has simply done what a lot of people do."

Phillips's eyes grew solemn. "An affair," he said matter-of-factly. "Is that what you mean?"

"It's always possible."

"With this, this . . . Powers?"

"Well, maybe not Powers," Frank said. "She visited someone else too."

Phillips's face grew very still. He did not speak.

Frank returned to the notebook. "She left home today at 12:25 P.M." he began. "She walked to Central Park." In his mind, he could see her once again, the tall, slender figure in the long red coat, the platinum sheen of her hair in the sunlight, the small black purse that hung from her left shoulder. "She took a cab to the Dakota," he went on. "I talked to the guy in the guardhouse there. He told me that Mrs. Phillips comes to see a man who lives there. She comes about once every two weeks."

"What's his name?"

"Preston R. Devine," Frank said. "Ever heard of him?"

"No."

"You're sure?"

"I've never heard of such a person," Mr. Phillips said. "Is that the man you think she must be seeing?"

"I know she sees him," Frank said. "I just don't know why."

"But you think it's an affair?"

Frank shifted about uncomfortably, closed the notebook and let it drop onto the top of his desk. "It's always possible," he said.

"Virginia?" Mr. Phillips said unbelievingly.

Frank shrugged. "It happens all the time." He glanced down at his notebook. "Does Mrs. Phillips go by her married name?"

"Yes, of course," Phillips said.

"Virginia Phillips?"

"Yes, yes," Phillips answered immediately. "Why?"

"What was her maiden name?"

"Harris."

Frank nodded.

Phillips looked at him intently. "Why are you asking about her name?"

"At the Dakota, when she sees this Mr. Devine, she uses another name."

Phillips's lips parted silently.

"Driscoll," Frank told him. "Miss Driscoll."

Phillips continued to stare at him astonished. "Driscoll?"

"Yeah," Frank said. "And after she left the Dakota, she walked into the park and I think she made some kind of drop."

Phillips eyes widened. "What are you talking about?"

"She had a purse with her when she walked into the park," Frank said. "She left it there. I followed her, so I don't know who picked it up."

"Are you sure it was—what do you call it—a drop?"

"No," Frank admitted. "It's only a possibility."

Phillips's eyes looked bewildered, then hardened. "I want you to find out everything you can about this man, this Preston R. Devine," he said vehemently. "And that doctor too."

Frank nodded.

"I don't care what it costs," Phillips added. Then he stood up. "No one betrays me, Mr. Clemons," he said darkly. "No one." He seemed to consider something for a moment, then act. "Virginia and I are going to be out of the city tomorrow morning," he said, "so you can work on the doctor and that other man."

Frank nodded.

Phillips looked at him. "And I suppose I should show you this," he said reluctantly, as he reached into his pocket and pulled out a slip of paper. "It was in her coat," he added. "I found it yesterday."

Frank took the slip and looked at it. It was a pawn ticket from a shop at Eighth Avenue and Forty-sixth Street, only a short walk from his office.

"It looks like she's been pawning things," Phillips said. "Probably her jewelry."

Frank sank the ticket into his jacket pocket. "I'll look into it," he said.

Phillips nodded. "Yes," he said crisply. "Thank you."

Frank walked him to the door, opened it and waited as Phillips walked past him and into the corridor. For a moment he faced the grim brick wall, then suddenly he turned back toward Frank. "Do you think she's having an affair?" he asked urgently.

"I don't know."

"Well, if she is," Phillips said, "what would pawning her jewelry and dropping something in Central Park have to do with it?"

Frank shook his head. "That's what I'm going to have to find out," he said.

The man behind the wire eyed him suspiciously as he came through the door.

Frank walked up to the counter and placed the lamp Karen had given him on top of it.

The man's attention shifted to the lamp. His hand moved gently up its long slender neck. "It's a nice piece," he said. "I wouldn't lie to you." He looked at Frank and shrugged. "But I don't get too many calls for something this nice."

"What's it worth?" Frank asked.

"At an antique store, you'd get more," the man told him. "I wouldn't lie to you. Over on the East Side, they can sell it. But here, the Avenue? People want guitars, knives, ashtrays from Atlantic City. This kind of thing, so nice, they don't know from something like this." He laughed to himself. "To the people who come in here, a lamp is something you use to see the bills with. You know what I mean? It don't mean nothing, but for light." He touched the lamp again, caressing its stained-glass shade. "This is more what you'd call an art piece, you see what I'm saying? You'd do better on the East Side."

"I don't want to go over to the East Side," Frank said. "What's it worth to you?"

The man looked the lamp over again, then shrugged. "I could go a couple hundred bucks."

"Okay," Frank said immediately. "But I don't want the money."

The man stepped back slightly. "What is this?" he asked darkly. "I got cameras all over this place. Don't try nothing."

"A camera's what I need," Frank said. "The one I was using got broken, and I need another one. I was thinking of a trade. For the lamp."

The man looked at him unbelievingly. "You want to trade me this lamp for a camera?"

"That's right," Frank said. "I need it for my work." He pulled out his card and gave it to the man.

The man read it, then smiled. "You know, I thought I seen you around. You eat up on the corner sometimes, that place with the funny name."

"La Femme Gatée."

"Yeah, that one," the man said. "The corn muffins are always from yesterday."

Frank smiled. "Can you help me with a camera?"

"I'll give you a two-hundred-and-fifty-dollar credit," the man said. "Fair enough?"

"Sounds good."

"I'm a fair man, that's the truth," the man said. "A lot of pawnbrokers, they're scum." He shook his head. "But not me." He thrust out his hand. "Lazlo Pipkin, nice to know you."

"Frank Clemons," Frank said as he shook his hand.

Pipkin smiled. "There used to be another gumshoe that hung out in the neighborhood," he said. "We're talking years back. Before the war. His name was Sanders, Sanderson, something like that, began with an S."

Frank nodded.

"Big guy," Pipkin added. "Big hands. I think he did a little bone-breaking for the shylocks." He shook his head. "I often thought, he must scare the shit out of people. They must pay up when they see him." He laughed to himself, then waved Frank over to another counter.

Frank spent the next few minutes making a choice, then swapped even for the lamp.

"One more thing," Frank said just before he left. He pulled the photograph of Mrs. Phillips from his jacket pocket. "Have you ever seen this woman before?"

Pipkin glanced at the photograph. "Yeah, I seen her," he said, as he returned the picture to Frank. "She pawned a few things over the last few months."

"What things?"

"Some jewelry. Nice stuff, too."

"Did she ever reclaim any of it?"

"No."

"Was she alone?"

"She always come in alone," Pipkin said.

"When did she come in last?"

Pipkin's eyes rolled toward the ceiling. "About two weeks ago, something like that."

"Do you have the dates?"

"Yeah, sure," Pipkin said. He disappeared into a small office, then returned. "Here are the tickets. They got the dates on them." He handed them to Frank. "See?"

Frank looked at them, took out his notebook and began to record the information that was on the ticket, the items, a watch and two gold bracelets, the date she'd pawned them, March 30, and the name she'd used, Elizabeth Lancaster.

"It's nice stuff," Pipkin said. "But it's jewelry, easier to sell. Not like a lamp. Worse comes to worse, you can always melt it down."

Frank smiled quietly as he continued to write.

"We get more rich types over here on the West Side than you'd think. They don't have no pawnshops over on the East Side."

Frank finished writing the information in his notebook and returned it to his pocket. "And that's the last time you saw her?"

"Yes."

"Did she mention why she was pawning her stuff?"

"No," Pipkin said. "But the ones from out of the neighborhood, they never tell you that kind of thing." He shrugged. "The other ones, they don't have to tell you. It's crack or the rent, or something like that."

"Did she say anything at all?"

Pipkin thought a moment. "She seemed real cold to me, business-like. She just wanted to pawn the stuff and get out. But you know how it is, you're in business, you like to talk to the people a little, so I started to talk to her. Nothing serious, just shoptalk, you know?"

Frank nodded.

"Anyway, I said to her, I said, 'I don't think you've ever pawned anything in here,' and her head shot up, and it was like her eyes closed down on me, like she was squeezing me, and in this real hard voice she said, 'There're a lot of things I haven't done before.' Then she just snapped up the money, and she was gone in a flash."

Frank took out his notebook and wrote down the remark, sharp, cold, terse, the only words he'd heard so far from her tightly drawn and silent mouth.

— 9 —

La Femme Gatée was only a few blocks away, and so after leaving the pawnshop, Frank walked up to it for a quick dinner. The man behind the counter greeted him as a regular, then took his usual order of ham and cheese on a roll.

"Be just a minute," the man said. "I'll bring it to you."

Frank nodded, took a Coke from the cooler across from the counter and headed for a table at the rear of the room.

It was nearly seven in the evening, and the place was empty except for a single couple, who sat drinking coffee in the back. While he waited for his sandwich, Frank watched them squabble quietly with each other.

"You can't beg 'em," the man said emphatically. "You look like a fucking creep, you do that."

The woman dropped her eyes. "I don't know how, Eddie." She was dressed in a soiled blouse, and an old blue sweater hung limply over her shrunken shoulders.

"Christsake," the man hissed at her. "You can't look like you ain't worth nothing, like they already said no. It don't work that way. You got to go after 'em, Frannie. You got to make 'em *see* you. Otherwise, they just go right by." He shook his head despairingly. "There ain't enough to you. You don't scare nobody, so they walk right through you, like you was air, like you was nothing."

The woman's eyes lifted toward him, her face broken but intent on his instructions. She fingered the napkin absently while she listened.

"You got to look 'em in the eye," the man told her. "You can't just

91

head away from 'em, like no matter what, they ain't gonna give you nothing."

The woman nodded meekly. "Okay, Eddie. I'll do better next time."

"We ain't got much time, Frannie," the man said hotly. "I ain't staying with you tonight, you don't get it straight."

"I'll get it straight," the woman said determinedly. She lifted her head. "I'll get it straight, no shit."

The man nodded, unconvinced. "Yeah, well, you got to. 'Cause if you don't come up with something, we'll be in the fucking park tonight, and I ain't staying there. You're gonna be on your fucking own, you understand?"

"I understand."

"It's fifteen bucks at the Mayfair," the man told her. "Fifteen fucking bucks, and you got to get it." He shook his head. "You got to do it, Frannie. Nobody'll get that close to me." His hand lifted toward his face. " 'Cause I got these spots on me."

"I'll do better, Eddie," the woman assured him. "I heard what you said. You got to come right up to 'em, look 'em straight."

"And mention kids," the man reminded her. He coughed into his fist, a hard, dry cough that he finally brought under control. When it was over, he looked half-dazed, as if he'd forgotten where he was.

"I'll look 'em straight, Eddie," the woman told him.

Her words seemed to return him to consciousness. "Yeah, yeah," he murmured weakly.

"And kids, too," the woman said, as if coaxing him back to earth. "I won't forget the kids."

"Right, kids," the man said. He drew in a long, feeble breath. "Like you got 'em in a hotel or something, you know what I mean?"

"Okay, Eddie."

The man nodded toward her coffee. "Well, finish it up, then. We got to get started."

Frank's sandwich arrived a moment later, and he ate it pleasurelessly while the man and woman stared mutely at each other before they finally struggled to their feet and headed out to the street. After that, he sat alone, his eyes moving continually toward the window, then beyond it, into the dark interior of the unfinished building that now towered over the neighborhood. Within a few months it would be finished, and the new residents would begin to take over, bringing their new demands for restaurants, clubs, boutiques. He wasn't sure what would be lost once the building was completed, only that something would, a rich, more concrete life of street scenes and loud music and something else that was even more important, but that he couldn't put his finger on.

He finished his sandwich, and headed down Forty-ninth Street toward his office. Up ahead, he could see a small, twisted figure staggering toward him, but the darkness concealed it until she came toward him in the grayish light of the single streetlamp which still shone between the avenues. It was the woman he'd seen in the restaurant only a few moments before, and she was moving toward him very firmly, her eyes fixed on his.

"Kids," she said as she came up to him, her hand outstretched. "I got to help my kids. They're in this hotel, and I got to get 'em out."

Frank said nothing. Not far away, he could see the man leaning against the wall, his head drooped forward as he coughed hoarsely into his fist.

"Things happen in them hotels," the woman said, "to them kids they got there."

Frank reached into his pocket for some change and came up with a couple of quarters. As he dropped it into her hand, he thought of the tower again, and realized instantly what would be lost when it was completed: the chance to see, every day, every hour, how much still remained to be done.

A black limousine was parked in front of his office, and as Frank approached it, a woman got out.

"Hi, Frank," she said.

It was Karen, his old lover, and suddenly, as he looked at her, a strange anger swept over him. It wasn't directed at her, he realized immediately, but at what had happened between them, the desert it had left behind, and as he looked at her, took in her sleek figure, her smooth skin, the lights that seemed always to be flickering in her hair, he knew with a sudden consuming emptiness how much he missed the old passion he had once felt for her, how dry his life had become without it.

"I guess you're surprised to see me," Karen said.

Frank nodded. "How you doing?"

"Fine," Karen said. She glanced toward his office. "May I come in?"

"Sure," Frank said. He led her down the stairs, through the corridor, then inside his office.

"Have a seat," he said after he'd turned on the light.

Karen looked at his desk. "Where's your lamp?"

Frank pulled the camera from his shoulders and placed it on his desk. "Somebody lifted it," he said. "It was all they took."

"I'm sorry," Karen said.

Frank smiled quietly. "Well, it speaks well for the lamp, right?"

Karen laughed slightly. "It's good to see you again, Frank," she said affectionately.

Frank shrugged. "What can I do for you, Karen?" he asked as he sat down behind his desk.

She looked faintly offended by his tone. "Does it have to be so businesslike?"

"You got married, didn't you?"

"Does that mean we can't be friends?"

"It means I can't."

"Why?"

"Because I can't think of you that way."

"Things change, Frank," Karen said. "They don't always have to be destroyed."

"I didn't pick you for a friend," Frank said. "For a friend, I picked an overweight, middle-aged Arab."

Karen laughed slightly.

"And when I'm with him," Frank said. "I never look at his legs or his neck or his mouth."

Karen's eyes darted away. "I thought we'd already lost that before you left."

"We had, but since then, there's been . . ."

Karen lifted her hand. "Please, Frank, I can't . . ."

"It's just the way it is, Karen," Frank said. "There's nothing I can do about it."

Her eyes watched him softly. "There's something about you . . . about us . . . that I will always miss."

"Me, too," Frank said with a slight shrug. "But so what?"

Karen looked at him coolly. "I think you've gotten a little harder than you were, Frank."

"A little older, that's all," Frank said impatiently. "You have less time to waste."

Karen straightened herself slightly. She looked faintly resentful, as if she'd been scolded and didn't like it. "I'd better go," she said. She smiled nervously as she stood up. "I'm not sure why I came anyway."

Frank remained in his chair. He said nothing.

For a moment, Karen lingered at the door, her eyes on him. "Actually, I do know. I just wanted to find out how you were doing." She looked around the room. "Are you still living here?"

"Yes."

"You just sleep on the sofa?"

Frank nodded.

A small smile fluttered to her lips. "So, I guess you don't have a woman in your life," she said.

For a moment, Frank thought she must be mocking him, then, almost instantly, he thought of the Puri Dai, and a wave of heat passed over him. He saw her arms as she had flung them upward under the hard light of the prison meeting room, saw her legs rise toward its bleak ceiling, and he realized that Farouk had been absolutely right that it had been a very long time.

He stood up immediately. "I have to go, Karen," he said. Then he swept by her quickly and headed through the door without so much as a backward glance at her astonished face.

She came into the room as she had the night before, with the matron at her arm. But this time she nodded almost imperceptibly when she saw him, then walked over and sat down at the table across from him.

He felt his body tense as she leaned toward him slightly, and for a moment, he wanted only to draw her into his arms, sit silently with her until he could sense the exact rhythm of her needs, then move determinedly to meet them.

"I talked to Leo Tannenbaum," he said finally. "Do you know who he is?"

She stared at him evenly and shook her head.

"He's the officer in charge of the investigation," Frank told her. "I'm sure he talked to you that night."

She made no response.

Frank smiled quietly. "Anyway," he said. "We went over the evidence against you. The blood on your sleeves, on the razor, under your fingernails, all that sort of thing."

She looked at him silently.

"I also went over to the place where it happened," Frank added. "I saw where the body was laid out." He stopped in the hope that she might speak.

She said nothing.

"It was laid out, wasn't it?" he asked. "She couldn't have fallen down that way."

She sat back slightly, her black eyes burning into him with a sudden anger. "Why are you doing this?" she asked vehemently, the words bursting out of her. So she could talk after all. Why now, he wondered, but did not dare ask, lest she stop again.

"Doing what?"

"Seeking out these things," she blurted. "Why can you not leave me alone?"

Frank shrugged. "Because," he stammered. "Because . . ."

"You must not do it," the Puri Dai told him.

Frank shook his head. "I have to."

"No," the Puri Dai said. Then she leaned over toward him. "No," she repeated adamantly.

"But I . . ."

She stood up and began to peer about.

Frank leaped to his feet. "What are you doing?"

She did not bother to look at him. "Matron," she called, "I am ready."

Frank looked at her desperately. "Don't go yet," he said. "I have a few things."

"Matron," the Puri Dai called, this time more loudly.

"Why are you doing this?" Frank demanded.

She turned to him. "Go," she said fiercely as she headed toward the door at the opposite end of the room.

"I've found out a lot," Frank called after her. "A lot." His mind raced to get out the details. "I know that Puri Dai couldn't possibly be your name."

The Puri Dai continued to move toward the door.

"It means Tribal Woman," Frank called after her.

She stopped and turned back toward him, easing her arm from the matron's grasp.

Frank looked at her squarely. "The Tribal Woman doesn't have a name," he said.

Her eyes were smoldering as she glared at him.

Frank jerked his notebook from his jacket pocket and flipped to the page he wanted. "This is a drawing I made. It shows the woman's body."

She did not look at the drawing.

"Her arms are stretched out," Frank went on. "What was she reaching for?"

The Puri Dai's eyes glistened for a moment, then turned dry again.

"What was she reaching for?" Frank repeated, almost tauntingly.

The Puri Dai said nothing.

Frank stepped toward her, pulled the bead from his jacket pocket and held it up to her. "If you hadn't wanted to see me, why did you send me this?"

Her eyes widened as she looked at it.

"Why would you have left this at my office?" Frank demanded.

Her eyes shot over to him. "I sent you nothing," she said in a swift, resentful whisper.

Frank stood his ground. "Well, someone did," he said. "I didn't steal it."

She stared at him fiercely. "It was not for you," she said. "The other."

"Other?"

"The one who came for his fortune."

Frank's lips parted wordlessly.

"The large one," she hissed under her breath, "who chose his destiny."

"Farouk," Frank murmured, his heart sinking, as if he'd lost something precious and could not regain it. "You wanted him?"

"Not I," the woman said. "Her."

"Who?"

"Salome."

"The dead woman?"

The Puri Dai nodded, her eyes lowering somewhat. "Salome," she repeated softly. "It was not I who sent for you."

She lifted her right hand slightly. It was very brown, and Frank found that he could barely control his urge to take it in his own. "Go," she said as she pointed toward the opposite door. "Go."

Frank didn't move. "Do you want me to get Farouk for you?" he asked.

She shook her head.

"What was Farouk to her?"

She continued to stare at him determinedly. "Go," she repeated.

Still, Frank remained in place. "Did she know Farouk?" he asked insistently.

The Puri Dai turned back toward the door just as the guard stepped through it. "I am ready," she said.

The guard opened the door and stepped back to let her pass through.

Frank continued to walk toward her. "What did she want from Farouk?" he demanded.

Silence.

"Was she afraid?" Frank asked. He could feel a strange desperation overtaking him, the sense that he was losing the slender grasp he still had on the Puri Dai.

He stepped forward quickly and touched her shoulder. "If I brought him here, would you talk to him?" he asked.

She stopped and once against turned toward him. "No," she said adamantly. "Not to him. Not to you."

She turned back toward the door, but Frank stepped around to block her path. "Please, you have to understand that I . . ."

She lifted her hand commandingly and silenced him. "It is not for you to do," she said.

Frank gazed at her quietly. He could feel her breath on his eyes.

"I think you'd better go, mister," the guard said sternly.

Frank did not seem to hear her. "Why did you dance?" he asked softly, his eyes fixed on the Puri Dai's shoulders. "The last time I was here. Why did you do that?"

The Puri Dai said nothing. Her hand pressed forward, palm out, as if easing him from her path.

"It was because you still have some reason to live, wasn't it?" Frank said. "What is it? What is that reason?"

The woman's eyes drifted from him.

"The razor," Frank added. "Whose is it?"

She stared at him lethally.

He felt something grow suddenly cold and empty inside himself. "A man," he said. "You must have a man."

Her eyes seemed to grow very small, the pupils to all but disappear.

Frank drew in a deep breath, nearly trembling when he spoke. "Is he your husband?"

She turned away from him.

"Your lover?"

Silence.

"Are you protecting him?" Frank demanded.

Her eyes shot back to him, dark and fiery, rocked by furies which seemed older than herself. "Never," she hissed in a voice that seemed to come from the depths of an ageless enmity. "Upon my mother's grave."

It was almost two in the morning before Farouk finally came through the door of the small after-hours place where they'd first met.

He saw Frank immediately, lumbered over and sat down.

"Good evening," he said quietly. He turned to the old man who had taken Toby's place at the bar. *"Café turco,"* he said.

Frank took the bead out of his jacket pocket and pressed it toward him. "I found out tonight that this was for you," he said tiredly.

Farouk looked closely at the bead. "For me?"

"Yes."

Farouk took the bead from Frank's hand and turned it over slowly. "It is from the Puri Dai?"

"No."

"But it is like the others," Farouk said. "The ones that made the curtain."

"Yeah," Frank said. "But it's from the other woman."

Farouk's eyes squeezed together slowly. "The one who told my fortune?"

"Yes."

"How do you know this?"

"The Puri Dai."

"She spoke to you?"

"A little."

"And told you that it was the fortune-teller who brought the bead?"

Frank nodded.

Farouk leaned back in his seat, suddenly studying Frank's face more closely. "She must have seen me coming from your office. She must have thought that it was where I lived."

"Probably."

Farouk's eyes continued to watch Frank intently. "So it was to me she came," he said slowly. "Not you."

"Yes."

The Turkish coffee arrived, and Farouk took a long slow sip, then lowered the cup to the table. "Well, now she has spoken," he said, "the Puri Dai."

"Yes, she has."

"And what else has she said?"

"Not much," Frank said. "But at least she said enough for us to know where the bead came from. The first time I saw her, she wouldn't talk to me at all." He shook his head, puzzled. "The only thing she did was dance."

Farouk's eyes brightened. "Ah yes, that is called the *baile jondo,* the Deep Dance."

"What does it mean?"

"It does not *mean* anything," Farouk said. "It only expresses."

"Expresses what?"

"Many things, I suppose," Farouk said with a wry turn of his lips. "For passions that cannot be released in any other way, the *baile jondo* speaks for such things, for primitive sensations, violence and desolation and sensuality, all these things in one."

"Why do they come out in a dance?"

"Because these things, they cannot be controlled once they are set loose," Farouk told him. "They are too dangerous, and if they are released, all things will change." He could see that Frank did not understand him, and so he elaborated a bit. "Men wish to be assured that tomorrow will be the same as today. But there are times when this need is endangered by other things. These things come from the blood, from the earth. They are as they have always been. It is how the Immortals live in us, through our passions."

"And what does the Deep Dance have to do with them?"

"It allows us to shake them off, so that we may be left to our drudgery," Farouk said with a sudden astonishing weariness. "But it also allows us to know that they were there, that they call to us in our sorrow." He took a quiet sip from the cup, then set it down and smiled very softly. "After the dance, she spoke, yes?"

"Only after I came back," Frank said. "And only a few words."

Farouk smiled knowingly. "They are not known for words, the Puri Dai."

Frank leaned toward him. "How do you know so much about Gypsies, Farouk?"

Farouk looked as if it were a question he had been waiting to answer for a long time. "Long ago, my grandfather traveled the Silk Road across the deserts of Arabia," he said. "When my father was a young man—really no more than a boy—my grandfather returned with a young girl, very dark, with black eyes." He turned away slightly and quickly put on his glasses, then returned his eyes to Frank. "She was to be a servant—actually, a slave."

"Slave?"

"She was won by my grandfather," Farouk said. "The wager, I believe, was over horses."

"A race?"

Farouk smiled knowingly. "No horse in the world can defeat an Arabian stallion. The Gypsy leader never had a chance."

"She was a Gypsy?"

"As beautiful a one as ever lived," Farouk said. "And she struck the heart of my father." He laughed quietly. "A circumstance upon which—to say the least—my grandfather had not planned. Imagine, that such a man's son should fall in love with a servant girl, that this servant girl should be a Christian, or at least, not a Moslem. Imagine."

"What happened?"

"They ran away," Farouk said. He lifted his arm in the shadowy light and moved it slowly in a wide angle. "Across the desert wastes. My father left the life of the caravan to run hashish in a small boat on the Mediterranean. But always they were together." The arm descended for a moment, then a single hand rose again, and drew the glasses from his eyes. He leaned forward, his face lit by the single candle on the table. "It was from her, my friend, that comes the blackness of my eyes."

Frank sat back. "Your mother?"

Farouk's face seemed to glow gently in the shadowy light. "She was one who remembered everything, all the customs of her people."

Farouk returned the glasses to his eyes. "Now," he said, "since all of this has come to light, how may I be of assistance?"

Frank shrugged. "To tell you the truth, Farouk, I don't know where to begin."

Farouk clapped his hands together softly. "Ah," he said. "Then we are already at the place where it is best to be."

— 11 —

From across the avenue, Farouk's eyes scanned the large window. He could see the blue curtain which covered it, but everything else was dark. "Perhaps she has left already," he said.

Frank shook his head. "According to Tannenbaum, she leaves at around three A.M."

Farouk glanced at his watch. "The Gitano have their own time."

"Let's wait a while longer," Frank said. "Just to be sure."

Only a few seconds later, the woman emerged from the dark first-floor landing, turned left and headed uptown. She wore a long coat, and her hair was bound up in a dark-red scarf.

Farouk watched her closely. "And she goes to Saint Teresa's?" he asked.

"That's what she told Tannenbaum."

"Every night?"

Frank nodded.

The two of them continued to watch the old woman as she headed north along Tenth Avenue, then crossed it and disappeared up Forty-eighth Street.

"Now, we can go," Farouk said happily.

They moved quickly across the street, Farouk's eyes surveying the upper floors. The windows were dark, as if the apartments above the fortune-teller's shop had already been abandoned.

At the window of the building Farouk drew Frank toward him, so that they both stood beneath the awning of the fortune-teller's shop.

"Just a moment," he said. His eyes moved along the door, then down along the side of the building. "If matters have not changed with the Gitano, there is always a key left for the wandering guest."

"You mean, on the outside?"

"On the outside, yes," Farouk told him. He shifted his attention to the top of the iron grate that covered the window. "Up there," he said. He walked a few feet to the edge of the grate, raised himself onto the tips of his toes and ran his fingers along the edge of the grate. "Nothing."

Farouk shook his head. "It is somewhere, the key," he said with certainty, as his eyes turned toward the awning itself. "Perhaps, there," he said after a moment. He pointed to the narrow rod which supported the cloth itself as his eyes shifted to Frank. "Look there."

Frank stepped over to it and ran his fingers along its edge. There was a very slender trough which stretched between the rod and the awning's steel supports. About halfway from the edge, he felt a loose piece of metal. He pulled it out.

Farouk smiled proudly. "Ah, you see. The ways of the Gitano do not change." He thrust out his hand and Frank dropped the key into it.

Farouk walked over to the door and inserted the key. The door opened, and they stepped into the dense interior darkness of the building.

Frank took out a book of matches and struck one. The room glowed in a faint reddish light, until Farouk found the light switch and turned it on.

Frank waved out the match, then allowed his eyes to move about the room.

The red bead curtains were gone.

"Maybe she's not coming back," Frank said.

Farouk glanced at the small table and the two metal folding chairs which still remained in the front room. "No, she will return," he said. "She would not leave these things behind."

He stepped into the second room and switched on the light. It was entirely empty.

Frank walked up alongside him, and for a moment they stood silently together.

"There was a white wicker chair right there," Frank said as he pointed to the center of the room. "That's where I saw the woman. And there was a small table beside it."

"And that was all?"

"There was some kind of statue," Frank told him. "And there was a candle and a medallion."

Farouk smiled distantly. "The Gitano are in love with ritual," he said matter-of-factly. "What did the statue look like?"

"It was a woman," Frank said. "She was dressed in robes and there was a hood over her head." He shrugged. "It looked like some sort of religious thing. Like in a church. Like the Virgin Mary, except . . ."

Farouk nodded casually as his eyes continued to scan the room. "Except what?"

"Except that she looked like she was walking in water, some kind of foamy water."

Farouk's eyes shot over to him. "Foamy water? You mean, like the sea?"

Frank nodded.

Farouk's face grew more concentrated. "And the medallion? What did it look like?"

"There was a scorpion on it," Frank told him. "That's all I remember."

Farouk walked over to the door that led into the next room and opened it. It was empty except for a large foam-rubber mattress.

"There were three beds in there," Frank said, as he walked up and glanced inside.

"Three beds in this one room?"

"Yes."

"So they all slept together, the women?"

"In the same room, yes."

Farouk nodded thoughtfully, then looked across the room to where the outline of the woman's body could still be seen on the unpainted wooden floor.

"That's where the body was," Frank told him.

Farouk walked over to the outline and studied it for a moment. "How was the body arranged?" he asked.

"She was facedown," Frank told him. "Lying on her stomach."

"And where was her head?"

"Near the door."

Farouk studied the outline a few more minutes, then nodded toward the third door. "It was open when the woman was killed," he said. "You can tell by the bloodstains. The bottom of the door is very near the floor. It would have made a pattern in the blood if it had been opened after the murder."

"Yes, it would have," Frank said.

Farouk thought a moment longer, then moved over directly in front of the now closed door. For a time, he stared at the door itself, then slowly, as if in response to some signal Frank couldn't see, he sank down onto his knees. "She was like this," he said quietly, "on her knees, facing the door."

"Yes, that's right," Frank said almost to himself.

"And the Puri Dai," Farouk added grimly as he got to his feet, "if it was the Puri Dai, she stood behind her, pulled her head back, exposing the throat, and then drew the razor across it." Farouk blinked rapidly, as if to bring himself back to earth. "And that was the end of it."

Frank thought a moment, his eyes fixed on the door lock. "Someone opened the door," he said, "so that . . ." In his mind he could almost see it, the woman on her knees, her head drawn back by the murderer's hand, and the door opening, slowly opening, so that whoever waited behind the door could see the old fortune-teller die.

Frank stepped over to the door and quickly opened it. A small table still rested at one corner, but the small square mat which had stretched out in front of it was gone. "This room is like I remember it," he said. "Everything's still here, except for a piece of foam rubber." He turned to Farouk. "It looked like a shrine, something like that."

Farouk stepped inside and looked around carefully. Then, suddenly, he cocked his head to the right and concentrated on the hook-and-eye latch that dangled from the jamb. For a few seconds, he stared at it carefully, then he raised his hand and touched it with his fingers. "Not a shrine, I think."

Frank looked at him quizzically.

"A cell," Farouk added. He drew the door closed and inserted the lock. "It was used to lock someone in the room."

"The Puri Dai?" Frank asked instantly. "You think she was some kind of prisoner."

Farouk didn't answer. Instead, he suddenly lifted his face upward and sniffed the air.

"What is it?" Frank asked.

Farouk glanced about, until his eyes settled on a few drops of brownish liquid that dotted the small tabletop. He dipped the tip of his index finger into one of the droplets, then brought it to his nose and sniffed again. "Raki," he said. "Just as I thought."

Frank stared at him wonderingly. "What?"

Farouk brought his finger to Frank's nose. "Do you smell that sweetness?"

Frank inhaled deeply. "Yes."

Farouk smiled wistfully. "That is raki. It is a drink, a liqueur made of raisins. It is a Turkish drink, not common in this country."

"Turkish?"

"Yes," Farouk said.

"You mean, they're not . . ."

"No, they are Gypsies, all right," Farouk said, anticipating Frank's question. He pointed to the odd-shaped instruments that hung from the wall. "Those are known only to the Gitano," he said. Then he shook his head quickly, and stepped out of the small room, edging his large belly carefully out the door. For a moment he seemed lost in thought, his large eyes strangely distant, as if he were seeing other worlds, vanished lands. Then suddenly he seemed to return to himself. "Where is the kitchen?" he asked.

Frank shrugged.

"Probably back there," Farouk said. He moved quickly out of the room, down a very short corridor to another small room. "Yes, here it is," he said as he stepped into it.

Frank stopped at the entrance. "What are you looking for?"

Farouk didn't answer. Instead, he moved quickly from one cabinet to the next, opening them one by one, then moving on to the drawers, the refrigerator, the small dark space beneath the sink.

When he'd finished, he stood near the center of the room, thinking to himself. "Three women," he said almost to himself. His eyes shot over to Frank. "Is that what you think? That there were three women in this place?"

"Yes."

"And no one else?"

"As far as I know."

Farouk shook his head. "I do not think so, Frank."

"Why not?"

Farouk brought his finger up to his nose again. "Because raki is not a woman's drink," he said. "And whoever drank it here last took the bottle with him."

Frank shrugged. "It could have been a guest. Someone passing through."

Farouk nodded. "That is possible," he said. Then he walked over to the small bathroom which adjoined the kitchen and turned on the light. He opened the small medicine cabinet, concentrating on the array of tubes and bottles which were crowded onto its three small glass shelves.

Frank ticked off the things he saw. "Toothpaste, perfume, hairpins."

Farouk continued to glance about.

"Lipstick, rouge, eyeliner," Frank went on. "I don't see anything that would belong to a man."

Farouk turned toward him. "Perhaps," he said. Then he drew a small pocket knife from his trousers, opened its slenderest blade and slid it into the tiny crevice where the sink's faucet met the basin. "Ah, yes," he said with sudden satisfaction as he brought the blade out once again.

Frank stepped over toward him and watched as Farouk brought the blade near his eyes. It was covered with tiny black flecks.

"Not the strands of a woman's hair," Farouk said, "but the leavings of a beard."

"A man," Frank breathed. "But why aren't there any other signs?"

"Because he does not live here," Farouk said, "but only comes to them in the night, yes?"

"And leaves in the morning," Frank added.

"After he has shaved," Farouk said. He glanced at his watch. "Come now, we must go."

They returned to Frank's office, moving down the nearly deserted sidestreets, their eyes searching up ahead for the old Gypsy. Finally they disappeared down the cement stairs, stepped over the old woman who was sleeping soundly at the bottom and made their way into the office.

Farouk sat in the old sofa by the window and watched while Frank retrieved the bottle from his desk and poured each of them a shot in a paper cup.

Farouk lifted his slightly, in a faint toast, then drank.

Frank sat down behind his desk. "What are you thinking, Farouk?" he asked bluntly.

One of Farouk's eyebrows arched gently. "Thinking? Many things, as you know."

"About tonight," Frank said. "That place."

Farouk considered the question for a moment, as if carefully weighing his answer. "I think that there is one who wishes his presence to be concealed. This person is a man, and for a time at least he has visited with the women."

"But where does that leave us?"

"Perhaps nowhere of importance." Farouk admitted. "But when one wishes to hide himself, it causes me to wonder why." He took another sip from the cup, then rested it on his large thigh. "You mentioned the statue," he said.

Frank nodded.

"Describe it for me again."

Frank shrugged slightly. "It wasn't much of anything. It looked religious, sort of like those plaster ones you see of Mary."

"You are a Christian?" Farouk asked.

"I'm nothing," Frank told him. "I was raised a Christian."

"Catholic?"

"No."

"But you said that it looked rather like the Virgin Mary?"

"That's right."

"*Like* the Virgin Mary," Farouk said emphatically. "It was not the Holy Mother herself?"

Frank shook his head. "It looked different somehow."

"In what way?"

"Well, like I told you, she looked as if she were walking in water."

"And it was foamy, this water? As if it were the sea, as if she were walking onto the beach?"

Frank nodded. "Yeah, that's the way it looked."

Farouk's eyes closed thoughtfully. "Was she carrying a child?"

"No."

"Was there a halo?"

"No."

"And you said she was wearing a purple robe, is that right? With a hood?"

"With a hood."

"And the hood was up?"

"Yes."

Farouk opened his eyes and smiled. "Forgive me these questions, but the more detail the description has, the better I can use it."

Frank took a sip from the cup. "Use it how?"

"To discover things," Farouk replied idly. "And there was also a medallion?"

"Brass," Frank said.

"Large? Small?"

"I'd say it was about four inches in diameter."

"And there was a scorpion, you said."

"That's right," Frank told him, "And on the Puri Dai, too."

"There were scorpions on her? You mean . . ."

"Embroidered on her blouse," Frank said quickly. "One over each breast."

Farouk sat back slightly, raised the cup toward his lips, then stopped and brought it down again. "I think it is now time for me to meet the Puri Dai."

Frank nodded.

Farouk glanced at his watch. "But not tonight," he said. "Toby has returned, and I must see her home." He got to his feet. "Tomorrow morning, then?"

Frank shook his head. "No, I can't," he said.

Farouk looked at him, surprised.

"The day case," Frank reminded him.

"Ah yes, the day case," Farouk said. "That which feeds the body and leaves the soul to starve."

— 12 —

Frank waited for the buzzer to ring, then stepped into the office's small reception area. The woman behind the desk nodded to him politely as he walked over to her.

"May I help you, sir?" she asked.

"I'd like to see Dr. Powers," Frank told him. He pulled out one of a collection of cards which Farouk had assembled for him over the past months. This one identified him as a professional tax consultant, and for a moment he tried to assume the manner of one: cool, professional, a man who could spot vultures from a great distance.

"Do you have an appointment?" the woman asked, after she'd glanced at the card.

"No, I don't," Frank said politely. "That's why I came so early. I thought that if the doctor had a moment, he might be willing to see me. I think he'd be interested in what I have to say."

"And you're a tax consultant, is that right?" the woman asked.

"Yes."

She didn't seem to doubt it, and Frank could feel himself assuming the role a bit more casually. Still, he could sense the overall stiffness of his manner, and for a moment he envied the way Farouk could pull it off, the way he could almost become the man he pretended to be.

"I know it's early," he said. "But I think Dr. Powers would profit by seeing me."

"I understand," the woman said. "Just a moment." She disappeared into the back of the office, and while she was gone, Frank dropped the tax consultant pose and looked the place over the way he always did, searching for that odd detail that would bring everything else into focus. He noted the small tables and chairs which dotted the waiting room, the spray of flowers in the corner, the overall elegance of the place, its antiseptic calm.

He drew in a deep, faintly weary breath and sat down in one of the small chairs near the front desk. His eyes ached slightly, and he rubbed them gently. They felt large and faintly sore, as if swollen with his long sleeplessness. He closed them for a moment, then opened them again and scanned the room a second time.

The walls were pale blue, and an assortment of framed Broadway posters hung from them, old broadsides advertising *Oklahoma!*, *Mame*, *The Sound of Music*. Aside from them, there was only one other picture, a very ornately drawn portrait of a woman whose eyes seemed to watch the world from behind a pale, gossamer screen. The eyes themselves were large and blue, and something about them disturbed him. For a time, he couldn't quite figure out what it was. Then, suddenly, he knew. Their color was the exact shade of the walls. Frank realized that either the walls or the eyes had been painted to match the other's color.

He was still looking at the eyes when the receptionist returned. "Dr. Powers will see you now, Mr. Clemons," she said. "But it'll have to be brief."

"Thank you."

"Just follow me, please."

She led him down a short corridor, then into the doctor's consulting room. Powers sat behind a large glass-topped desk, his back to the window. He rose immediately. "Good morning, Mr. Clemons," he said. He smiled brightly and offered his hand.

It was a fat little hand, very pink and pudgy, but Frank pumped it enthusiastically, as he thought a tax consultant would.

"Good morning, Dr. Powers," he said.

"Please, sit down," Powers told him. The smile stayed on his face, as if someone had pasted it there because without it there would have been no face at all.

Frank took a seat in front of Powers's desk. He crossed his legs primly, like he'd seen men do in ads for expensive suits, and folded his hands in his lap. "Thanks for seeing me without an appointment," he said.

"Happy to do it," Powers said. "Would you like some coffee?"

"No, thanks."

The smile flexed a little, as if Powers were testing his lips for longer service later on. "So, tax consultancy," he said cheerfully. "Tax avoidance, not evasion, I hope."

He was a large man, but the longer Frank observed him, the more light and buoyant he seemed. He looked swollen and overweight, but like a beachball—puffed out, yet empty.

"Like everyone else, I'm always interested in saving money," he said. "So, what exactly do you do?"

Frank brought himself to attention. "I provide advice and assistance, particularly to people in private occupations." It sounded exactly like something Farouk would have come up with, and he felt vaguely pleased by it. "Sometimes in difficult matters," he added without elaborating.

"Mostly doctors?"

"Quite a few doctors."

"So you know the particular kinds of expenses we have?"

"Yes," Frank said. Then he guessed. "Transporting specimens, for example."

"No, I use a local lab, Pentatex, over on Second Avenue," Powers said. "They're very good."

"Yes, they are," Frank said authoritatively. "You send all your lab work from this office?"

Powers looked at him quizzically.

"I mean, you have only one office?" Frank explained.

"Yes."

"You don't work out of your home?"

"No."

"Other deductions apply for work out of the home," Frank told him, in a voice that sounded as if he actually knew what he was talking about.

"Well, I'm afraid they wouldn't apply to me," Powers said.

"So you use this office exclusively?"

"Yes."

"And a hospital, of course."

"Hospital?"

"Well, there are always certain costs which are involved in hospital affiliations," Frank added.

Powers said nothing.

Frank smiled disarmingly. "Which hospital do you work with?"

Powers hesitated for a moment, then answered. "Fifth Avenue General."

Frank nodded appreciatively. "That's a fine hospital," he said.

"Yes, it is," Powers said. "Now, about your service, advice you said?"

"Well, the new tax code is very complex," Frank told him. "There are a great many deductions that aren't as obvious as they should be. And the guidelines aren't as precise as people think."

"Which means?"

"That you have to know what you're doing," Frank said. "And that many people are too busy to do the kind of study they need to use the new code to their advantage."

"You mean, even skilled accountants?"

"Even very skilled accountants."

"But you've studied it all very well, I suppose?"

Frank nodded. "Particularly for people who have a net income of more than half a million dollars."

Powers smiled proudly. "Like me?"

Frank nodded. It had been a good guess. "Have you practiced medicine in New York State for a long time?" he asked.

"Only a few years."

"Before that?"

"Pennsylvania," Powers said.

"Is that where you went to school?"

"No," Powers said. "Boston."

"Harvard?"

Powers shook his head, shifting the smile left and right. "I only wish. With a Harvard medical degree, I'd have probably gotten to Fifth Avenue a lot faster." He cleared his throat softly. "No, I went to Tufts. I graduated in the class of '68."

Frank smiled amiably. "Did you like Boston?"

"It was all right," Powers said. "But I wanted to get back to New York."

"So you've lived here before?" Frank said, trying for a tone of small talk to hide the needle of interrogation.

"Oh, yes," Powers said. "When I was a wild young thing. You know, like so many others, trying to make it in the big city, make your mark."

"But you left," Frank said.

"Yes, and most people don't come back once they do that," Powers said. "But not me. As you can see, I've returned."

Frank decided it was time to throw him a bone. "And very successfully," he said.

"Yes," Powers said. "That was also part of the dream. To return to New York on my own terms." The smile stretched a little. "I never got it out of my blood, I guess," he added, "the city."

"Well, it looks like things have gone well for you."

Powers cocked his head slightly. "You know, you don't exactly sound like a native yourself."

"No, I'm not."

"Southern accent, of course," Powers said thoughtfully. "But not Virginia, and not Mississippi." He laughed. "I'm quite good at doing accents. It was one of my strong suits." He glanced toward the window, the sweep of Manhattan. "Anyway, I had to get back to New York," he said. "I love the atmosphere. The pace, you know, the excitement. It's my kind of town."

Frank grinned back at him. "Absolutely."

Powers looked pleased. "Well, I'd like to talk to you about this again," he said. "Shall we set up an appointment?"

Frank took out his notebook, flipped to a blank page and pretended to study it. "How about Saturday?"

"That sounds good," Powers told him. "Providing it can be early in the evening."

Frank glanced back at the empty page. "Well, I have another appointment at four that afternoon, but I should be free by six."

"Six would be fine," Powers said. He stood up. "Do you know Broadway Lights, the restaurant?" Frank nodded. "Shall we meet there?"

"Good," Frank said. He offered his hand and Powers shook it pleasantly, then escorted him back to the outer office.

"Well, thanks for coming by," Powers said.

"Thanks for seeing me on such short notice," Frank told him. He glanced about the office again. "The place looks nice."

"Broadway," Powers said dreamily as his eyes drifted from one poster to the next. "It's so romantic, don't you think?"

Frank nodded.

"I just love it," Powers added rapturously, as if it were a holy word. "The Great White Way."

Frank smiled pleasantly. The Boulevard of Broken Dreams, he thought.

It was exactly the sort of thing he knew he'd do badly, and so after leaving Dr. Powers's office, Frank walked to the nearest telephone and called Farouk.

"Yes?" Farouk said, using the only word he ever used to answer the phone.

"It's Frank, I have something for you."

"About the Puri Dai?" Farouk asked quickly. "I thought that you couldn't . . ."

"No, it's not about her," Frank told him. "It has to do with the day case."

"Ah, yes," Farouk said.

"I haven't mentioned much about it."

"It has not been worthy."

"Well, the thing is, it's taken a turn you can help me with."

Farouk gave a short laugh. "So now it involves a little paperwork, yes?"

"That's right."

"Where shall I meet you?"

"Well, as it turns out, I'm not too far from the library."

"The one on Fifth Avenue?"

"Yeah."

"I'll be there in twenty minutes," Farouk said.

* * *

He made it in only fifteen minutes, walking briskly up the stairs, then groaning slightly as he lowered himself onto the cement steps beside Frank.

"The summer, it is coming soon," he said. He pulled a white handkerchief from his jacket pocket and wiped his great bald head. "So, the day case."

Frank nodded.

Farouk returned the handkerchief to his pocket. "How may I be of assistance?"

"The whole thing revolves around a woman," Frank began. "The husband noticed that his wife has been acting a little strangely, and that some of her jewelry has been disappearing."

Farouk nodded. "I see."

"The wife has been hocking jewelry at that little place near us on Eighth Avenue," Frank added.

"You spoke to Lazlo?"

"Who?"

"The old man who runs the shop," Farouk said. "Lazlo Pipkin."

"Yeah, I talked to him."

"From him, you get the truth."

"That's the way it sounded to me."

Farouk's eyes drifted toward the street, following a tall woman as she made her way northward up Fifth Avenue. "So you want to find out about the jewelry?"

"The husband's more concerned about the woman than the jewelry."

Farouk continued to watch the woman. "Are you certain of this?"

"I think so."

Frank's answer seemed to satisfy him. "All right," he said. "And what have you discovered about the woman?"

"I've followed her for a couple of days," Frank said. He took out his notebook. "On Monday she went to the Pierre Hotel. She belongs to a group that wants to save the rain forest. She stayed there a couple of hours, then took a cab to see a gynecologist named Kevin Powers. She got out at his house, or at least I guess it's his house. Anyway, it's in the Village."

"And the address?"

"One-twenty-four West Twelfth Street."

Farouk nodded.

Frank looked at him curiously. "Don't you ever take anything down?"

"Everything," Farouk said. "But not on paper."

Frank shook his head, then looked back down at his notebook. "The next day she went to the Dakota and saw a man named Preston R. Devine. He runs some sort of import business. Allied Global-East. The offices are in the diamond district. On West Forty-seventh Street. She goes there fairly often, and she uses a false name at the door."

Farouk looked at Frank knowingly. "Then it is perhaps an affair of the heart, yes?"

"It's possible," Frank said. "They never leave the man's apartment."

Farouk smiled sadly. "Betrayal, I am afraid, is often a matter of small rooms and drawn shades." He turned to Frank. "How long was she with this man?"

"Couple of hours," Frank told him. "She uses the name Driscoll when she sees him. And after she left him, she took a walk in the park. But there was a reason for that. I think she used it for a drop-off."

Suddenly Farouk seemed slightly more interested. "Drop-off?"

"She left her purse near the Alice in Wonderland statue."

"For whom did she do this?"

"I don't know."

Farouk looked at him reproachfully.

"By the time I got back to the statue, the purse was gone," Frank explained.

"I see," Farouk said. "Anything more?"

"This morning she's with her husband," Frank told him. "But I'll be trailing her this afternoon. He said they'd be back home by around noon."

Farouk nodded.

. "So since she was covered for the morning," Frank went on, "I decided to check up on the doctor."

Farouk leaned forward, his eyes rising up the long gray line of the business tower which rose across the street. "And learned what?"

"Nothing," Frank told him.

Farouk drew himself back slightly. "Which is why you are in need of my assistance," he said with a wry smile.

"That's right," Frank said.

"Good," Farouk said. "Now, tell me what you know of this person?"

Frank turned the page of his notebook. "His name is Kevin A. Powers. He says he went to Tufts for his medical degree. He graduated in 1968."

Farouk nodded. "Good. Anything else?"

"He's associated with Fifth Avenue General," Frank added. "And he gets his lab work done at a place called Pentatex." He closed his notebook and returned it to his pocket. "That's all I've got."

Farouk looked satisfied. "It is enough," he said.

"Well, what I'd like for you to . . ."

Farouk raised his hand to silence him. "If what I bring you is of no assistance, then you owe me nothing." He pulled himself to his feet. "I will see you tonight."

"Do you want to meet at my office?"

"That is fine."

"When?"

Farouk shrugged. "It is best for you to decide."

"Well, Phillips usually comes home at around six," Frank said. "I should be back on Forty-ninth Street not long after that. We can go over what you've found out."

Farouk nodded. "Yes," he said. "I should have discovered certain things by then." He smiled quietly. "I shall not take up too much of your time."

Frank shrugged. "Take as long as you need."

Farouk shook his head determinedly. "No," he said. "By then it will be late."

"Why would that matter?"

"For the night case," Farouk said, as if reminding Frank of some ancient and incontestable duty which could not be denied.

13

Frank continued to sit on the steps of the library for a time after Farouk had gone inside. It was almost noon, and the lunchtime crowds swarmed all around him. At the bottom of the steps, a skinny man in a black leotard had tied himself up in loops of chains and was busily entertaining the people with his escape. They applauded each time another length of the chain fell free, and after a while, Frank found their celebration of such meaningless liberation oddly discomforting and walked away, heading north up Fifth Avenue until he reached Sixty-fourth Street.

From the corner, he could see the Phillips brownstone, and so he remained at some distance, trying to vary his positions day to day in the hope of keeping his cover for as long as he could. Across the avenue, the borders of Central Park had begun to take on the faintly greenish tone of early spring, and as he looked out into it, his mind shifted back to the light-blue walls in Powers's reception area, and then the portrait that hung from one of them, the matching color in the woman's strangely distant eyes. After a while, he could feel himself becoming lost in such pointless concentration, and so he blinked hard and drew his eyes away from the park, his mind away from the portrait, and fixed them on the brownstone which stood near the middle of the block, perhaps a hundred feet away.

He was still watching it nearly an hour later when a car stopped in front of it. Mr. Phillips got out and walked to the passenger side. He opened the door and Mrs. Phillips stepped out as well. He kissed her lightly, then got back in the car.

Frank shrank back slightly as the car moved toward him very

slowly until it halted at the corner, and he saw Mr. Phillips's eyes sweep over to him, then nod slightly as he pulled away.

Mrs. Phillips remained on the street, glancing quickly at her watch once Mr. Phillips had turned the corner. Then, instead of going inside, she headed east toward Madison Avenue, and Frank went after her, walking as quickly as he could to keep her in sight, but holding himself far enough back to be nothing more than a distant figure, should she glance over her shoulder.

But she never glanced back. Instead, she moved forward hurriedly, her slender figure weaving in and out of the scattered pedestrians who surrounded her.

As Frank continued after her, he took out his notebook jotted down the time, and then the few observations which struck him as he walked. She was moving faster, as if hurrying somewhere, until she finally reached the corner of Madison Avenue. She stopped abruptly, glanced at her watch, then looked downtown, as if searching for a cab. But instead of raising her arm to hail one, she turned right, headed down the avenue for several blocks, then abruptly turned on her heels and walked to a shop window. For a moment, she stood at the window, facing it silently. Then she turned again, walked to the curb and glanced southward a second time.

Even from a distance, Frank could make out a certain strained quality in her posture. Her head was held high, but she moved it in quick, birdlike jerks, and her skin seemed to tighten around her bones, as if trying to squeeze out their dark-red marrow.

Then suddenly, her whole body slumped slightly, her shoulders dropping like someone who'd just released a long-held breath, and she trudged a few yards down the avenue to a telephone booth and stepped inside.

Frank continued to move toward her, but slowly. He could see her fumbling edgily in her purse for a moment before she drew out a silver telephone credit card. Then she picked up the receiver, read off the card number and waited while the operator made the call.

Frank closed in slightly, but only near enough to tell that she never spoke into the receiver. After a moment, she returned it to its cradle, then straightened herself and backed out of the booth. For a time, she looked oddly disoriented, as if she didn't know exactly what to do. Then she simply started walking back.

When she was far enough away, Frank rushed into the booth. He pulled out his notebook to the page where he'd written down all the important numbers Mr. Phillips had given him, and dialed the operator.

"New York Telephone," the operator said. "May I help you?"

"Yeah, thanks," Frank said quickly. Up ahead he could see Mrs. Phillips's body moving farther and farther away from him. "I just made a credit card call, but I think I may have given you the wrong number."

"What is your card number, sir?"

Frank read the number.

"And how can I help you?" the operator asked.

"I was wondering if you could tell me the number that was called."

"I can if it was completed," the operator said.

Frank took a guess. "Yes, it was completed," he said.

"Just a moment," the operator told him. She left the line for a few seconds, then returned. "I show a credit call made just a moment ago."

"Yeah, that's it," Frank told her. "Can you tell me the number?"

"It was a local number, sir," the operator said, "five-five-five, seven-one-five-four."

"Thank you very much," Frank told her, as he wrote the number down in his notebook. Then he hung up and stepped out of the booth.

Mrs. Phillips was barely visible as she continued to walk uptown, so he started after her immediately, moving at a quick pace, shifting in and out of the thickening pedestrian traffic until he was near enough to keep her easily in view. Then he slowed down and kept his distance, idly strolling along the sidewalk, his mind going back over what the operator had told him. Mrs. Phillips had completed her call. But he knew that she hadn't spoken into the receiver, which meant that she'd probably gotten an answering machine. But whose?

Mrs. Phillips continued uptown until she got to Sixty-fourth Street. Then she turned west until she reached the brownstone and disappeared inside.

For the rest of the afternoon, until Mr. Phillips returned at six,

Frank waited outside the building, sometimes pacing slowly up and down the street, sometimes taking up various positions and simply standing very still, like a figure painted onto an urban landscape. His eyes continually drifted over to the small wrought-iron gate, then up along the building's silent, shuttered windows, the sightless eyes of its upper floors. Somewhere behind them, he thought, Mrs. Phillips might be preparing to come out again, preparing her face, her lips, her hair, the whole mysterious mask, so that she could come back through the little gate, lead him here and there, dropping dark hints like bits of paper as she went, messages which he would instantly snap up, but which, when opened, returned nothing to him but his own blank stare. Still, if she came out, he would follow her anyway. And so he waited for the door to open. But it never did.

The first shades of evening were already darkening the air by the time Frank got back to his office, and as he neared it, he found his pace quickening somewhat, as if he were finally getting close to something that would lend an edge to the day case, some element of compelling attraction. It was the sort of thing that kept the evil bubble from growing in him, that kept his days from seeming like a long, uneventful blur. It wasn't the same kind of piercingly beautiful edginess which fatherhood had given him or, from time to time, a woman. But it was edginess of a kind, the sense of something poised threateningly behind a curtain, and in barren times, it was enough.

Once in his office, he strode quickly to his desk, sat down behind it, and pulled out his notebook. He flipped through the pages until he came to the one that held the number the operator had given him. It was possible that everything resided in that number, and that the day case would suddenly, abruptly, find its solution. He picked up the receiver, then tapped out the number and waited.

It rang three times, then Frank heard the receiver click, and after that, the short purr of the tape as the answering machine spun out its answer: "You have reached the offices of Business Associates. At the sound of the beep, you will have one minute to leave your message."

The small beep sounded immediately, and Frank hung up the

phone. He took out his notebook and wrote the name of the company down in it, then opened the bottom drawer of his desk, took out the Manhattan telephone directory and looked up the address. Business Associates wasn't listed. He closed the book and returned it to the drawer, trying to imagine what Business Associates did, that they'd chosen such a deliberately nondescript name for it. Then slowly, meticulously, he went back over the notes he'd made during the day, trying once again to figure out some pattern that would make things clear. He smoked one cigarette, then a second, a third, until a dense white cloud hung around him, one too thick for occasional waves of his hand to disperse.

After a while, it was too much for him to take, and so he walked outside and stood silently on the street, his body slumped against the railing which led to his basement office. He stood there nearly an hour before he returned to his office and waited for Farouk to arrive.

—14—

Farouk knocked at the door of Frank's office, then walked in without waiting for an answer. He was wearing a black double-breasted suit with a white shirt and dark-red tie. He fingered the small red rosebud he'd inserted into his lapel. "How do I look?"

"Like you're going to a show or something," Frank said.

Farouk smiled happily. "That is close enough, I suppose," he said as he sat down in the chair in front of Frank's desk.

"To what?"

"The look I intended."

"What did you intend?"

"To give myself an air of opulence," Farouk told him. "But with a touch of risk."

Frank walked to the small coffeemaker, poured Farouk a cup in a short paper cup and handed it to him. "It's Turkish," he said. "I had it ground up."

Farouk took a quick sip. "Good. Very good."

Frank sat down behind his desk. "Who are you made up to be?"

"A man of substance," Farouk said with a wry smile. "One who cannot easily be turned aside."

"Where are you going?"

"To see a man of means. A certain Mr. Preston R. Devine."

Frank rolled his own cup of coffee between his hands. "You found out something?"

"About Powers first. Then also, Mr. Devine."

"Go ahead.

131

"I begin with Powers," Farouk said. "And I must say that my first suspicions were not confirmed."

"What suspicions?"

"I thought perhaps that he was not a doctor," Farouk said. "But he is. Not only that, but the 1968 degree from Tufts University, it is genuine. A Dr. Kevin Austin Powers was graduated in that year."

Farouk took out a small square of paper and handed it to Frank. "The final confirmation will be yours."

Frank looked at the paper. It was a grainy photocopy of a page from a university annual.

"Do you see your Dr. Powers?" Farouk asked.

Frank's eyes scanned the page until he found the face, younger, but still somewhat pudgy, with more hair, but not a lot more. "That's Powers," he said.

Farouk nodded. "Then the first area is closed," Farouk said. "To discover if a man is who he says he is, this is the first thing one must know."

Frank handed him back the page. "So Powers is a legitimate doctor."

"Undoubtedly," Farouk said. "But a man of broader interests as well." He took another sheet of paper from the breast pocket of his jacket and handed it to him.

Frank looked at it closely. It was another page from the same university annual; this time all the last names began with D. On the third column down, a face was listed as belonging to Preston Robert Devine.

Frank glanced up from the page. "Old college buddies."

"Companions of the mind," Farouk said. "If one would wish to put the best light on it." He smiled quietly. "But in any event, it is our first connection." He raised his hand and wagged his finger. "But I am pleased to tell you that it is not the last."

Frank returned the page to Farouk. "Go on."

Farouk stuck the paper back into his jacket pocket, then folded his large arms over his chest. "Something you said interested me," he began. "About the pictures in Powers's office. They are not the usual decorations in such places, and when a man makes such a choice, he betrays himself."

"What did it betray in Powers?"

"A love of the theater, of course."

Frank was unimpressed. "So, he's a theatergoer," he said. "Broadway's clogged with them at night."

Farouk shook his head. "Ah, he is a good deal more than that, my friend. To sit and enjoy, this is not enough for Dr. Powers. For him, there is a wish to be more involved in it. He wishes to make theater."

"Make theater?"

"His desire is to produce plays," Farouk said. "In this pursuit, he has spent a great deal of money." He shook his head mournfully. "But he has not made any, I am afraid." He plucked his ear dramatically. "As they say, he does not have the knack of the street."

"So you're telling me that Powers has lost a lot of money producing unsuccessful plays?"

"Yes."

"But he's also made a lot of money in his practice, right?"

"Without doubt."

"So what's your point exactly?"

"That this money he spends on producing plays, it is spent with all his heart," Farouk said.

Frank looked at him quizzically.

"His medical practice is only a profession. He does it differently. For what is called in German only the *Geschäft*. For the business, but not the love of it."

"I see," said Frank. "But what does that mean?"

"That to the making of plays, as the poets say, there is no end."

Frank smiled quietly. "You mean, no end to the cost."

Farouk nodded.

The smile broadened. "So Powers is in debt."

Farouk now smiled as well. "To Mr. Devine, the companion of his youth, through one of Mr. Devine's companies. Business Associates."

Frank leaned forward instantly. "Business Associates?"

"Yes," Farouk said, already reading Frank's suddenly intensified interest. "You have heard of it?"

"Mrs. Phillips called there this afternoon," Frank said. "She got an answering machine."

Farouk nodded. "So she was seeking Mr. Devine?"

"That's the way it looks."

"Who is himself associated by matters of debt to Dr. Powers."

"How do you know about all this?" Frank asked.

"Public debt is a matter of record, my friend," Farouk told him. "It is written down, as they say, in the Book of Life."

"So it's a legal debt, completely public?" Frank asked, surprised. "Signed contracts, the whole thing?"

"Entirely," Farouk said. "Except for the amounts."

"What do you mean?"

"Two years ago, Dr. Powers lost a great deal of money on a play," Farouk said. "He had many creditors. To pay them off, he did what is often recommended, he consolidated his debts. He went to Mr. Devine and borrowed a large amount of money. The terms of this indebtedness were publicly recorded."

"And with the money he got from Devine, Powers paid his other debts?"

"All of them," Farouk said. "Clearing all indebtedness from his credit report." Farouk leaned forward slightly and snapped his fingers. "As they say on the street, 'Like that.' "

"But if it's all legal, all public—this debt, I mean—what does it tell us?"

"Well, for one thing, the debts were more than the amount he borrowed from Devine," Farouk explained. "That is interesting, in itself. But more interesting is the fact that Powers only paid Devine back a part of the money he owed. The remainder of the debt is still outstanding," Farouk said.

"How much?"

"Two hundred thousand dollars."

Frank whistled. "Powers still owes Devine that much?"

"Unless it was forgiven," Farouk said pointedly.

"Forgiven?"

"In lieu, as they say, of something else?"

"Like what?"

"Forgiveness of debt can come for many reasons," Farouk said. "Sometimes it is a matter of the blood. A father forgives a son's indebtedness. Sometimes it is a matter of the heart. Friendship, for example. But sometimes debt is forgiven in lieu of other forms of payment."

Frank considered it for a moment. "Such as?" he asked finally.

Farouk shrugged. "Well, it is always possible that Dr. Powers is providing some kind of service to Mr. Devine." He took out his handkerchief and wiped his forehead softly. "To know this, I will have to discover certain things about Mr. Devine himself."

"Devine," Frank repeated softly, almost to himself. "Did you find out anything about his business? The other one, that Allied Global-East place on Forty-seventh Street?"

"That I do not know as yet," Farouk said. "But I will soon discover it."

Frank took a sip from the coffee. "I like Turkish," he told him.

"Because it does what it claims," Farouk said matter-of-factly. "That is why."

Frank thought a moment longer about the connection between Powers and Devine. He came up with nothing but what Farouk had already stated.

"But what about Mrs. Philips?" he asked finally. "What do you think this relationship between Powers and Devine has to do with her?"

"She goes from one to the other," Farouk said. "More than this, I cannot say."

"Could she be carrying the bag?"

"That is possible."

"Or maybe she's just an investor, along with Devine."

"Another factor in Business Associates," Farouk said. "This is also possible."

"Or she could be anything," Frank added. "Anything at all."

Farouk smiled. "And thus, the third alarm."

"The what?"

"In a fire, the third alarm is the bell that signals when all hands must be applied," Farouk said. "It is sounded when the flames are beyond control." He stood up, his hands plucking at the rosebud again. "I must go now to meet Mr. Devine."

"How'd you get an appointment with him?"

Farouk smiled knowingly. "By relying upon the secret of all allure," he said. "The promise that you alone may grant a man the full force of his dreams."

"What was his dream?"

"Money," Farouk said crisply.

Frank looked at him pointedly. "That must have made it easy for you."

Farouk nodded. "Very easy, yes," he said. Then he smiled quietly. "When the dream is simple," he added. "It is simple to deceive."

It was still faintly light when Farouk trudged up the cement stairs, and after a few minutes of lingering in his office, Frank went up them too, then turned right and headed down the street. He walked first to La Femme Gatée and had a sandwich. After that, he walked down Eighth Avenue to Smith's Bar and ordered his nightly Irish. He sipped it slowly while the bar's old-time habitués drifted in and out. They had the hard, leathery look of people who'd managed to see the whole thing through, and for a while, Frank felt a certain envy of the way they'd managed to make it to the end, snap the ribbon which still fluttered at the finish of their long, impossible run.

He ordered a second Irish and sipped it slowly, like the first, his mind drifting back as it always did, to those moments in his life which still struck him as worth remembering, soaring hopes, searing losses. Beyond these, it was a long flat plain, and it was too late for him to deny that he'd been living on that plain for more years now than it made sense to remember. He imagined that there must be a way back to the mountains and the valleys, but the only one he'd ever found—drink—had led him to places that were even worse. Everything else was an episode, a little love affair with Karen, a case that first burned him to the core and then brought Farouk to him like a large, lumbering angel. Still, for all that, none of it was enough to keep the wolves at bay, and for a moment he tried to imagine what would actually be able to do that for him. Then suddenly the Puri Dai came back to him in a vision of dark hair and flashing eyes, and he found himself yearning for time to pass quickly so that he could see her again, join her in the night. He was still anticipating it as he left the bar and headed back toward his office. Night had fallen entirely by then, and the darkness seemed only to intensify the yearning that he could feel building within him. It was nearly unbearable, his need to see her, so that he seemed almost in a haze by the time he reached Forty-ninth Street.

Deegan was waiting for him, leaning impatiently beside his car. "I've been here for two hours," he said irritably. "She wouldn't leave until she saw you."

"She?"

"The woman, your client, or whatever she is," Deegan said. "She made a full confession, and they released her into my custody." He shrugged. "No priors, and no resources to escape. The jails are full." He smiled mockingly. "I made an eloquent plea, and so they gave us the day."

"What happens after that?"

"A halfway house," Deegan said. "Minimum security. For now."

Frank glanced about. "Where is she?" he asked quickly. Then he glimpsed her, astonishingly free and only a few yards away.

She was standing in the dark corridor, her back pressed against its bare brick wall. There were bits of paper and old bottle caps at her feet, and for an instant Frank felt the impulse to sweep down and clear them away, to tidy things up a bit, the littered walkway she stood in, the rumpled sofa in his office, the cluttered desk and dank, stuffy closet. But it was too late, and so he simply nodded to her coolly, kept himself in check.

"I'm surprised to see you here," he said.

Her eyes were only partially visible in the shadowy light, but Frank still had no problem sensing how lethally they rested on him.

"When did you get out?" he asked.

The Puri Dai watched him cautiously as he approached her, then passed by and stepped over to the door.

"This morning," she said crisply after he'd started to open it.

"What was the bail?" Frank asked casually as he inserted the key and swung open the door.

"Only that I must return," the woman said.

Frank looked back at her, surprised. "For murder, that's all they asked?"

The Puri Dai shrugged. "A document was delivered, that is all I know."

"Where are you staying? At the halfway house?"

She didn't answer, and Frank decided not to pursue it. He stepped into the office.

"Come in," he said as lightly as he could.

She followed him into the room, then watched him warily as he took off his hat and walked over to his desk.

"I haven't had much time to work on your case," Frank said. "Just a little at night." He gave her a determined stare. "But I want you to know that I'm not giving up on it."

The Puri Dai stepped toward him. "That is what I have come to tell you," she said. "You must end this. You must not continue."

"Why not?"

"Because it is over."

"What is?"

"There is no defense," the woman said. "I have made my confession."

"Yeah, Deegan told me. Frank sat down behind his desk. "When did you make this confession?" he asked.

"Last night."

"Did you make it without him?"

"He is nothing to me."

Frank leaned back into his chair. "What did you say in the confession?"

"That it was I."

"That you killed the other woman?"

The woman lowered her eyes slightly, but didn't answer.

"You must have given them quite a few details," Frank said. "They don't automatically accept confessions."

"What I knew," the Puri Dai said, "that is what I told him."

"Him? Who did you confess to?"

"One of the men who was there."

"At the prison?"

"That night."

"Tannenbaum?"

She shook her head. "The other one. The one who is like you in the way he speaks."

"Southern? McBride?"

She nodded. "He listened for a long time."

"You told him everything? All the details?"

"Everything."

Frank leaned forward slightly. "Tell me."

She glared at him, as if he'd asked her to do something obscene.

"I need to know," Frank said immediately.

She looked at him doubtfully.

Frank made up a reason. "For my records," he said. "So I can close the case."

The Puri Dai was not convinced.

"That's what you want, isn't it?" Frank asked. "For me to close the case?"

"Yes. That is what I want."

"Then just answer a few questions," Frank told her, "and it'll all be over."

Her eyes squeezed together determinedly. "It is over now," she said. "As I have told you. I do not want you to go on with this."

"I heard you," Frank said coolly. "But it's not that easy. Not for me."

She turned away slightly, her face a dark profile against the front window of the office.

Frank took out his notebook. "Were you alone when you killed her?"

She did not answer.

"Was anyone else in the room?"

She turned to him. "No one," she said hotly. "No one. Is that enough?"

"Not quite," Frank said. "I'd like to know why you did it."

She did not answer.

Frank kept his pen pressed onto the open notebook. "I need a motive."

The Puri Dai did not speak.

"Was it some kind of argument?" Frank asked.

Silence.

"If it was an argument, what was it over?"

She did not answer.

"Money?"

She glared at him resentfully, but still remained silent.

"Where were you when you killed her?" Frank went on insistently.

She stood up. "I must go."

"Were you in front of her?" Frank demanded. "Did you stab her?"

The Puri Dai's face grew rigid.

"What did you use to do it with?"

"A razor," she shot back angrily. "A razor."

"Where'd it come from?"

"I must go."

"Three women lived in that place," Frank said. "What were they doing with a straight razor?" His eyes bore into her. "Who else was living with you?"

She seemed suddenly frightened, stricken. "No one."

"Then what was the razor for?"

She did not answer.

"There was hair on it," Frank said, playing his trump card. "From a man's beard."

Her eyes ignited. "There was nothing on the razor," she said with absolute certainty. "Nothing. Nothing."

Frank sat back slightly. "Because you washed it," he said confidently. "You took it into that little bathroom, and you very carefully washed it."

She shook her head. "I washed nothing," she snapped.

"You washed everything," Frank told her determinedly. "You even washed that little bathroom. But not well enough." He stood up. "Look, I'll show you."

The Puri Dai did not move.

Frank walked to the small bathroom in his office, switched on the light and looked back at her. "Come here, I'll show you."

She remained rigidly in place, but Frank could tell that she was watching him intently.

Frank took out his pocket knife, slid the blade under the crevice between the faucet and the basin and brought it over to her. "See those little hairs," he said as he pressed the small blade toward her. "We found the same kind in that sink on Tenth Avenue." He took his handkerchief and slowly wiped the blade clean. Then he leaned toward her, his face very close to hers. "Who is he?"

She did not answer.

"Who is he?" Frank repeated insistently.

She drew back from him. "I do not want you," she said icily. "I have come to tell you that."

Frank's eyes bore into her. "I can't close this case yet," he said emphatically.

Her eyes took on a strangely pleading softness. "You must," she said.

"Why?"

She did not answer.

"Who are you protecting?" Frank asked.

The softness disappeared instantly, and she turned and started toward the door.

Frank wheeled around to block her. "What is all of this about?"

She pressed toward him, and he stepped back slightly, then back again and again, until they were near the door. When she moved to open it, he took her hand.

"Whatever it is you want," he said, "I'll help you get it."

For a moment, the anger dissolved from her eyes. It was replaced by something that looked like pity.

She drew her hand from his. "You are like the rest," she said. "Even when you give, you take."

Frank stared at her longingly. "Take what?"

She shook her head silently, resignedly, as if the truths she knew were impossible to teach.

Frank touched her arm gently. "Take what?"

"I must go."

"Where?"

She didn't answer.

"The Women's Center?" Frank asked.

She raised her hand and placed it softly against his face. "You must close the case."

"I can't."

A single finger traced the outline of his jaw. "I will give you what you want," she said.

Frank took her hand and drew it away from him. He had never wanted anything more, or been less able to accept the way that it was offered. "Whatever this man is," he said, "he's not worth that."

Her face hardened suddenly, and she leaned forward and kissed him roughly, contemptuously, so that her lips seemed to leave on his the taste of dirty money.

He stepped back from her and wiped it from them with his sleeve.

Her eyes were very cold when he glanced toward them again. "Why did you do that?" he asked.

Her smile was like an iron bar stretched across her face. She let it hold there for a moment, then turned and walked away.

—16—

Two hours later, Frank walked directly into Deegan's office, swiftly and unannounced. "I want to see the confession," he said sharply.

Deegan's head jerked up from the stack of papers he'd been poring over. "Where the fuck did you come from?"

"The confession," Frank said edgily, his voice almost quaking, "was it detailed?"

"I'm not sure it had to be," Deegan said. "They've got a lot on her. The night cashier at that little bodega across the street saw her go into the storefront just a few minutes before the murder. A delivery boy spotted her standing over the body with the weapon in her hand." He shrugged. "Shall I go on?"

Frank didn't answer.

Deegan sat back and folded his arms over his chest. "You know, according to Miss Cortez . . ."

"Who?"

"Cortez," Deegan said, "that's the woman's last name."

"When did she tell you that?"

"She told me everything, Mr. Clemons," Deegan said proudly. "But it looks to me as though she hasn't exactly taken you into her confidence."

Frank whipped out his notebook. He could feel the cells in his body firing like millions of tiny pistons. "What was the full name?" he demanded.

Deegan eyed him suspiciously. "What's the matter with you?"

145

"Nothing," Frank replied coldly.

"You strung out on something?"

"The name," Frank said hotly. "Just give me the name."

Deegan shook his head. "She doesn't want you on the case any-more," he said. "That's why she dropped by."

"She told me."

"Well, then you also know that I don't have to give you a fucking thing."

Frank kept his pencil poised on the page. "Do you believe that confession?"

"I have no reason not to."

"It's a lie. All of it."

"How do you know?"

"She said she was in front of the old woman when she killed her," Frank said. "That couldn't be true."

"Why not?"

Frank stared at him, astonished. "Haven't you read the medical report?"

Deegan looked embarrassed. "I haven't had time," he said defensively. He nodded toward an enormous stack of folders that rested in front of him. "I'm not just working one case, you know."

Frank didn't feel like arguing the point. "Well, the woman was killed with a razor."

"Christ, I know that."

"And the way it was drawn across her throat," Frank added, "it had to have been done by someone who was standing behind her."

Deegan seemed to consider it.

"And there was a man living in that little storefront where the woman was killed," Frank said. "And he hasn't surfaced yet."

"How do you know there was a man living there?"

"We found hairs from his beard."

"We?"

"I have an associate."

"And where'd you find these hairs?"

"In the bathroom on Tenth Avenue."

"When did you go there?"

"Last night."

"With Tannenbaum?"

Frank shook his head.

"Who went with you?"

"Just my associate."

Deegan's eyes widened in horror. "Are you out of your fucking mind?" he yelped. "You just broke into the private apartment?" He laughed. "And you're questioning my professional competence? They'd pull your license in a second if they knew about that break-in."

Frank stepped toward him. "I want to see her confession," he said.

Deegan stared at him arrogantly. "And what makes you think I have to give it to you?"

Frank glared at him. "Look, the fact that you didn't even bother to read the goddamn medical report in a murder case before you let your client plead guilty, that fact can be just between us, or it can . . ."

Deegan stood his ground. "And that little break-in on Tenth Avenue can just be between us too, pal."

Frank started to fire another salvo.

Deegan lift his hand to silence him. "Now wait a minute," he said. "Let's just calm down for a minute, okay?"

Frank nodded.

"Now," Deegan said after a moment, "you're basically saying that Miss Cortez is pleading guilty to a murder she didn't commit. Is that right?"

"Yes."

"Why do you think she's doing that?"

"I don't know."

"In my experience, there are usually three reasons for such a thing," Deegan went on. "Number one, the guy wants publicity. Number two, the guy's crazy. Number three, to protect the real killer." Deegan smiled. "Are you with me so far?"

"Yeah."

"So, what do you think the situation is with Miss Cortez?"

"The last one," Frank said. "Protection."

"For the guy with the beard, right?"

"That's my guess."

Deegan sat back and thought about it. "So who is he, her husband?"

"Maybe."

"Could be a friend, a relative. Or maybe something a little more interesting—a lover."

Frank felt stricken by his answer. "Probably," he said.

"You think you can find this person?"

"I can try."

Deegan nodded. "Can I count on you to pass all the information you find about this case to me?"

"Yes."

Deegan smiled. "You see, Frank, we can behave like gentlemen with one another."

Frank said nothing.

Deegan took a deep breath. "Okay, then on the basis of what you've told me and our other agreement, I consider it my professional duty to give you a copy of Miss Cortez's confession, along with any other information which I deem relevant."

Frank pressed his pencil toward the open notebook. "Let's start with her name," Deegan said. He pulled her confession from a stack of other documents. "Her whole name," he said, as he handed it to Frank.

It was Magdalena Immaculata Cortez, and Frank pronounced it very clearly, trying to keep the long, lazy southern vowels out of his voice as he said it to the man who ran the bodega down the block from the storefront on Tenth Avenue.

The man behind the counter blinked rapidly. "Holy shit, that's a mouthful, huh?"

Frank nodded.

"You a cop?" the man behind the counter asked. He was short, and very thin, with black curly hair. His fingers were long, and he drummed them continually along the edge of the counter to some beat that was only in his head.

Frank took out his identification.

"Oh," the man said. "Private dick. Ain't that what they call you guys?"

"Sometimes," Frank said. "My name's Clemons."

"Frankie Betonni."

Frank smiled crisply. "About the woman," he said.

"Woman, yeah," Betonni said. He swayed his hips slightly to the inaudible beat. "Magda . . . whatever. Which one was she?"

"Tall, dark," Frank said. "She sometimes wore . . ."

"Oh yeah," Betonni said excitedly. "The really hot one."

"Hot?"

"A sizzler, you know what I mean? A good-looking piece of pie, man. Very sharp, great-looking ass." He moaned lustily, and Frank felt like slapping his face, but managed to control himself.

"I understand you saw her the night of the murder," he said.

"Yeah, I seen her," Betonni said lightly. "I told the cops all about it."

"When was that, do you remember?"

"I told them that, too," Betonni said. "It was three A.M. sharp."

"You can be that precise?"

"Cause my shift ends at three, and Felix was late relieving me. He's a real fuck, that guy. Never on time."

"So you saw the woman pass in front of the store," Frank said. "And you glanced at the clock."

"Yeah."

"Did she come in?"

"No."

"Was she carrying anything?"

"She had a bag with her," Betonni said. "I don't know what was in it."

"What kind of bag?"

"Like a shopping bag, something like that," he said. "With handles."

"Did it look like she had groceries in it?"

Betonni shook his head. "There was cloth sticking out of it," he said. "Like a sleeve or something."

Frank took out his notebook and wrote it down. "Do you remember the color?"

"Red," Betonni said. He smiled proudly. "I got a good memory, don't I?"

"Yeah," Frank said. He looked up from the notebook. "So you saw her pass by," he said. "Then what?"

"What do mean, then what?"

"Where'd she go?"

"Right across the street."

Frank glanced out the front window. The small light-blue FORTUNES TOLD sign was blinking softly. "Over there?"

"Yeah."

"And she went directly inside the building?"

"That's right."

"And you didn't see her go out again?"

Betonni shrugged. "I left a few minutes later."

"How about the guy who replaced you," Frank said. "Did he see her go out again?"

"That fuck?" Betonni screeched. "That fuck never did show up that night."

"So no one took over your shift?"

Betonni shook his head. "No. So I waited till around three-fifteen, then I just fucking closed the place."

Frank glanced back at his notebook, wrote it down, then returned his attention to Betonni.

"The woman," he said, "did she shop in here much?"

"We're still talking about the sizzler, right?"

"Yeah."

Betonni grinned. "Sometimes she did. I kept hoping I'd get lucky."

Frank let it pass. "Did the other women shop here too?" he asked.

"Yeah, they all come in once in a while."

Frank took a chance. "And the man?" he asked casually.

Betonni went blank. "Man?"

"Yeah," Frank said as offhandedly as he could. "The guy who was living with them."

Nothing registered in Betonni's face.

"You must have seen him," Frank insisted.

Betonni shook his head. "I don't remember no guy," he said. "Young or old?"

Frank tried to judge from the color of the hair. "On the younger side."

"Younger, huh?" Betonni said. "So he'd be the one slamming the sizzler, right?"

Frank could feel his eyes narrowing. "You see a guy or not?"

Betonni shook his head. "I don't think I ever seen no guy around." He smiled playfully. "That's why I kept hitting on her."

Frank felt one of his hands ball up into a fist. "You were always hitting on her?"

"Sure, it don't cost me nothing," Betonni said airily. "And shit, man, maybe one time in ten, I actually hit the jackpot."

Frank swallowed hard, then forcefully drew his eyes away from Betonni. "When she came in to buy things, what sort of stuff did she buy?"

Betonni's eyes roamed the store. "Odds and ends, mostly. Soap, paper towels, that sort of shit."

"How about shaving cream?"

Betonni looked at Frank curiously. "Shaving cream? Why would a bunch of . . ." He stopped. "Oh, I get you. You're after that guy again."

Frank smiled thinly.

"Shaving cream," Betonni asked himself thoughtfully. "Shaving cream . . ."

"Cigars?" Frank added. "Pipe tobacco?" For a moment, he balked at the last item, then decided to go on with it. "Prophylactics?"

Betonni smiled. "Rubbers, yeah," he laughed. "That would be a sure sign, wouldn't it?" Again, he thought it over. "But I don't remember any of that kind of thing," he said finally. "It could have been they bought stuff like that, but I don't remember any of it."

Frank put away his notebook. "Thanks, anyway," he said.

"Hey, no problem, man," Betonni said. He looked him up and down. "You guys always carry a piece with you?" he asked. "I mean, like cops do."

"Not always," Frank said as he stepped to the door. When he glanced back, Betonni had shaped his hand into a pistol, his thumb used as a cock, his index finger a long, fleshy barrel. Slowly, the thumb fell forward. "Boom," he said playfully, as Frank turned back toward the door.

Once outside, Frank drew in a deep breath, then headed north toward Toby's. It was nearly two in the morning by then, and the avenue was entirely deserted. As he walked, he tried to imagine where the Puri Dai would have gone on the avenue at about the same time several days before. Betonni had seen her walking south hastily, carrying nothing but a single shopping bag.

He stopped and stared up the avenue. It was a long dark corridor of closed shops, their protective shields of corrugated tin securely in place over their glass storefront windows. Still, far in the distance, almost to Fiftieth Street, he could see a single lighted space, and he made his way toward it quickly.

It was an all-night laundry, and it was almost entirely deserted except for an old woman who sat near the back, idly thumbing through a magazine.

She glanced up listlessly as Frank approached her.

He nodded, then took out his identification and showed it to her.

The woman stared at it a moment, then glanced up at Frank. "I don't read so good since I broke my glasses," she said. She lifted the magazine slightly. "Even this, I just look at the pictures."

"I'm looking into a murder that took place down at Forty-Seventh Street a few days ago."

The woman nodded. "Yeah, I heard something about that."

"It was a Sunday night, actually," Frank added. "Is this place open Sunday nights?"

"It don't never close," the woman said. "I'm here seven nights a week."

"So you work here?"

"Every night, 'cept on Christmas."

Frank glanced about. "Is it usually this deserted around this time?"

"Yeah. We don't do much business past two in the morning."

"Do you happen to remember if anybody came in last Sunday night around this time?"

"Some old geezer come in," the woman said. "Had palsy in his hands." She laughed hoarsely. "He'd pull a pair of shorts out of the drying, and Christsake, it looked like he was waving bye to the Queen Mary, you know?"

Frank smiled. "How about a woman?"

The woman giggled. "I'm more interested in men, myself."

Frank allowed himself a small laugh. "I mean that night," he said, going on quickly. "Did you notice a woman come in here Sunday night?"

The woman thought about it. "Like a model, almost?"

Frank felt his breath stop. "Yes."

"In a costume?"

"A Gypsy."

"Yeah, I seen her," the woman said.

"What was she doing?"

The woman shrugged. "Just doing her clothes, like you'd expect. You know, wash a batch, then dry them." She thought a moment. "She just had one load."

"Did you notice what kind of clothes they were?"

"Kind? What do you mean, kind?"

"Men's clothes?"

The woman shook her head. "Women's I think. Bright colors. The only thing I really noticed was that they was still sort of wet when she pulled them out of the dryer."

"Wet?"

"Yeah, they needed another spin."

"But she didn't do that?"

The woman shook her head. "She was in a hurry, I think. She didn't look like she had the time."

"Did she say anything?"

"No."

"Was anyone else with her?"

"Anyone else?"

"I was thinking, perhaps a man?"

"No, I didn't see nobody else," the woman said. "Just that woman in a costume, you know." She smiled. "Like she was trying to be something that wasn't really her."

* * *

Frank walked directly to Toby's after-hours joint after leaving the laundromat. He took his usual table at the back of the room and ordered an Irish from Teague, the waiter-bouncer whose name he'd only recently learned.

The drink came fast, but he didn't drink it that way. Instead, he sat back and sipped slowly, while his eyes perused the place through its perpetually shadowed light.

Toby was behind the bar, silently serving drinks to the few people who sat slumped over it. She looked a bit tanned by her trip, but otherwise she appeared the same, utterly silent as she dried glasses or mopped the nightly spill from the top of the bar. Farouk had not spoken of her very often, except to say, long ago when they worked the Covallo case together, that he'd married her "to keep her from oppression." He'd never said what he meant by that, and Frank had never asked.

After a while, Toby wandered over to his table and said the first words he'd ever heard from her. "Farouk, he no here."

"I know."

She stared at him with dim, unblinking eyes. "Farouk, he no come tonight."

"You mean, at all?"

Toby continued to stare at him while her hand massaged a glass with a white cloth. "Farouk, he no come tonight," she repeated. "Farouk say, he no here."

Frank nodded. "Okay, thanks."

Toby finished the glass, then returned to the bar, plucked another one from a tray and began drying it.

Frank leaned back, edging his chair against the wall behind him, and closed his eyes. For a time, he saw the Puri Dai as he imagined her in the laundromat, hastily, perhaps frantically, doing her clothes. Then he recalled that Betonni had said that she was moving quickly down the avenue as she'd passed the bodega only a few minutes later, that she'd moved very quickly across the street, the single shopping bag dangling from her hand, and disappeared into the building. It was as if that particular night had demanded nothing so much as speed, and as he thought about it, it seemed to Frank that everything was connected to this speed, this accelerated pace, as if she were falling through some kind of vertical space, plunging toward murder at a steadily increasing velocity.

He closed his eyes more tightly and kept them closed, breathing more slowly, trying to get what rest he could. But as the minutes passed, he could see that the world beyond his eyes was growing brighter and brighter, that the day case was now breaking over him like a wave.

— 17 —

He rubbed his eyes wearily as he took up his usual position outside the Phillips brownstone about four hours later, edging his shoulder up against the brick wall, his eyes peering steadily at the little wrought-iron gate, and then the building which rose behind it.

Mr. Phillips left first, moving obliviously down the street, his eyes never once darting toward Frank as he headed for work. For a time after that, the door to the brownstone remained closed. Then suddenly, it opened, and Mrs. Phillips made her way to the gate, opened it and stepped out. She was dressed in a long blue coat, and wore black high-heeled shoes. Her hair was drawn back and curled into a tight bun at the back of her head. She wore the same gold-framed dark glasses, but there was no hat, as there had been on Tuesday. For a moment, she stood very still, as if taking in the early-morning sunlight, then she turned right, as Mr. Phillips had, and walked eastward.

Frank shoved the bagel he'd bought a few minutes before into his jacket pocket, then took out his notebook and scribbled down the time: 8:37 A.M.

At the corner of Madison Avenue and Sixty-fourth Street, he began to close in on her, still carefully keeping his distance. He followed slowly, edging himself around the same corner a minute or so later. He could see her standing at the same shop window she'd stopped at the day before. She was facing the window, but even from a few yards away, Frank could tell that she was not looking at the merchandise behind it. Instead, she was glancing down, peering into her purse as one of her white hands riffled through it. For a moment, Frank supposed that she was preparing for another drop, but almost immediately, her hand drew up from the purse. She was clutching a long black comb. She looked up, staring at her own reflection in the mirror, as if studying it, the same way he'd seen her do it before. She seemed to concentrate upon it, as if trying to figure something out. Then her hand shot back behind her head and released the clasp which held the coiled hair. A blond wave fell over her back and shoulders, and she combed it violently in quick, anxious strokes, then returned the comb to the purse and turned toward the street.

A large black Mercedes limousine drew alongside the curb almost immediately, and she strode directly toward it, opened the door herself, and disappeared inside.

Frank stepped forward quickly, wrote down the license number as it moved away, then hailed a cab and followed the limousine as it made its way up the long avenue, past luxurious boutiques and expensive antique shops until it turned west again, reached Fifth Avenue and turned south. From there, it headed directly to Fifty-seventh Street, turned east, and drove into the parking garage in the basement of Trump Tower.

"Just pull over here," Frank said.

The driver drew the cab over to the curb. Frank paid him quickly and got out. He walked around the corner, turned left and headed toward the entrance to the building. The usual crush of people filled the lobby of the Tower, gawking wide-eyed at the immense marble walls and interior waterfall that cascaded over it.

Frank took up a position across from the bank of elevators along the opposite wall, watching the floor lights while he waited for each of the elevators to descend to the basement garage, then rise again. Inevitably, the doors opened again once the elevator reached the lobby, and Frank kept a close eye on each one, trying to spot Mrs. Phillips. First one elevator rose, then another, but Mrs. Phillips was never in any of them, and after a time, Frank decided that she must have used some other entrance into the building.

There were several security men in the lobby, all of them easily identified by the small gold-plated lapel pins they wore. The pins were microphones which fed information into a central security headquarters, and according to his own count, at least fifteen men in the lobby were wearing them. He picked the one nearest to him, a tall man in an elegant blue suit, and walked up to him.

"My name's Clemons," he said. He showed him his identification. The man nodded. "Is there a problem?" he asked.

"I was following a limousine that went into the Tower's underground garage," Frank said. "Someone in it, I was wondering if they could get into the building by using anything but the elevators in the lobby."

"They could take the stairs," the man said.

Frank thought of Mrs. Phillips's spike-heeled shoes. "I don't think so," he said. "Any other way?"

"Not unless we're talking about a resident of the building."

"And what if we are?"

"Well, there are private elevators," the man said. "But you wouldn't be allowed down there."

"Private?"

"They go directly to the residences," the man said.

"Without stopping at the lobby."

"That's right."

"Could a visitor use those elevators?"

"Only if they passed a security station."

"Which would be where?"

"In the garage."

Frank smiled quietly. "Could I get down there?"

"You could go to the security station," the man said. He eased himself away from the wall. "Come, I'll show you."

Frank followed the man through the crowded lobby, then down a flight of stairs to a large office filled with screens and elegantly dressed guards.

One of the guards met Frank and the security man at the door. He was tall and very slender, as if honed down to a sharp angle by too much hard experience.

"What can I do for you, Ray?" he said to the security man.

The security man nodded toward Frank. "This gentleman's interested in the private elevators," he said.

"Really, why?" the man said. He wore a sterling silver name plate that said "Schaeffer," but he introduced himself anyway. "Charles Schaeffer," he said.

Frank nodded. "Like Ray said," he began, "I was just wondering . . ."

"Nonsecurity personnel aren't allowed in the central office," Schaeffer said to the younger man. "Don't you remember that from your orientation?"

"Well, yes, sir," the other man sputtered. "But this man, he's a . . ."

"I don't care what he is," Schaeffer snapped. "You don't bring people to the central security office."

The other man's face paled. "Yes, sir."

Shaeffer's small blue eyes shifted over to Frank. "What can I do for you?" he said with a surprisingly sudden politeness.

Frank took out his identification.

Schaeffer looked at it very closely, then took out a pad and copied down the private investigator's license number. When he'd finished, he handed it back to Frank and looked at him with eyes that had suddenly gone dead.

"A limo came in here a few minutes ago," Frank said. "I was wondering who it belonged to."

"We have a great many limousines in this garage," Schaeffer told him. He took Frank gently by the arm and began to move him away from the security station.

"It was a black Mercedes," Frank added. "I got the license plate."

"Why were you following it?"

"I was following somebody who got into it."

"I'm afraid I can't help you," Schaeffer said, once the two of them were alone by the elevators. The politeness had disappeared, and Frank realized that his identification card had fixed him in Schaeffer's mind as nothing but a two-bit shiny-suited gumshoe who was probably poking his nose into things the big guys at the top of the building weren't interested in having brought out.

"I'm afraid you're not allowed down here," Schaeffer said. "Reynolds shouldn't have brought you down."

"The woman had long blond hair," Frank said. "She must have passed the guard station."

Schaeffer reached around Frank's body and pressed the up arrow of the elevator. "The people in this building are very security-conscious," he said.

"Do I look like a threat to their security?" Frank asked coldly.

The elevator doors opened behind him, but Frank did not get in.

Schaeffer's jaw tightened. "You are technically trespassing," he said.

Frank thought of his license, how, with his record, it could easily be revoked. He stepped back and held open the elevator door. "I'm not interested in bothering anybody," he said. "I was just following a woman."

"But you lost her, didn't you?"

Frank said nothing.

"So, technically, that's the problem, isn't it? That you lost her."

Frank could feel the rubber safety door growing warm in his hand. "Did you see her, or not?" he asked sharply.

Schaeffer pressed his hand lightly against Frank's chest, urging him into the elevator. He didn't answer.

"Did she go to a private apartment here?" Frank demanded.

Schaeffer was staring at him silently as the two doors moved smoothly toward each other.

Just as they came together, Frank could see him smile.

He couldn't cover all the entrances to Trump Tower, so he decided to pick the one he'd seen her disappear into, the one that led out of the garage. He waited, pleasurelessly finishing off the bagel he'd stuffed into his jacket earlier in the morning, while his eyes stared at the black square of shadow that penetrated the building's enormous foundation. Schaeffer had been right. There were a great many limousines, and for the next hour, Frank watched them as they came out of the garage—Cadillacs and Lincolns, a single white Rolls Royce, even another black Mercedes, but one with a different license number than the limousine which had picked Mrs. Phillips up on Madison Avenue.

Frank glanced at his watch restlessly, then, fifteen minutes later, glanced at it again. He could feel the evil bubble growing in him, the one that made everything a little emptier than it already was. It had started with Sarah's death, deepened with his divorce, then deepened more as his love for Karen had gone dry and passionless. It drifted toward him from out of nowhere now, as if it no longer needed to be called up by any particular thing, but simply occupied its place as a steadily darkening presence, filling him with hissing accusations about the way he'd lived his life. There were times when he suspected that everyone must have such a specter, but then he'd see a couple laughing in a restaurant or a father playing with his daughter in the park, or even some solitary old woman contentedly reading a newspaper on her bare cement stoop, and they would strike him as people who'd somehow escaped the grasp of a merciless pursuer, had closed the door and thrown the bolt just in time to leave the shadow breathless in the hall.

Another car emerged from the underground garage, but as it broke into the light, Frank saw that it was dark blue, rather than black, another Cadillac rather than a Mercedes. He leaned back against the wall of the building and continued his long vigil. He knew that there was no way he could be sure that Mrs. Phillips was still inside the Tower. She could easily have left it by another entrance, taken a cab and gone to her next destination. Or she could simply have been driven out of it in a different car, one of those Cadillacs which had passed practically under his nose as it made its way back onto the street.

He lit a cigarette, fanning the smoke from his eyes to keep the garage in view. No cars were coming out and a steady stream of pedestrians walked back and forth across the dark entrance. They were mostly business people and office workers who labored in the immense buildings which rose over the avenue and along the surrounding streets, stretching river to river across the granite backbone of Manhattan.

Another hour passed, then another.

Schaeffer had gotten it right. He had lost her. There was no point in waiting any longer. The only thing to do now was return to the Phillips apartment so that he could at least find out when she got home.

He walked back up to the corner of Fifth Avenue, then northward to Sixty-fourth Street and took up his usual position by the wall.

Time continued forward with a maddening slowness, flowing over him like a thick, turbid river, choked and currentless.

He drank a cup of coffee, then another and another, crushing each paper cup in turn, then tossing it listlessly into the wire receptacle a few feet from where he stood.

One by one, he went through his cigarettes.

The bright midmorning air darkened into blue.

He looked at his watch. It was nearly five o'clock. He took out the last of his cigarettes and lit it, then glanced to his left, his eyes half-fogged with boredom, until in a sudden, stunning instant he realized that she was shooting toward him, that she was practically upon him, so close that the sound of her high-heeled shoes as they clicked against the cement sidewalk were as loud as pistol shots.

Reflexively, he pulled his eyes away from her, fixed them on a single seam of mortar in the brick wall which faced him, and let her pass, his breath held tightly in his lungs. A flash of blond hair swept across his field of vision as she whisked by, and he could feel a slight breeze from the air her body displaced as she swept past him. A very subtle sweetness surrounded him in her wake, and as he drew his breath again, his eyes watching as she disappeared behind her door, he realized, with an aching sense of something deeply out of place, that she'd seeded the evening air with her perfume.

—18—

"There's something wrong, Farouk," Frank said immediately as Farouk came through the door.

Farouk sat down at his usual place in the chair opposite Frank's desk and lifted his hands, palms up. "Something wrong? Well, that is the way of it, yes?"

"No, I mean about this case."

Farouk glanced toward the window. A hint of light still remained. "You mean, the day case?"

Frank nodded. "I followed her again this morning," he said. "She walked to Madison Avenue, but not to shop. It was too early for the stores to be open."

"What did she do then?"

"She stopped in front of a window and sort of looked herself over, that's all."

"At her face?" Farouk asked.

"Yes. Then she stepped over to the curb and got into a limousine."

Farouk stroked his chin. "A moment, please. She walked from her home on Sixty-fourth Street to Madison Avenue. That is but a single block."

"Yes."

"And that is when she stopped to look at her face in the window?"

"That's right," Frank said.

Farouk said nothing, but Frank could tell that things were moving through his mind.

"Then she let down her hair and . . ." he began again.

Farouk raised his hand to stop him. "You did not say this, about the hair. She let down her hair?"

"Yeah."

"And then she did what?"

"She started walking over to the curb, and a limousine pulled up."

"Which she did not lift her hand to signal."

"No.

"Which she signaled with her hair."

"What?"

"When she let down her hair, that was the signal."

Frank reviewed the scene in his mind. "Yes, that's possible," he said.

"And so the limousine pulled up to the curb and she got in, yes?"

"That's right."

"And went where?"

"To Trump Tower," Frank told him. "Into the garage of the building."

Farouk's face stiffened. "Trump Tower?"

"Yeah, why?"

"It is what I learned from Mr. Devine last night," Farouk said, "that he has an apartment in Trump Tower."

"But I thought he lived at the Dakota?"

"Lives there, perhaps," Farouk said. "But he also owns an apartment in Trump Tower."

"He just happened to mention that?" Frank asked.

"He let it drop at the right moment," Farouk said. "To demonstrate that he is a man of means."

"Did he say anything else about it?"

Farouk shook his head. He thought a moment longer, his eyes drifting up toward the ceiling for a few seconds before they fell back sharply toward Frank. "And how long did she stay at the Tower?"

"I don't know."

Farouk looked at him unbelievingly. "You don't know? Why is this?"

"Because I lost her."

Farouk continued to stare.

"She must have taken something other than the usual elevators to get to the upper floors," Frank explained quickly. "They have private elevators for the residents."

"And you think she took one of these?"

"Yeah, I think so."

"To visit Devine?"

"I don't know," Frank said. He took out his notebook. "I was able to get the license number of the limousine she got into on Madison Avenue, and I . . ."

"A moment, please," Farouk interrupted. "We have only a little time left for the day. Will this be short?"

"I'll make it short," Frank said. He ripped the page out of the notebook. "Here's the license number. I'd like to know who the car belongs to."

Farouk took the paper, glanced at the number, then handed it back to Frank. "You need this more than I."

Frank returned the page to his notebook, then the notebook to his jacket.

"What happened after you lost her?"

"I don't know."

"You did not see her again?"

"Not until she got back home," Frank admitted. "She practically bumped into me on the street."

Farouk's face grew solemn. "Perhaps you have burned your cover, yes?"

"I don't think so."

"How did she look when she returned?"

"The same."

"I mean, her hair," Farouk added pointedly.

In an instant, Frank saw her again, her white face coming toward him like a puff of ghostly smoke. "It was up," he said. "She'd put it back up again."

Farouk drew in a deep breath. "You are right," he said. "There is something wrong."

Frank nodded. "What about you, what else did you find out?"

"On the day case, you mean?"

"Yes," Frank said. "You had an appointment with Devine."

Farouk smiled. "It is my hope that the following may be of some assistance," he began. "Mr. Devine received me with great kindness." He pulled out a small business card and handed it to Frank. "This is what is called "the hook.' "

Frank glanced at the card. It listed Farouk as an official representing something called the United Middle Eastern Consortium.

"A hook must hold the bait," Farouk said. "In this case, the bait is in the words."

"'Middle Eastern,'" Frank said. "'Consortium.'"

Farouk smiled. "Does it not seem appropriately modest?"

"Yes, it does."

"But also appropriately wealthy, yes?" Farouk added. "Appropriately, as they say, discreet."

Frank handed him back the card. "So he was happy to see you."

Farouk nodded. "He is one of those for whom the making of money holds the delights of the flesh," he said.

"Where'd you meet him?"

"At his office on Forty-seventh Street," Farouk said. "It was quite lavish. But not so lavish as to make Mr. Devine appear as one who spends money unwisely."

"What did you say to him?"

"In his office, very little," Farouk said. "He did not wish to remain there." He smiled. "He is a large man, like myself, and the hour was late."

"He was hungry."

"Dinner was quite extravagant," Farouk said. "A four-star restaurant which caters only to those who wish to be seen eating well. Mr. Devine was well known to the staff." He smiled. "Yellow pike in a light pepper sauce, very tasty. And Devine has excellent taste in wine as well." He rubbed his hands together softly. "The atmosphere was very cordial, but the conversation, as they say, was quite down-to-earth."

"What did he say?"

"That he was always pleased to discover new business associates," Farouk said. "I told him that I represented a number of people who were interested in investing in theatrical productions."

"How'd he react?"

"As if a cold wind had come through the window," Farouk said. "He said—and these are his words precisely—he said 'You should tell your associates that they would do better to burn their money and enjoy the heat.' " He smiled. "I, of course, immediately expressed my appreciation for such honesty. My associates are not interested in burning money, I told him, but in acquiring more and more of it. I asked if perhaps Mr. Devine might be of some assistance in this pursuit." He took out his ivory cigarette holder and tapped a cigarette into it. "At this remark, as you might imagine, the cold wind grew warmer, and Mr. Devine appeared to glow." He lit the cigarette. "He spoke a great deal, and I learned that in addition to those activities which I mentioned at our last meeting, he is also what is called a 'packager.' "

"Packager? What does that mean?"

"He packages things, puts deals together. It might be anything," Farouk said. "With Dr. Powers, for instance, he was packaging a theatrical production."

"But that's not his main business?"

Farouk laughed. "With this man, it hardly rates as a sideline."

"What else, then?"

"Jewels, furs, oil," Farouk said. "His dealings are international, and quite varied. His connections run very deep among my own people, in fact."

"What does he sell to them?"

"He does not sell," Farouk said. "He does not buy. Remember, my friend, Mr. Devine is a packager. He brings together the people who have something with the people who want it, you see? When money is spoken of, Mr. Devine rises from a bottle, like a genie."

"Has he ever had any dealings with Harold Phillips?"

Farouk shook his head. "Not that I have been able to discover," he said. "But, as far as I have been able to determine, in all matters, his dealings have been quite legal."

"So it's a dead end," Frank said dully.

"Not exactly dead," Farouk said. "I was not satisfied with what I had discovered, and so I returned to the question of theatrical productions. I told him that I and others were still interested in financing such enterprises. Mr. Devine did not seem interested. So I told him that this was surprising to me, since I'd heard his name mentioned as regards a company known as Business Associates."

Frank leaned forward slightly. "How'd he react to that?"

"Rather strangely, I think," Farouk told him. "He simply smiled."

"He didn't say anything?"

"After the smile, came the words," Farouk went on. "He said, 'Ah, I see. Well, if all goes well, that can certainly be arranged.'"

"That's all?"

"Yes."

"You didn't pursue it?"

"It was my opinion that I could not pursue it at that time without betraying myself."

Frank eased himself back into his seat. "No, I don't think you could," he said disappointedly.

Farouk smiled. "But much time remained for other inquiries," he said. "And I was pleased to make them."

"What did you find out?"

"That Mr. Devine is a man of various philanthropical interests."

"Charities?"

"And in this, I discovered a new connection," Farouk said. "One between Devine and Mrs. Phillips."

"What is it?"

"I believe that you told me Mrs. Phillips was involved in a group which wishes to save the rain forest of South America, yes?"

"That's right."

"This played in my mind," Farouk said. "And because of that, I visited the offices of this group." He smiled. "They were happy to give me a certain amount of material on their cause." He drew a single sheet of paper from his jacket pocket and handed it to Frank. "Including a letter detailing their concerns, complete with a letterhead that was kind enough to list the members of their board."

Frank opened the letter, read it quickly, then glanced up. "Devine is on the board."

Farouk nodded. "A recent member. He joined earlier this very year."

Frank glanced back down at the letter, his eyes moving down the short list of names which moved in a column down the left side of the paper. "So Devine and Mrs. Phillips sit on the same board."

"Precisely," Farouk said. "Which makes it all the more unusual that she would use a false name in visiting him."

"Unless our first guess was right."

"An unfaithful wife."

Frank nodded.

"With a single odd twist, however," Farouk added quickly. "Dr. Kevin A. Powers."

"What does he have to do with anything?"

"He turns the circle into a triangle, do you not think?"

"I don't know."

"He is the odd thing," Farouk said. "He must be looked at again. He is the piece that does not exactly fit."

"Unless he's just her doctor."

"Whom she does not visit in his office," Farouk asked doubtfully, "but in his private home?"

Frank said nothing.

Farouk shrugged. "Still, you could be right," he said. "And if I discover nothing of importance between them," he added, "then I will proceed with this." He tapped the side of his head. "The license number."

Frank nodded. "Since that's all we've got for now," he said.

"Oh, not at all, my friend," Farouk said. He glanced toward the window as he got to his feet. The last deep blue had darkened into black. "There is always much to discover for those who work the night."

—19—

But the day case had now begun to linger too, and Frank was still going over its various connections and disconnections when Mr. Phillips knocked at his door.

"I don't mean to bother you," Phillips said, as Frank opened the door, "but I've been feeling very anxious."

Frank stepped back to let him pass. "Come in."

Phillips walked immediately to the seat opposite Frank's desk and sat down. "As I told you, Virginia and I went away night before last."

"Yes."

"I think I should tell you that she seemed even worse," Phillips added. He looked curiously drained, as if his worry had been steadily intensifying since their last meeting.

Frank sat down behind his desk. "Worse? In what way?"

"As I told you, she's been distant for several weeks. But Tuesday night it was as if I didn't even exist. I'd have to say something three or four times before she'd acknowledge my existence, and then it was as if she was surprised to see me there." He shook his head. "I don't know what to do," he added quietly. "I'm like some pathetic figure in a play."

"Did she say anything at all?" Frank asked.

Phillips shook his head. "Nothing."

"Did you ask her about anything?"

"I asked her how she was doing," Phillips said. "I told her she didn't look well."

"What'd she say to that?"

"She said she had some pain."

"Pain?"

"In her stomach."

"Anything else?"

"She said she didn't want to stay on at the country house," Phillips added. "She said she had to get back to New York."

"When was this?"

"When I told her that I'd like for us to stay through the afternoon, maybe even an extra day."

"She didn't want to do that?"

"Absolutely not," Phillips said. "We were going to drive up to our house early that evening. It's only an hour or so outside the city. Then we were going to spend the night and come back in the afternoon. Normally, of course, we would have stayed longer, but I had a rather important meeting that afternoon, and so we'd only planned the trip for one night and then for a few hours the following morning."

"So she was expecting to be back in the city by the afternoon?"

"Yes," Phillips said. "But when I saw how she was, her condition, I told her that I would cancel the meeting and that we'd stay the whole day, then spend another night. I thought it would help to relax her, but she wouldn't hear of it. She insisted on returning to New York by noon."

"Maybe she had some kind of business."

Phillips shook his head determinedly. "No, she didn't," he said darkly. "I know. I checked her appointment book." He looked vaguely ashamed of himself. "Here," he said as he drew a small leather book from his coat pocket. "I thought you might want to see it, too."

Frank took the book and leafed through it quickly.

"Stealing her appointment book," Phillips said mournfully. "I never thought I'd have to do that to her."

Frank continued to go through the book, noting one appointment after another, most of them with organizations whose functions appeared to be charitable.

"She's been very active," Mr. Phillips said weakly.

"Was she working with these groups when she married you?" Frank asked.

Phillips shook his head. "Virginia didn't have any money when I met her. She wouldn't have had anything to give them."

Frank turned to the first day he'd followed her and noted that she'd recorded her morning appointment with the Friends of the Rain Forest, but not her afternoon one with Dr. Powers. "Have you ever heard of a group called Business Associates?" he asked.

Phillips thought a moment. "I don't think so. Why?"

"It's one of Devine's businesses. Your wife made a call to him there the day you came back from the country."

Phillips looked puzzled. "What sort of business is it?"

"It puts people together, a sort of broker for various investors. Did your wife ever mention it?"

"No."

"Did she ever mention investing some of your money in anything?"

Phillips shook his head. "We never talk about money. Only when we talked about the will."

"The will." Frank's eyebrows went up. "What will? Yours?"

Phillips nodded.

"What about it?"

"Well, originally, Virginia would have been provided for, of course, but we'd had a prenuptial agreement that limited her inheritance. It was drawn up on my lawyer's advice. Because things had gotten so complicated with my first marriage, he thought it would be a good idea to have things very clearly stated this time."

"But something changed?"

"The more I thought about it, the more unfair I thought it was. So I made a simple right of survivorship document, which means that when I die, everything goes to her."

"And you told her about this?"

"Of course."

"When?"

"About six weeks ago."

"How did she react?"

"There wasn't much of a reaction," Phillips said. "She kissed me. That was all."

Frank glanced down at the appointment book. "What did your wife do before you met her, Mr. Phillips?"

"She was a consultant, a kind of free-lance money manager."

Frank flipped to Tuesday. She had nothing listed for that day, despite the fact that she'd seen Devine, then strolled through the park.

"But you never used her to manage your money?"

"No, of course not," Phillips said. "I married Virginia, I didn't employ her."

"Do you know who any of her clients were?"

"No, we never discussed her work much. She didn't seem to care for it, really, so she was glad to give it up, she said."

Frank flipped to the next page. She'd jotted down her trip to their country house, and had even listed the time when she expected to be back in the city: twelve noon.

"You wanted to stay over Wednesday afternoon, right?" Frank asked.

"Yes."

"And she wouldn't do it?"

"Absolutely not," Phillips said. "She simply wouldn't hear of it. I'd never seen her so adamant about anything."

"Did she give you a reason why she had to get back?"

"Business, she said. One of her charities. Something about cancer research."

"But you didn't believe her."

"I wasn't sure."

"So you grabbed the book."

Phillips nodded silently.

Frank turned the page to see what she'd scheduled for Thursday morning. Nothing. The trip to Trump Tower was a mystery. He let his eyes drift farther down the page. "She had something listed this afternoon," he said.

Phillips leaned forward slightly and looked at him very solemnly. "Yes, I know. But not until almost four in the afternoon."

Frank nodded, his eyes still on the open appointment book.

"Did she go there?" Phillips asked.

Frank glanced at the page. "You mean to what she has listed here, the Cancer Research Group?"

"That's right."

"I don't know."

Phillips looked at him quizzically. "What do you mean?"

"I lost her, Mr. Phillips," Frank admitted.

"Lost her? How? Where?"

"At Trump Tower."

"Trump Tower?" Phillips asked wonderingly. "What was she doing there?"

"I don't know," Frank said. "But whatever it was, she didn't list it in her appointment book."

"Who did she see there?"

"I'm not sure," Frank told him. "Devine, maybe. He has an apartment there, I know that much."

"But you don't know if she went there?"

"Not for sure, no," Frank admitted. "But I do know that a limousine picked her up and took her to Trump Tower."

"A limousine?"

Frank nodded. "I got the license number. I'm having it traced."

"You think it belongs to Devine?"

"It's possible."

Phillips stared at Frank mournfully. "It is an affair, that's what you think, isn't it?"

"I don't know," Frank said. "It's possible. But why would she be pawning her jewelry over something like that? Why would she be making drops in Central Park?"

"You make her sound like a criminal," Phillips said, a little angrily.

"I'm just asking questions."

Phillips shook his head. "No, somehow I just don't think that's it. Look, I know what a love affair is like. I'm not as entirely innocent as I seem. I've seen people in love, and it doesn't make you look the way Virginia looks. You make her behavior sound . . . I don't know . . . furtive, and that's not how she appears to me."

"How does she appear to you?"

It took Phillips a moment to find the right words, but when he did, they were good enough. "Like her blood has turned to ice," he said.

Frank looked at Phillips pointedly. "How much did you know about your wife before you met her?"

"Not much."

"This consulting work," Frank said, "are you sure she never gave you any details?"

"Not many. She always acted as if I wouldn't want to hear about it, as if it were boring."

"So you didn't press her on it."

"I didn't see any reason to," Phillips said.

"And she just dropped her business entirely after she got married?"

"Yes."

"Did she ever mention working for two people, partners, something like that?"

"No, why do you ask?"

"Well it's the only connection I have between Devine and Dr. Powers. A business connection. They've had some mutual investments, you might say, and I thought that maybe your wife might have worked for them before you met her."

"She never mentioned working for anybody."

"Never mentioned any of her clients?"

"No."

"Did you ever see any business stationery, business cards, any paperwork on her job?"

"No," Phillips said, almost curtly. "What are you suggesting?"

"I'm just wondering about what your wife did before she met you."

"But I've just told you."

"And you've also told me you don't know much about it. If you look at her appointment book, you see nothing but charities, but she goes other places, Mr. Phillips. Places she doesn't bother to record in her book, and I was thinking that they might have something to do with her past, with her old job, that maybe she still has a few clients from before."

Phillips shook his head slowly, his eyes growing more intense as he stared at Frank. "These investments that Powers and Devine have, what are they in?"

"Everything from oil to jewels to Broadway shows," Frank told him.

"That's quite a varied portfolio."

"I guess they put money in anything that seems like a good investment."

Phillips almost laughed. "Broadway shows? A good investment?

I've never had anybody advise me to put my money in a show unless I needed to generate a big loss for tax purposes."

Frank said nothing.

Phillips looked at Frank pointedly. "Is there anything illegal going on with these two?"

"I haven't found anything illegal yet."

"Are you suspicious?"

"I'm always suspicious."

Phillips's eyes darkened. "My will, the changes I made, Virginia started acting strangely right after that."

Frank nodded. "Yes, she did."

"Do you think there's a connection?"

Frank shrugged. "Not necessarily," he said. But I wouldn't bet my life on it, he thought.

Frank sat at his desk for a long time after Phillips left. For a while, he went back over the sketchy details of what he'd been able to gather so far. He tried to put it together with the information Farouk had brought him, but that was sketchy, too, and so he did what he always did at such times. He went back to his own notebooks, staring at names, addresses, times of arrival and departure, until all of the small elements of the case swirled chaotically in his mind.

He stood up, stretched and glanced at the small wall clock which hung like a bleak trophy from his wall. Farouk had given it to him not long after Riviera's death. It was faded white, with a single blue eye staring out of its center, the red hands circling it like bulging veins. For an instant, it seemed to glare at him angrily. Then, as he watched it a bit longer, the single eye appeared to soften and grow faintly sad, as if in response to some increasingly melancholy tale.

He sat down again and lit a cigarette, his eyes scanning the room as they always did, taking in its impossible disarray. Outside his window, the cement stairs remained empty for the time being. He knew that the old woman would take her place soon, but at least it was spring now, and as the weeks passed, she would sleep snugly in the warming air.

He leaned back, drew in a deep breath, and tried to look forward to that warmth. For a moment, it seemed to him that that was everything, just a certain deep, deep warmth, and he thought of the times he'd had it and the times he hadn't, and how different those times were. If Virginia Phillips was growing cold, then her husband was not only doomed to lose her, but to remember that she'd once been with him, full and rich and warm.

You are like the rest. Even when you give, you take.

The Puri Dai's voice suddenly went through him as wrenchingly as a scream. He sat up, the cigarette still dangling precariously from his mouth. He could see her as clearly as if she stood at his door, tall and dark and furious, her fingers curled into fists, her eyes like small glowing coals.

You are like the rest.

What had she meant by that?

You are like the rest.

It was a terrible accusation. But of what crime? What had he done to her that she could despise him so?

He pulled himself to his feet, walked to the window and stared out into the thick spring night. The air seemed cool, and after a moment he walked out into it and looked up. Far above the cruelly pointed spires of the tallest man-made things, he could see a few badly tarnished stars as they shone through the thick corruption of the upper air, and as he watched them, they seemed to accuse him too, demand certain things that they had never asked of any other man.

20

It was nearly midnight when he found Sam McBride lounging against an unmarked car a few yards from the entrance to Manhattan North. He wore a baggy dark-green suit that seemed a size too large for him and an old straw hat with a wide plaid band. He was munching a sandwich casually as Frank approached.

"You're Sam McBride, right?" Frank asked.

McBride nodded. "Who're you?"

Frank realized instantly that the Puri Dai had been right, that McBride did have the same accent he did, only a little deeper, less misshapened by his years in the North.

"My name's Clemons," Frank told him. He took out his identification.

McBride gave it a quick glance, then took another bite from his sandwich. "What can I do for you?"

"I was talking to Leo Tannenbaum about a case you have in the precinct," Frank said. "And he told me you were the first man on the scene."

"What case was that?"

"The murder of a woman on Tenth Avenue."

"There's been more than one of them," McBride said flatly.

"This one happened early Monday morning," Frank said. "At a fortune-telling operation."

It registered in McBride's mind, and Frank saw his eyes light up slightly. "Them Gypsies, you mean?"

"That's right."

"Yeah, I took the dime on that one," McBride said. "It was right near the middle of my tour."

"You work the graveyard shift, then?"

"Midnight to eight," McBride said. "Always have."

"I'm trying to piece some things together on this case," Frank said.

McBride looked at him quizzically. "How come? Who you working for?"

"The woman."

McBride looked at him doubtfully. "That's bullshit."

"She doesn't want me to work for her," Frank admitted. "But I'm doing it anyway."

"How come?"

Frank shrugged. "I don't know," he said. "Maybe because I think she's innocent."

McBride finished off what was left of the sandwich, then crumpled the paper it had been wrapped in and tossed it into the street garbage can a few feet away. "She gave me a full statement when she finally decided to talk," he said. "You know what I mean, a full confession?"

"Yeah, I know."

"But you figure she didn't do it?"

"It think it's possible that she didn't."

"Well, all I can tell you is that she claims she did it," McBride said.

"Did she tell you why?"

"Family trouble."

"Is that all?"

"It's been known to be enough."

"But what about the murder itself?"

"She says it was her that did it."

"I mean the details."

"She don't remember the details."

"I read her statement," Frank said. "Does it have pretty much everything in it?"

"Everything she said."

"So it wasn't a very detailed confession?"

McBride shook his head. "No, but she hit the big points."

"There were a few things that don't add up."

McBride shrugged. "They's always a few things like that," he said. "Like I said, she got the big points pretty good."

"Well, she's a smart woman," Frank said. "She could figure the big points out. The little ones would be tough, though. I mean, she couldn't make up a murder she didn't really know about, could she?"

"What makes you think she don't know about it?"

"Because she's already lied about a few things," Frank said. "And I think she's covering up for somebody."

"The real killer, you mean?"

"It could be," Frank told him. "I don't know."

McBride eased himself from the car and rolled one shoulder. "Arthritis," he said. "I ain't got that many good strokes left." His eyes cut away suddenly, settling on a single little girl who played by herself on the sidewalk, oblivious to the few drunken men who eyed her only a few yards away. "All alone in the middle of the night," he said as he continued to watch her. "It makes me sick, the way people let their kids run wild." He shook his head. "If her daddy knew what was on these streets, he'd never leave her to play like that." He looked at Frank. "Past midnight, can you believe it?" He shook his head. "Maybe he just don't give a shit."

Frank nodded, his eyes studying McBride's face. There was a terrible weariness in it, but it was strangely animated despite that, as if the tiredness came from inside, but had not yet gripped his body, made him useless for the kind of sudden, annihilating action which might still flow from it.

"If I had a little girl," McBride said, "I'd never let her out of my sight." He looked at Frank. "I guess that'd make me a pretty bad daddy, right?"

"It depends."

"You married?"

"Divorced."

"Any kids?"

"I had a daughter."

"Had?"

"She died," Frank said as quickly as he could, then went on immediately.

McBride looked at him, but not brokenly as other people often did. Something in him still trembled with resistance, and for a moment Frank saw that still-living cell as the bedrock of his hope.

"About this case," he said quickly, "I'd like to go over the confession with you. You know, sort of line by line."

McBride settled back against the car. "It was pretty short," he said. "Like you already figured out, there wasn't much to it."

Frank nodded quickly, his mind still on his daughter. He felt exposed, as if he were naked beneath the grayish light of the street lamp, which shone not far away. He wanted it to darken around him, the spaces to draw in and enclose him.

"Maybe we could go someplace," he said edgily. "Get a cup of coffee, a beer if you want one."

McBride shook his head. "Not a beer," he said. "I don't drink. But I could use a Coke."

They ended up at La Femme Gatée, at a small table near the back. Frank pulled out his cigarettes and offered one to McBride.

McBride shook his head. "No, thanks."

Frank smiled quietly. "You're a clean liver."

McBride shrugged. "It ain't that I don't want one," he said. "But I got to live as long as I can. 'Cause of my wife. She's an invalid, you might say. Nobody else to see after her."

Frank nodded. "I understand."

"As for drinking," McBride said with a short smile, "I just like to keep clear-headed, you might say, keep my judgment clear and all that."

Frank lit a cigarette. "Where you from?"

"Mississippi. How about yourself?"

"Alabama."

McBride smiled. "Two old country boys."

"Yeah."

"What brought you up here?"

"A woman," Frank said ruefully.

McBride shrugged. "I come for my wife. She needs a lot of treatment, and there's a group up here that takes care of people in her shape."

Frank nodded.

"I don't much like it, though," McBride added. "You?"

"It's all right," Frank said. He glanced toward the window. "Good as anyplace else, I guess." He took another draw on the cigarette, then crushed it out. "About the confession, it was pretty short."

"Yeah."

"She didn't give many details."

"Maybe they didn't matter to her."

"Maybe she didn't know them."

"It's possible," McBride said. "Or maybe she just wanted to get it over with."

Frank took out his notebook. "Did you take her through the whole thing?"

"Yeah."

"Starting where?"

"With why she did it."

"What'd she say?"

"That she'd gotten into an argument with the other woman, and that the old lady had called her names."

"What names?"

"She didn't remember, just bad names."

"Had they always lived together?"

"Always."

"The three women."

"That's right."

"Did she say anything about the third woman?"

"That she lived there, that's all."

Frank wrote it down. "Did she mention any men?"

McBride shook his head.

"Any relatives or friends?"

"Nobody," McBride said. "From everything she told me, it was like those three were the only people in the world." He took a quick sip of Coke. "They even slept in the same room."

"Yeah, I know."

"You do? You been there?"

"Yeah," Frank said quickly, then hurried on to the next question. "So it was just a family argument? That's the way she told it?"

"That's right."

"That got out of hand."

"There was probably a long buildup," McBride said. "There usually is."

"But she didn't talk about that."

"No."

"What about the murder?"

"I took her through it," McBride said. "She said that she came home early that morning and that the other woman was waiting for her."

"Where had she been?"

"To buy groceries."

"At four in the morning?"

"That's what she said," McBride told him. "And it checked out, too. We talked to the people in the store. It's not too busy at that time of day, and the woman, she had a look about her. Everybody remembered her."

"And she had them delivered, right?"

McBride nodded. "The delivery boy, he actually saw her with the razor in her hand."

"Was the door open when he got there?"

"Yeah, I think so," McBride said. "Anyway, he called for somebody to come to the door, and when nobody come, that's when he stepped on in and saw her."

"With a razor in her hand?"

"That's right."

Frank looked at him skeptically.

McBride shrugged. "That's his story. It's her story, too."

Frank tried to get everything in order. "So she comes home from grocery shopping, gets into an argument with the other woman, kills her, then leaves the door open when the delivery boy shows up?" He looked at McBride pointedly. "Did she give him a tip?"

McBride shook his head.

Frank decided to cut to the bone. "During the whole time she was making her statement, did she say anything that didn't match the murder?"

"You mean the physical facts?"

"Yeah."

"No. She didn't say anything that went against what we already knew."

"How about anything that struck you as odd in some way?"

"No."

"How about the place itself?" Frank said. "Did you give it a good toss?"

"A routine toss."

"Did you find any clothes around?"

"Clothes?"

"Yeah."

"Sure we found clothes," McBride said. "Hell, they was three women living there."

"I mean, in a paper bag. A big brown shopping bag. Sort of damp."

McBride shook his head. "No, why? Should we have found something like that?"

"Well, just before the murder, she went up to that laundromat at Fiftieth Street and did some laundry."

"You sure about that?"

"The old lady who keeps the place remembered her," Frank said. "And that little shit who runs the bodega across the street from the building, he saw her go in with the bag."

McBride shrugged. "Maybe she put 'em away."

"Wet clothes? Wouldn't somebody have noticed? I mean, unless they just disappeared."

McBride seemed unimpressed. "Well, the delivery boy said he left the groceries right in that front room, and we never found them." He drew in a weary breath. " 'Course, anybody could have taken food that was setting there like that."

"But not wet clothes," Frank said.

"Okay," McBride said, giving in slightly. "What's your idea about what happened to them?"

"I think it's possible that somebody took them," Frank said. "That maybe she was doing laundry for somebody."

"You mean, a man?"

"That's right."

McBride smiled slyly. "You mean, like the real killer? The one she's protecting?"

Frank could tell he wasn't buying it. "Maybe," he said with a quick shrug, then went on to something else. "How about anything else like that? Some little thing that got you to thinking."

McBride considered if for a few seconds. "Well, I don't remember nothing very important along them lines," he said finally. "Not the kind of thing you're looking for."

"But something?" Frank asked hungrily. "What?"

"Well, when we were going back over everything, I asked her where she got the razor," McBride said. "You know, just to pin that down."

"What'd she say?"

"She said, 'Off the floor.' "

"Those were her exact words?"

"Exact words."

Frank wrote them down.

"And I said, 'You mean, the razor was on the floor?' " McBride added. "And she said, 'The bathroom.' And I said, 'You mean, off the bathroom floor?' And she said, 'Yes.' "

"Did she look nervous when this was going on?" Frank asked. "Like she'd missed something?"

McBride snapped his fingers. "For just that long she had that look," he said. "She just went right back to herself."

Frank wrote it down quickly, then looked back up at McBride. "When she gave the confession, how'd she seem?"

"Seem?" McBride asked.

"Did she look like she was having trouble with her story?"

"You mean, like she sort of making it up as she went along?" McBride asked.

"Yeah."

"No, she didn't look like that," McBride said. "The only thing I can say is, she seemed mad as hell." He took a sip from the Coke. " 'Course, she's had a few bad days, I can't deny that. But the way she'd look at you, it was like she wanted to blow your head off right there, set the whole world on fire." He shook his head. "The whole time, she looked like she just wanted to haul back and spit right in my face."

Frank could see her face in his mind, the stark, threatening eyes, as if all the world had become the object of her vengeance. *You are like the rest.*

"And to tell you the truth, that's one of the things that made me think she did it," McBride said. "I mean, besides being caught right there, and the blood and the fingerprints and all that kind of thing. I'm talking about the, what you might call, the *will* to do it. I could see it in her, that if she really got into it, she could pull it off."

"Kill somebody?"

"Kill anybody," McBride said. "It's not everybody that can actually take something to the limit that way." He grew silent for a moment, his face growing somewhat red as the seconds passed. "A woman can get mad," he said finally. "Real mad, but most times it don't amount to much, don't amount to nothing a man ever has to really be afraid of." Suddenly his eyes glistened and his voice became a fierce, vehement whisper. "And more's the pity for that, Frank," he said. "More's the fucking pity."

— 21 —

Farouk arrived at Frank's office just as he was heading up the stairs the next morning.

"You are going to Mrs. Phillips's home, yes?" he asked.

"Yeah," Frank said as he mounted the final step.

"Perhaps, you wish to have a companion?"

"Why? Do you want to come along?"

"There is something that interests me," Farouk said. He nudged Frank forward and the two of them began walking east on Forty-ninth Street.

"The license number which you gave me," Farouk said. "I worked on it this morning."

Frank glanced at his watch. It was only a little after eight. "You must have gotten on it pretty early," he said.

"Like you, I do not always sleep."

"Well, what did you find out about the limousine?" he asked.

"First of all, it does not belong to Mr. Devine," Farouk told him.

"Who does it belong to?"

Farouk smiled darkly. "Winston Burroughs."

"Who's that?"

"A most important man," Farouk said. "But one who is not known for his charitable acts."

They reached the corner of Eighth Avenue and waited for the light to change. Frank glanced back at the delicatessen on the corner. "I could use a cup of coffee," he said.

Farouk nodded. "Yes, good. I will join you."

They walked inside and took a table at the back. The waiter came and they both ordered coffees.

"Coffee, regular," Farouk said unhappily after the waiter had disappeared. "It is all they have in such places."

Frank lit a cigarette. "What do you know about this Burroughs guy?"

"That he is powerful," Farouk said. "He moves in great circles. A British citizen, but an international businessman, and he also has diplomatic status. He would not be subject to the laws of this country."

Frank looked at Farouk pointedly. "Is there any reason to think he's broken a few of them?"

Farouk shook his head. "None at all," he said. "But to one who lives so high, the law seems far below."

"You don't like him, do you?"

"I do not like his kind. People who live beyond the fear of consequences."

The coffees arrived, and the two of them drank silently for a moment.

Farouk was the first to speak. "Burroughs has had important dealings with Devine."

Again, Frank thought about asking him how he knew such things, but stopped himself. "What kind of dealings?" he asked instead.

"Mostly it has been in oil and real estate," Farouk said. "He is a man of many investments."

"But everything looks legal?"

"Yes."

"How about charities?"

"As I said, he is not a generous man."

"But he must give away something."

"He funds political parties," Farouk said.

"What kind?"

"Those which would serve him well."

"How?"

"Open their countries up to him," Farouk said. "Markets. Resources. As we say in Arabic, 'Buying and selling are the wind and rain.'"

Frank put out his cigarette and glanced at his watch. "We'd better get going."

The two men got to their feet and headed toward the cashier at the front of the delicatessen.

Farouk walked out into the street and lingered there while Frank paid the check. He was looking at the delicatessen's name when Frank joined him on the street a few seconds later.

"Do you know what it means," he asked, "'La Femme Gatée'?"

Frank shook his head.

Farouk thought a moment, struggling for the right translation. "The unruly . . . no, not exactly." He considered it again, his eyes perusing the words a second time. "Yes," he said finally. "That is it." He looked at Frank. "The ungovernable woman," he said. "She who cannot be ruled." As he said it, something seemed to strike him suddenly.

Frank leaned toward him. "What is it?"

He didn't answer. Instead, he closed his eyes very slowly, then opened them.

"You must go alone today," he said solemnly. "I have changed my mind. There is something else I must work on." Then he turned and headed back down Forty-ninth Street, moving away so quickly that Frank didn't have time to ask him if he'd meant the night case or the day.

Frank had barely arrived at his usual place across the street from Phillips's brownstone when he saw her emerge from the building. She walked east to Madison Avenue, but this time crossed it and headed farther east, all the way to Park Avenue. Then she turned south, walked to the corner of Park and Sixtieth Street and stopped.

There was a large building just behind her, and after a moment, she walked behind one of its large black supporting columns. For a time, Frank couldn't see her. Then she came into view again, her hair still in place, her shoes the same, along with her dress, but with a red silk handkerchief dangling loosely from her hand.

She looked as if she'd used it to daub her eyes, but instead of returning it to her purse, she walked once again to the curb, then let it drop to the ground beside her.

Almost immediately, another limousine pulled up to the curb. This time it was a white Cadillac, and Frank recorded its license number quickly as Mrs. Phillips disappeared into its dark interior.

After it had pulled away, Frank walked over to where Mrs. Phillips had been standing. Her red handkerchief was fluttering gently on the sidewalk, and he bent down and picked it up. It was soft and very delicate, and he unconsciously ran it through his fingers while he watched the white limousine move slowly southward through the thick Park Avenue traffic. It was almost out of sight before he stuffed the handkerchief into his pocket and hailed a cab.

The white limousine went directly to Trump Tower, drove into the parking garage and disappeared, just as the black one had the day before.

Since there was no need to go into the building, Frank decided to maintain his surveillance from just outside the building. He slumped against the wall and watched as people moved in and out, whirling through the large bronze revolving doors. Most of them were tourists, since the building itself had become one of the city's most spectacular sights. Whole families stood gaping at its impressive exterior, then trudged inside to take pictures of the marble walls, greenery and waterfalls.

As he watched them, Frank thought of his own early days in the city, of the long walks with Karen, then the longer ones by himself, a rogue figure stalking through the city's twilight streets. Now more than ever, it was this that struck him as his appointed fate, to be forever the solitary night crawler that Tannenbaum had called him, wifeless, childless and, except for Farouk, utterly alone. It was not a fate that struck him anymore as entirely dreadful. He had come to accept it the way he accepted death, along with a vast number of deep, unrightable wrongs. And yet, there were times when this acceptance seemed like something broken in him, not a sign of strength or resignation, but of an old resistance that had lost its will.

He was still thinking vaguely of these things, smarting slightly under their invisible lash, when a black limousine pulled up in front of the Tower. Reflexively, he glanced at its license plate and realized that it was the same as the one he had written into his notebook the day before.

Two large men got out and took up positions on either side of the passenger door. One of them snapped a radio up to his mouth and said something. Then the other man bent forward and opened the door.

A short, somewhat stocky man got out of the car, moving awkwardly, as if he were pulling a heavy sack behind him. Almost immediately, another man stepped up to him and thrust out his hand. "Good to see you, Mr. Burroughs," he said.

Burroughs smiled happily and shook his hand. "I am sorry," he said, "but I have only twenty minutes."

"Plenty of time, I hope," the other man said cheerfully. "Please, come in."

With that, the two men walked quickly into the lobby of Trump Tower, turned to the right and entered a luxury jewelry shop which glittered with diamonds and rubies, and which had been cleared of its usual number of gawking tourists.

Once Burroughs was inside, the two men from the limousine took up their positions on either side of the door and smiled sweetly as people passed them, glancing inside to watch Burroughs make his purchases.

It seemed only seconds before Burroughs stepped out of the shop and hustled back to his limousine, but it was enough time for Frank to confirm Farouk's impression, that he was a man who knew no consequences.

Frank stationed himself beside the revolving door once Burroughs's limousine had pulled away. If Mrs. Phillips left by the front door, instead of being whisked away in the limousine that had picked her up on Park Avenue, then he would be able to resume his surveillance. It was a chance he had to take, since he couldn't cover both places at the same time.

Almost an hour later, the risk paid off, and Mrs. Phillips came through the revolving door. He was only a few feet from her, and as she lingered a moment on the sidewalk, he was able to get a long, concentrated look at her face. Her eyes were light blue and strangely moist. Her lipstick was bright red, and in contrast to her smooth, white skin, it made her mouth look like a wide gash. From a distance, she might have looked like a sleek East Side model, someone who knew how to wear clothes, how to stand with an elegant defiance amid the pedestrian traffic that swirled around her. But she was very near to him now, and all of that looked like nothing but a pose that was less grand than the woman who assumed it. He could feel a curious power in the way she stood very still and let her eyes stare out across the moving crowds as if they were troops under her command. She seemed as if she were the focus of her own concentration, as if some kind of spotlight beamed down upon her constantly, singling her out from the mass, and as Frank continued to look at her, it was easy for him to imagine her raising money for her charities, ordering wine from the respectful sommelier, or conducting complex deals in a room full of cigar-chomping men who never for one moment doubted her right to stand among them.

Suddenly, in a quick, darting movement, she turned to face him, her eyes concentrating on him with an unmistakable intensity, bearing in like the twin barrels of a cold blue shotgun. "The time," was all she said.

Frank quickly glanced at his watch. "It's ten-fifteen," he said.

She nodded quickly. "Thank you." Then she turned and headed down the avenue.

Frank stepped forward, then stopped, realizing that he could not follow her now, that she had held him in view too long not to recognize his face. So he simply craned his neck above the swirling crowd and watched her disappear into its sea of gently bobbing heads.

22

Farouk looked at him, astonished.

"The thing is, this time I'm pretty sure she made me," Frank told him. "Yesterday, across from her place, I'm not sure she noticed me. But today, she looked right at me."

Farouk thought about it. "Perhaps she had already made you, Frank."

"I've thought of that, too," Frank said. "It's possible. But I don't know when or how."

Farouk fell silent, his eyes drifting toward the ceiling. "And she said only, 'The time,' yes?" he asked when they dropped toward Frank again.

"That's right."

Farouk smiled at the mystery of it. "A woman of codes."

"Codes?"

"Codes. Passwords."

"What do you mean?"

"It is possible, is it not, that she thought you were someone else."

"Someone else?"

"A contact of some kind. As they say, a secret agent."

"A contact," Frank repeated, almost to himself. "But for what?"

Farouk lifted his hands, palms up. "I do not know."

Frank took a moment to consider the possibilities. "She could be some kind of middleman."

Farouk nodded.

"A go-between, or something."

"It is a world of go-betweens," Farouk said. "And Mrs. Phillips could be such a person."

"Or just a packager, like Devine."

"Always possible."

"But of something secret, illegal."

Farouk smiled faintly, but with an obvious delight. "The day case is taking on something of the night, yes?"

"Enough for me to need your help on it," Frank admitted.

"I am pleased to be of assistance," Farouk said matter-of-factly. "What is it that you wish?"

Frank handed him the license number he'd recorded from the white limousine. "For starters."

Farouk glanced at the paper, then handed it back.

"And some legwork, too," Frank told him.

"Because you cannot follow her now," Farouk said.

Frank nodded. "All I can do is go through this," he said as he held up the copy of Mrs. Phillips's address book, which her husband had given him.

"But the woman's address," Farouk said. "What is it?"

Frank gave it to him.

"When do you usually arrive?" Farouk asked.

"She's never left before eight-thirty."

"From what place do you observe?"

"There's a little brick wall almost directly across from her house. I usually stand there."

"Then I will avoid it."

Frank nodded. "Yeah, I think you should. I'd have changed positions again myself, if I were going there tomorrow." He opened the drawer of his desk and pulled out the camera. "If you see her with anybody, I'd like a picture."

Farouk took the camera. "Very well."

"That's all," Frank said. "Just keep track of her and let me know where she goes, who she sees, everything."

Farouk nodded quietly. "And what are you to do?"

"I'll do some work on Powers," Frank said. "Try to find out what her connection to him is."

Farouk did not seem entirely satisfied. "About the night," he said. "About the Puri Dai."

She strode into Frank's mind, tall and furious, inexpressibly in need, but utterly beyond him also, as if she lived on a distant planet which only once in a thousand years aligned itself with him. "She still doesn't want me to work the case," he said quietly. "But I still believe she's innocent."

"Then that is the thing that you must prove."

"I'll try," Frank said. "But it's really closing down. I only have one more place to go."

Farouk looked at him very seriously. "Then go there right away," he said.

The Food Palace was located on Forty-third Street. Its night manager was a large black woman whose hair stuck out in a thousand different directions, as if she'd just been hit with forty thousand volts.

"Private eye?" she asked incredulously as she stared at his identification. "For who?"

"A private client," Frank said.

"This got something to do with the store?"

"One of your deliveries," Frank said.

Her face filled with recognition. "Oh, you mean Pedro. How he seen that woman that killed her mother. The police already axed him a million questions about that."

"I got a few more," Frank said. "Is he here?"

"Maybe so," the woman said. She lifted her head slightly and called the cashier, who stood at a register a few feet away. "Hey, Angela, you seen Pedro?"

"He's on delivery," Angela called back, without ever taking her eyes off the cash register.

The manager looked back at Frank. "He should be back pretty soon. You can wait for him."

"Thanks."

"He's a little short guy," the manager added. "Seventeen, something like that. Sort of wiry-looking, with bad skin." She looked repulsed. "Oily hair, too," she said with a short mocking laugh. "Gives me the creeps."

Frank smiled. "Thanks a lot."

"No problem," the manager said. She stepped back into the small raised booth from which she could observe the entire store and pointed to the far right-hand corner. "He'll probably show up over there," she said. "By the dairy section."

Frank walked down the nearest aisle, then wheeled to the right and stood by an enormous cooler of milk and cheese. There were two double doors to the left of the cooler, and he kept his eyes more or less focused on them. Other customers passed him, pushing grocery carts before them. Sometimes they gave him a wide berth, as if sensing something dangerous in him, contained, but potentially explosive, a creature who lived by different rules.

Pedro came through the double doors about fifteen minutes later. He was wearing blue jeans, cut out at the knees, and a fishnet shirt to display the pectorals he'd clearly been working to develop.

Frank stepped over to him, blocking his movement down the aisle. "Are you Pedro Ortiz?" he asked.

Ortiz's body tightened, as if he were preparing to receive a blow.

To ease the young man's mind, Frank quickly pulled out his identification. "My name's Frank Clemons," he said. "I'm a private investigator."

Ortiz continued to look at him apprehensively, as if the line that divided a private investigator from a cop had never been made clear to him. "Hey, man, I ain't done nothing," he whined. "Why you bustin' on me, man?"

"I'm not busting you," Frank assured him. "I just have a few questions, that's all."

Ortiz didn't look as though he was buying it. "Questions? What kind questions you got, man? 'Cause I ain't done nothing." He raised his hands and waved them back and forth. "No way, man. I'm clean." He'd began to sweat. "No way, man. I mean it. I'm clean."

Frank had seen that kind of sweat before. He knew where it came from. "How much time have you done, Pedro?" he asked.

"I did two years, that's all," Ortiz said. The whine was still in his voice, but had taken on a childlike, petulant edge. "It was a bummer, too, man. A rush job, tha's right."

"Where'd you do it?"

"Allentown, man."

"That's federal."

"Fucking post office, man."

"Two years?" Frank said. "For mail fraud, or something like that? You must have copped a plea."

Ortiz said nothing. He hunched his shoulders resentfully.

"You must have sent Uncle a package, Pedro," Frank said pointedly.

Ortiz's eyes shifted about nervously.

"There must be some people you'd rather not see," Frank added. "But let me tell you something, I'm not working for them."

Ortiz's eyes suddenly settled on Frank. "Who you working for, man?"

"Nobody you need to hear about," Frank said. "But I have a few questions for you."

Ortiz shifted from one foot to the next. "Not here, man. I got a job, you know. I mean, you got to see how it is, you understand what I'm saying?"

Frank said nothing.

"I mean, you looked at yourself in the mirror lately?" Ortiz asked. "You got a look to you, man. It ain't normal."

"Where do you want to go?"

"I'll meet you when my shift's over."

"When's that?"

"I got second shift today." Ortiz told him. "I'll be off at midnight."

"Okay," Frank said. "Smith's Bar over on Forty-seventh and Eighth."

"Yeah, okay, man, tha's good."

"Don't hang me up, Pedro," Frank warned him. He gave him a psychotic stare. "I don't like that."

"No, no way, man," Pedro sputtered. "You'll see me, man. I'm stand-up, you know?"

Frank smiled thinly. "I'm sure you are," he said. *On your mother's grave,* he thought.

23

He was on his second shot of Jameson's by the time midnight rolled around. The usual crowd was mulling over the day's losses, mostly old-timers staring listlessly at themselves in the mirror that stretched out across the full length of the dark, splintery bar.

Frank sat at a table in the back. He could see the traffic along Eighth Avenue very easily, despite the grayish clouds that rose from the steam cart at the front of the room. A small white-haired man was standing behind it, cutting two-inch thick slices of corned beef while an old woman waited for it, her small red tongue flicking hungrily as she watched.

The old woman was about halfway through her sandwich when Ortiz finally came through the door. He stared around a moment, craning his neck until he spotted Frank at the back of the room. He looked disappointed to find him there, hunched his shoulders slightly and sauntered back to him.

"So, I'm here," he said gruffly as he sat down.

Frank took out his notebook.

"Christ, you ain't even gonna spring for a drink?" Ortiz said.

Frank signaled for a barman, and he stepped over immediately.

"Gimme a margarita," Ortiz said. "Straight up, with salt."

The barman looked at Ortiz as if he were some creature from another species. "We don't have mixed drinks."

"You don't have mixed drinks?" Ortiz squealed. "What kind of fucking bar is this?"

The barman's eyes squeezed together, and the tattooed belly

dancer on his upper arm did a quick bump and grind. "We don't have mixed drinks," he repeated grimly.

"He'll have a beer," Frank said quickly, to ease the tension.

"Beer?" Ortiz blurted. "I don't want a . . ."

"Beer it is," the barman said crisply. Then he spun around and disappeared.

"Classy fuckin' place," Ortiz muttered.

Frank opened his notebook. "This has to do with a woman," he said.

Ortiz laughed. "Don't everything."

"This one is accused of murder," Frank added.

"Oh, so tha's what this is all about," Ortiz said happily. He looked relieved. "That killing over on Tenth Avenue."

Frank nodded.

"Jesus, man," Ortiz said excitedly, "I ran right into that fuckin' thing. I was right in the middle of it."

Frank turned to a blank page and moved his pen into position. "I want you to tell me everything you know about that night."

"I told it all to the cops."

"This time it's to me," Frank told him. "Maybe you'll remember something."

Ortiz began, but spotted the barman walking toward him with the beer. He waited until after the first long drink to begin.

"Well, I was working the third shift that night," he said.

"Midnight to eight?"

"Tha's it," Ortiz said. "We call it the 'suicide shift,' because you're out on these fuckin' streets, you know, when you gotta be crazy to be out there." He shrugged. "But in this neighborhood you got a lot of people that don't do nothin' 'cept at night. They sleep the fuckin' day away, and at night, tha's when they get goin'. So we got deliveries from midnight to eight. It ain't a lot of 'em, but enough to matter to the store, you know, so they got to provide the service and all, 'cause if they don't, they lose these night types."

"When did you get the call from the woman on Tenth Avenue?" Frank asked quickly, trying to keep him focused.

"It wasn't no call."

"What do you mean?"

"She come in, that woman," Ortiz said. "She didn't call for nothing."

"She came into the store?"

"Tha's right."

"Had she ever done that before?"

"I ain't never seen her in there," Ortiz said. He grinned. "And I woulda noticed her. Because she was real fine, you know?"

"What time did she come in?"

"Musta been around three-thirty in the mornin'."

"Was anybody with her?"

Ortiz shook his head.

"Are you sure?"

"She was alone," Ortiz repeated. "I woulda noticed if she been with somebody."

Frank nodded. "So she came in the store. Then what?"

"She did some shopping," Ortiz said. "I seen her scooting around the aisles, you know, gettin' this and that. She was movin' real fast, like she was in a big hurry."

"You watched her the whole time?"

"Well, the store was empty, and it gets boring. So, when a fine thing like that comes in, it sort of gets you workin' at it again, you know?"

"How long was she in the store?"

"Maybe fifteen minutes."

"So she didn't buy very much."

"No," Ortiz said, "just a few things."

"And she looked like she was in a hurry?"

"Moving real fast, yeah."

"What happened when she finished getting whatever she needed?" Frank asked.

"Well, Gloria run it through the register, like always. Then the woman paid, and Gloria done what she was supposed to do next."

"Which was?"

"She bagged the stuff."

"Where were you?"

"I was standin' at the end of the counter," Ortiz said. "Sort of watchin' the whole thin', Gloria doin' the baggin', and that woman. She was the one I was watchin'."

"What was she doing?"

"She was puttin' her change away."

"But she didn't take her groceries," Frank said.

"No, she didn't," Ortiz said. "She looked at Gloria and she asked if the stuff could be delivered. Gloria said yeah, okay, that was good, and the woman gave her the address."

"Then she left?"

"Tha's right," Ortiz said. "And I didn't see her again 'til I brought the stuff over."

"How long did that take?"

"About ten minutes."

Frank wrote it down, then looked back up at Ortiz. "When you got to the place on Tenth Avenue, what happened?"

"I went on in."

"You went in?"

"Tha's right, like I said."

"You didn't knock at the door."

"Didn't have to," Ortiz said. "It was already open."

"She'd left the front door open?" Frank asked doubtfully.

Ortiz shrugged. "Hey, man, I thought it was funny, too, but I said to myself, I said, 'Hey, man, she probably knows you're right behind her with the stuff, so tha's how come she just left it open.' "

"So you just went in?"

"Tha's right," Ortiz said. "I sort of poked my head in there and I guess I said something. You know, called something, like, 'Hey, delivery's here,' something like that. Then I walked on in."

"What did you see?"

Ortiz shivered. "Man, it was *weird*," he said. "Like from *Nightmare on Elm Street,* you know?"

"What was weird?"

"Just her, you know, standing there." He shivered again. "She'd just done it, you know. The blood was still dripping from the razor. And she was just standing there, with her arm raised up over her head, like she was about to slice her again."

Frank nodded and wrote it down. "Standing where?" he asked when he'd finished.

"Over that other woman, the dead one."

"Tell me exactly how she was standing."

"*Over* her, like I said," Ortiz told him. "With this weird look on her face."

"Her face?" Frank said immediately. "She was facing you?"

"Yeah, facin' me."

"And you were standing at the front of the room?"

"Behind some kinda curtain."

"A beaded curtain, right?" Frank asked. "Red beads?"

"Yeah, red beads."

"And she was facing you with her arm in the air?"

"And the razor in her hand, you know, and it was drippin'," Ortiz said. He laughed dryly. "It's funny what you notice. I noticed it was still drippin'."

Frank wrote it down. "Where was the body?"

"It was on the floor," Ortiz said. "And like I told you, she was standin' over it."

"Where were her feet?"

"Sort of spread apart," Ortiz said, "one on each side of the other woman's head."

Frank's pencil stopped. "Head?"

"Tha's right."

Frank tried to picture it. "So she was facing you with her arm in the air and the razor in her hand?"

"Yeah."

"And her feet were on either side of the other's woman's head?"

"Tha's the way it was," Ortiz said flatly.

"Did she see you?"

"I think so."

"What did she do?"

"Nothin'."

"Did she come toward you?"

"No."

"How about her arm," Frank said. "Did she lower it?"

Ortiz shook his head.

"So she just stood in place, and let you look at her?"

"Yeah, for just a second," Ortiz said. "Then I got the hell out of there."

"And called the police," Frank said.

"Tha's right," Ortiz told him. He took a sip of the beer. He looked pleased with himself. "So tha's the story."

"What'd you do with the groceries?" Frank asked.

"Huh?"

"The groceries," Frank repeated. "They weren't in the room."

"In the room?"

"The woman's place," Frank said. "The cops checked out everything. They never found any groceries."

Ortiz suddenly stiffened. "What are you talkin' about, man? The cops didn't find no groceries?"

Frank shook his head.

"But I dropped 'em, man," Ortiz said insistently. "Like I told them cops, I dropped the bag, man. I dropped it right by that curtain."

Frank gave him a withering stare. "Well, nobody found them, Pedro."

"Tha's why them cops kept coming back to me, then," he said, almost to himself.

"They fingered you at first," Frank told him, "because of the groceries, because they were missing."

"But the woman confessed," Ortiz said. "So I'm off the hook, right?"

"Except that the groceries are still missing," Frank said darkly.

Ortiz took a quick nervous gulp of the beer. "I dropped them by that fuckin' curtain. Tha's all I know, man."

"Well somebody got rid of them," Frank said.

"Not me, man," Ortiz said edgily. "I didn't do nothin' to them groceries."

"Do you remember what they were?"

"They was groceries, tha's all."

"Well, you were standing right there when Gloria bagged them," Frank said.

"I seen what they was," Ortiz told him. "They was the usual thing." He went through the list. "Some tuna, some bread and mustard and stuff like that. Some peanut butter and crackers. She had some fruit, too, apples and shit. She started to buy a quart of milk, but she decided not to, and just left it in her basket. And she had a

magazine or something, and one of them little car games, and
a . . ."

"Car games?"

"Yeah."

"What's that?"

"They sell them on a rack beside the checkout counter," Ortiz
said. "It's in a little plastic packet and it's full of little games and
puzzles for kids to play with when they're on a trip. I seen her grab
it."

Frank remembered them now, remembered buying the same
sort of thing for his own daughter when she was nine or ten, remembered how she would sit silently in the backseat of the car as they
all drove toward his hometown, the sound of her fingers as she
played, the calm whirr of her breathing.

"And the woman took one of those games?" he asked intently.

"Yeah, she did."

"And it was put in the grocery bag like everything else?" Frank
asked excitedly. "With all the other stuff she bought that night?"

Ortiz nodded. "Yeah, I seen Gloria put it in there. It was stickin'
out of the bag when I got to Tenth Avenue." He smiled at the irony
of it. "Just a little game, you know, like for a child."

Suddenly Frank saw the little room with its small chair and tiny
square of foam rubber, then the hook-and-eye lock, which had been
screwed too loosely into the doorjamb to hold an adult inside, but
which would have worked just fine if the prisoner was a child.

24

The Women's Center was only a few blocks from Smith's Bar, and Frank walked to it within a matter of minutes. It was nearly one in the morning, and the mood of the avenue had darkened considerably during the last few hours. The bridge and tunnel crowd had abandoned Manhattan for the wide green safety of the suburbs, and the edginess of the people they'd left behind had slowly begun to take over the street's still-bustling atmosphere. A few crack zombies slumped against the iron metal gratings of the closed storefronts, and here and there, a prostitute from one of the slum hotels threw a whispered remark at a quickly passing stranger: *Hey, babe, wanna date?*

During all of his short walk to the center, Frank tried to think of exactly what he was going to say to the Puri Dai once he saw her again. It was easy for him to imagine her dark eyes watching him steadily as he went through what he'd learned from Ortiz, but her reaction was beyond him, and something in its unpredictability seemed to draw him instinctively toward her, as if she were the lure he could not avoid.

"Why do you want to see her?" the woman at the desk asked as Frank returned his identification to his pocket.

"She made a confession," Frank answered. "I'm checking on the details."

"Is she expecting you?"

"No."

"I'll need to let her know," the woman said. She was wearing a sturdy, corduroy jacket and pleated trousers. Her hair was long and fell in brown strands to her shoulders. Her voice was very crisp and self-assured, not a woman who might fall easily before a disingenuous tale.

"She won't see me, if you do let her know," Frank told her bluntly.

The woman looked at him suspiciously. "Well, that's her choice, isn't it?"

"I'm trying to help her," Frank said.

"And she doesn't want you to?"

"That's about it."

The woman glanced back down at the name. "Magdalena Immaculata Cortez," she said. She looked at Frank. "What is she anyway?"

Frank gave the only answer that struck him as entirely accurate. "A woman," he said.

The woman laughed. "Well, I know that," she said. "All we have here is women."

"The thing is," Frank said, "she may have confessed to something she didn't do."

"She's up for murder, right?"

Frank nodded.

"Yeah, I read her sheet," the woman said. She smiled. "I read all the sheets. I'm in law school. Fordham Law." She put out her hand. "Ruth O'Keefe."

Frank shook her hand lightly, then smiled as amiably as he knew how, a technique which Farouk used very well, but which always gave him a faint, insistent ache. "Can you help me out?" he asked.

Ruth studied him a little longer. "I'm not really sure."

"Well, there's no law against me just dropping by her room, is there?"

"That depends."

"On what?"

"Whether you're on the visitor's list," she said.

"Could you check?"

"Sure, no problem," Ruth said. She pulled out a small stack of papers and flipped through them until she came to the one that referred to the Puri Dai. "Well, you're in luck, Mr. Clemons."

Frank gave her another smile. "Frank."

"Anyway, you're on the list."

Frank was surprised. "I am?"

"Yeah," the woman said. She turned the folder toward him. "You and somebody named Deegan."

"That's her lawyer."

Ruth turned the folder back around. "Anyway, you're on the list."

"So I can go on up?"

Ruth hesitated.

"I'm trying to save her life," Frank said, "even though she doesn't want me to."

Ruth considered it a moment, then made her decision. "All right, I'll let you go up unannounced," she said. "But if she asks for you to leave, you'll have to."

"I understand."

"She's on the sixth floor. Room 603. You can take the elevator at the end of the hall."

"Thanks," Frank said.

"Actually, I'm glad you dropped by," she said. "You can save me some steps."

"How?"

Ruth handed Frank a small blue envelope. "This is for Maggie," she said.

Frank took the envelope and glanced at it. It was addressed to Magdalena Cortez. There was no return address, no stamp or postage mark.

"Would you mind taking it to her?" Ruth asked.

Frank lifted the envelope toward her slightly. "Somebody must have delivered this," he said.

"Yeah."

"Who?"

Ruth shook her head. "I don't know."

"You didn't see anybody?"

"I guess it came while I was away from my desk."

"When was that?"

"About an hour ago," Ruth said. "I had to go to the bathroom." She looked at him curiously. "Why, you don't want to take it to her?"

"No, I'll take it to her," Frank said quickly. "I was just wondering who it was from."

Ruth looked at him knowingly. "Well, I guess you'll just have to ask her, won't you?"

The Puri Dai was not in Room 603 when Frank got to it, but another woman was, a girl with blond hair who whirled around instantly as he entered the room.

"Who are you?" she blurted.

"My name's Clemons," Frank told her. "Are you in this room, too?"

"Why?" the girl asked nervously. She raised one of her arms defensively. "Why do you want to know?" Her eyes were light green, and they were bulging fearfully. She was very thin. The skin over her face was drawn tightly over her skull, so that the structure of her bones could be seen behind it. She had a wide, flat forehead and high, rounded cheekbones that gave her a primitive, hunted look, which nothing in her manner did anything to offset.

Frank eased himself out the door so that he no longer blocked it. "There's another woman in this room," he said. "I was looking for her."

The girl said nothing. She covered her stomach with one of her arms, its fingers grasping shakily at the waist of her dress. "She went down to the common room," she said.

"Where's that?"

"End of the hall," the woman told him. "It's got double doors."

Frank offered a quick smile. "Okay, thanks," he said. He nodded politely. "Sorry if I disturbed you."

He eased himself out into the hallway, then walked to the common room.

The Puri Dai was sitting in one of its empty corners, her body very erect in a red plastic chair. She had combed her hair, and it fell over her shoulders in long black tresses. Her skin was very dark in the half-light of the deserted corner.

Frank took off his hat as he stepped over to her. "This is for you," he said as he handed her the envelope.

The Puri Dai's eyes had regained their light, as if something remained inexhaustibly alive within her. She took the note, but did not look at it. Instead, her eyes remained almost imploringly on Frank. "Will you do as I ask?" she said.

Frank shook his head again. "You didn't kill anybody," Frank told her bluntly. "And one way or the other, I'm going to prove it."

She didn't deny it, but only turned away, her eyes now set on the street below.

"You went to a grocery store," Frank said. "You did that only a few minutes before the murder."

The Puri Dai kept her eyes turned toward the window.

"You bought a few things, and then had them delivered," Frank added. "The guy who brought them over was named Pedro Ortiz."

She drew in a long, deep breath, held it for a moment, then let it out it a quick rush.

"He's the one who talked to the cops," Frank said. "The sole eyewitness, right?"

Silence.

Frank took out his notebook. "Do you know what he saw?"

The Puri Dai didn't answer.

Frank opened the notebook. "I spoke to him only a few minutes ago. He went over everything very carefully."

The Puri Dai rose to her feet, but continued to look toward the window.

"He said the door was open, but that he didn't go in at first," Frank said. "'The door was open,' he said." He looked at her penetratingly. "Open," he repeated.

Silence.

"On Tenth Avenue."

Silence.

"At four o'clock in the morning."

Her eyes drifted over to him, but still she didn't speak.

Frank stared at her a moment, her stare searing him around the edges, until he pulled away, and let his eyes drop back to the notebook.

"He called to you. You heard him, didn't you?"

The Puri Dai said nothing.

"He said, 'Hey, delivery's here.'"

One arm rose slightly, then drifted down to her side again.

"There was no answer," Frank continued. "So after a while, he stepped inside." His eyes followed his notes carefully, concentrating on the smallest details as he went on. "He called to you again after he stepped into the building. But you didn't answer. He didn't go very far in, but from just inside the door, he could see the curtain." He looked up at her. "You know the one I mean, the one with the red beads."

Her eyes shifted away from him, locked onto the dark window once again.

Frank looked at his notebook again. "He walked over to the curtain, and looked through it." He stopped, hoping that she might say something. When she didn't, he continued. "That's when he saw you."

The Puri Dai's eyes closed slowly and remained closed until Frank spoke again.

"This is what he saw," Frank said. He hesitated, hoping that she would take up the narrative. "He saw you," he began again after a moment. "No one else. Just you."

She opened her eyes and turned her head toward him, her face strangely mobile, as if lights were passing over it.

"Just you," Frank repeated, this time with a slight edge to his voice, as if he knew it all now, and was merely waiting for her confirmation. "With the razor," he added, then hesitated again. "Standing over the old woman," he said finally. "With the razor in your hand."

Her eyes studied him closely for a moment, then a kind of visible relief swept into her face. "That is all," she said. "That is all he could have seen."

"Yes, that's all," Frank admitted. "But there are a few details that still interest me."

The relief disappeared from her face.

"Why was the door open?" Frank asked.

There was no answer.

"It was open because you wanted Ortiz to come in," Frank said. "You wanted him to see you."

Silence.

"But what he saw, there's a problem with it."

The Puri Dai's eyes filled with an intense concentration, but she did not speak.

Frank lifted his arm high above his head, the fist clenched. "Your hand was in the air like this," he said. "That's a stabbing motion." He brought his hand down in a rapid slice. "Like that." He looked at her closely. "But she wasn't killed like that. She wasn't stabbed at all. Her throat was cut."

The Puri Dai said nothing.

"And it was cut from behind," Frank added. "The killer had to have been standing directly behind her, and she was probably on her knees."

Her eyes began to glisten, as if she were seeing it.

"She was on her knees," Frank repeated, "and she was facing that little room."

Her hands began to tremble slightly.

"That little room that someone was kept locked up in," Frank added.

Her fingers began to scratch mercilessly at her thighs.

"And the killer took the woman by the hair, and pulled it back," Frank said in a hard, relentless voice. "And he brought the blade across her throat."

Suddenly, the Puri Dai's face grew stony. "Go now," she said. "I do not want you."

"You were standing with your feet on either side of her head," Frank continued relentlessly. "You couldn't have killed her in that position."

"Go," she repeated, with a sudden, unexpected tenderness, almost pleadingly.

"And the groceries," Frank said, as if he had not heard her. "Peanut butter. Bread. Fruit. Do you know what they all have in common?"

The Puri Dai did not answer.

"They don't need to be put in a refrigerator," Frank said. "You'd also bought a quart of milk, but suddenly you didn't take it. You couldn't take it, because you weren't going to have a refrigerator, were you?"

"Go," the Puri Dai said softly. "You do not know what you are doing."

Frank looked at her very pointedly. "And then, there's this," he said. He reached into his jacket pocket, pulled out the little car game he'd bought on the way to the center and tossed it onto the sofa where she'd been sitting.

The Puri Dai's eyes flashed toward it, then back up at Frank, where they fixed on his desperately.

"You were going to run away," Frank said determinedly. "But not alone. You were going to take someone else with you." He looked at her intently. "A child."

One of her hands drew in around the blue note, crushing it completely.

"You were going to take the person who was kept locked up in that little room, where the latch is high and loose, so that only a child couldn't get out if it were locked."

The Puri Dai pressed her hands flat against her legs.

"Is it your child?" Frank asked.

She didn't answer, but Frank could tell that it was. "Where were you going to take her?"

Silence.

"Is it a boy or a girl?"

Silence.

"How old?"

The Puri Dai stared at him angrily, but didn't answer.

"Where is it now?"

Suddenly, something seemed to break in her. "Safe," she said.

"Safe? From what?"

"She is safe now."

Frank took a small step toward her. "She? A little girl?"

The Puri Dai turned away from him.

"Safe now?" Frank asked.

"Yes."

"Why?"

Silence.

"Why is she safe now?"

The Puri Dai didn't answer.

Frank moved closer to her. "Tell me."

She was shivering slightly, but beneath those small movements, Frank could see a will of iron.

"How old is she?" he demanded.

Silence.

"Why is she safe now?" Frank demanded. "From what?"

Her eyes drifted over to him. "She is safe," she told him. "Let her be safe."

"Why is she safe now?"

There was no answer.

"Why is she safe now?" Frank repeated loudly.

The Puri Dai hesitated for a moment, then began. "Because," she said, then stopped. "Because . . ."

Frank was very near her now, his face nearly touching hers. "Why?" he whispered with a sudden, shuddering desperation. "Why is she safe?"

"Because the *errate*—the blood—has been fouled," the Puri Dai told him in a quick, passionate whisper. "Because her blood—the pure blood of our line—has been made impure."

"What are you talking about?"

"Her blood," the woman said coldly. "In her veins."

"Impure? How is it impure?"

She stared at him mercilessly.

Frank took her by the shoulders. "Where is she?" he demanded. He could feel his allegiance to the Puri Dai suddenly and miraculously shifting to someone else, a little girl he had never seen, but whom he imagined now as she must have sat in the little chair, facing outward in inexpressible terror as the old woman sank to her knees, stretched out her arms as her head was pulled back and stared at her in unspeakable horror as the razor was drawn across her throat.

"Tell me where she is," he demanded hotly. "Where is your daughter?"

"Safe," the Puri Dai replied coldly. "The only one who ever has been."

For a moment he started to ask another question, but the look in her eyes had hardened to an absolute solidity, and he realized that there would be no more answers, that she had told him the last of what she would ever tell.

25

It was nearly three in the morning when Frank finally stumbled wearily into Toby's after-hours place. He could still see the eyes of the Puri Dai, utterly firm, as if the mind behind them had turned to cold blue steel.

Farouk was already seated at his table in the back of the room. He'd already ordered Frank his usual, a Jameson's, straight up, and he slid it over to him easily as he sat down. "The night is warm," he said.

Frank nodded, then took a drink. He could feel his own eyes burning slightly in the smoky air, as if growing softer and more pliant as the Puri Dai's turned to stone.

Farouk watched him closely. "You do not look well, Frank. Perhaps it is time you slept on something besides that sofa in your office."

Frank shrugged. "It's just me," he said. "I don't need anything else."

"A man does not always know what he needs," Farouk told him firmly.

Frank nodded, then drew in a deep breath. The Puri Dai was still in his mind, just as she had lingered in it insistently during all the long silent walk he'd taken by the river after leaving her. But now she was no longer alone in the place she occupied. Now there were two of them with him, so that when he saw the Puri Dai in his mind, there was also a child standing beside her, a little girl with long dark hair, like her mother's, and the same black eyes.

Farouk took a long pull on his drink, his eyes staring over the rim of the glass.

Frank watched him drink. It wasn't his usual, either scotch or Turkish coffee. It was a clear liquid that seemed to move down the glass slowly, like a thick syrup.

"Raki," Farouk said. "Would you like one?"

Frank shook his head.

"The smell in the Gypsy's house," Farouk said. "It brought back many things." He placed the glass on the table. "It is odd, what the mind displaces." He smiled. "The only thing more odd is what may return to occupy its forgotten place."

Frank suddenly looked at him pointedly. "You found something, didn't you?"

Farouk nodded. "It may be of assistance."

"What?"

"Three words," Farouk said. "Though not in your language."

"What words?"

"La Femme Gatée."

"You told me what they mean."

"'The ungovernable woman,'" Farouk said. "'She who is master of herself.'"

"Yes."

"This brought something back."

"A memory?"

"More a sense of things, my friend," Farouk said. "Of lost connections."

"Go ahead."

Farouk leaned back slightly and took another sip of raki. "The Gitano believe that sudden ideas do not come from inside us, but from the *duende*, the wandering ghost." He smiled. "It enters through the soles of our feet, and shoots up into our minds, and that is when we feel something which we could not have guessed before."

Frank nodded, already laboring to follow Farouk's slowly unraveling connections.

"The *duende* is the source of all sudden, passionate inspiration," Farouk told him. "It is she who gives the Gitano the power to tell fortunes, to know what others cannot know." He smiled again, but this time with a distant, eerie seriousness. "She is, herself, a *femme gatée,* and only music lures her."

Frank instantly thought of all the odd instruments which hung from the wall of the Gypsy house. His lips parted silently.

Farouk seemed to know what he was thinking. "The *gusla,*" he said. "And the *tiple.* These are the traditional instruments of the Gitano. They are used to summon her, and when I remembered these instruments, and saw the words 'La Femme Gatée,' that is when, as they say, the *duende* entered me."

Frank leaned forward slightly, his hand squeezing tightly around his glass. "And told you what? Something about the woman?"

"About *them,*" Farouk said, as if gently correcting him. "About the three women."

"The three of them?"

"Yes," Farouk said. "It made me think of another three women my mother used to speak of."

"Who were they?" Frank asked.

"They are known as the Seaborne Marys," Farouk said quietly.

"The Seaborne Marys," Frank repeated, almost to himself.

"They come from a tale my mother told me of a strange Gitano sect," Farouk went on. "As you know, my father was a Moslem, but my mother, she was from the Christian world." He smiled. "But a different Christian world, a Gypsy Christian world, and so, like everything with the Gitano, this world was like no other. It had its own sense of things." He inserted a cigarette into his ivory holder and lit it. "The Gitano take what they want, and add what they want. This they do in their food and drink. This they do in their songs. And this also they do in their religion."

"Religion?" Frank asked unbelievingly. "They believe that there were three Marys?"

Farouk nodded. "Known to them sometimes as the Three Marias, and other times as the Seaborne Marys."

Frank continued to stare at him incredulously.

"Let me explain," Farouk said. "For the Gitano, there were three Marias, three Marys, besides she who was Christ's mother, the Holy Virgin. These three Marias were all beloved of Christ. Two of them, Maria Salome and Maria Jacobe, these were the sisters and helpmaids of the Holy Virgin."

Frank looked at him penetratingly. "Those were the names of the women on Tenth Avenue."

Farouk smiled. "Yes, they were."

"So the Puri Dai . . ."

"Is the Third Maria," Farouk said. He took another sip of raki, then continued. "According to this small sect of the Gitano, which my mother sometimes spoke of, the Three Marias did not remain in the holy land with the Virgin. After the Crucifixion, they fled by sea from the fires of Palestine."

"All three of them," Frank said quietly, trying to keep it all straight in his mind.

"All three," Farouk said. He listed them again. "Maria Jacobe and Maria Salome, the two sisters of Christ's mother. And with them, the Third Maria."

"The Third Maria," Frank said. "Who was she?"

Farouk smiled knowingly, and in an instant, Frank knew who the Third Maria was. "Magdalene," he said softly, "Mary Magdalene."

"Maria Magdalena," Farouk said solemnly. "The whore whom Christ adored."

"Yes," Frank said. He remembered all the sermons his father had preached about her, loudly and incessantly preached, as if he too had from time to time fallen beneath her enigmatic spell.

"Maria Magdalena," Farouk repeated, "whom Christ saved, and who followed him as one of his disciples."

Frank nodded.

"And it was she who first discovered the Resurrection," Farouk added, "found that the stone had been rolled away from Christ's tomb."

"Yes."

"To most of the Gitano, Magdalena was beloved of Christ just as his mother was. Just as were the other two Marias."

"Most of the Gitano?" Frank said quizzically. "But not all?"

Farouk nodded slowly. "No, not all," he said. "There is a small sect, very old, which carries forth another idea."

"Which is?"

Farouk's eyes darkened solemnly. "That the Third Maria was a woman whom God not only loved," he said slowly, "but in His fleshly shape . . . desired."

Frank's eyes widened. "Desired," he repeated.

"It is she of all women whom Christ loved as a man is said to love a woman," Farouk said.

"With his body," Frank said.

"By flesh and blood," Farouk said. Then his words became more measured as he went on, as if they were leading him into a treacherous land. "And it was also the Third Maria, according to this one small sect within the Gitano faith, who lived to bear Christ's only earthly child."

Frank sat back slightly. "Christ's child?" he asked unbelievingly.

"So that such holy blood would not be lost to man," Farouk said, as if by way of practical explanation.

For a moment, Frank felt as if the *duende* had entered him as well. "The *errate*," he said.

Farouk nodded. "Holiest of blood. She who has it must live a secret, blameless life. She must be kept apart from the world of the *gorgio,* so that her blood can be handed down from one generation to the next, mother to . . ."

"Daughter," Frank whispered, his mind whirling wildly, moving from the small game the Puri Dai had bought for her, to the open door where she must have sat, her small eyes filled with horror, as the old woman slowly dropped to her knees before her.

"The blood flows through the generations," Farouk said, "passed, as you say, from mother to daughter." His voice grew low, somber, tragic. "And at the age of ten the child is bound over to the Gypsy Father. She is bathed in raki and adorned for him, so that she is fit for his pleasure, and for the passage of the *errate.*"

Frank's lips parted silently. "You mean, for him to . . ."

"Yes," Farouk said.

Frank's eyes fled to the bar for a moment, then snapped back to Farouk. "She was trying to save her daughter," he said. "She was going to run away with her, but it was too late."

Farouk nodded.

"Someone killed the other woman," Frank went on, "and took the little girl."

"For her holy blood, yes."

"And the only way she could save her was to confess to murder?"

"To poison the blood, that is true," Farouk said. "To make it

useless for all time. To do it publicly, as they say, to enter the world
of the *gorgio*."

Frank stood up instantly. "I've got to go talk to the Puri Dai," he
said worriedly.

"Why?"

Frank stood up. "Because now I know why she's been trying to
get me off the case," he told him. "I've been trying to prove her
innocence. To build a case for not accepting her confession."

Farouk nodded.

"Which would mean that her daughter's blood . . ."

"Would still be pure in the eyes of the Gypsy Christ," Farouk said.
He stood up. "I will go with you," he said.

They hailed a cab and went directly to the Women's Center. It
was almost four in the morning, and the front desk was empty. The
small lounge to the right was also vacant, except for a single figure
who sat, curled up at one end of the sofa, her arms wrapped around
her knees. She was smoking a cigarette while she peered out the
window, and she didn't bother to look around when Frank walked
up to her.

"I need to see one of the women here," Frank said.

"Go ahead," the woman answered dully.

"She's on the sixth floor," Frank said. "You know where the desk
clerk is?"

The woman shrugged. "She pees a lot," she said. "She's probably
in the john."

"Would you mind getting her for me?"

The woman suddenly whirled around to him, her body seemed to
grow red around the edges. "Go get her your fucking self," she
screeched. "I'm not your fucking maid!"

Frank stepped back slightly, nearly bumping into Farouk. For an
instant, he started to reply, then felt Farouk's hand drawing him
away. "No need, my friend," he said softly. "No need."

Together they walked to the desk. The desk clerk returned almost
immediately. It was Ruth, and she smiled cheerfully as she came
down the corridor.

"You're back?" she asked.

"Maybe for the last time," Frank told her.

"To see Maggie?"

"Yeah."

She looked suspiciously at Farouk, "Who's he?"

"He works with me," Frank explained. "On the same case."

"Actually, I'm with Social Services," Farouk said. He pulled out one of his fake identification cards. "The woman has been assigned to me."

"You guys work late, too, huh?" Ruth said. Then she shrugged. "Well, okay, you can go on up."

They turned and walked to the elevator. Frank stepped in first and pressed for the sixth floor.

Farouk remained silent for a moment, his eyes staring steadily at the lighted number. "We must think a moment," he said.

Frank looked at him. "About what?"

"We cannot change her, my friend," Farouk said. "She is still the Puri Dai."

"What do you mean?"

"To save her daughter, she will do anything."

"That confession won't hold together, Farouk."

"Then we must put something in its place."

"What?"

"Her daughter," Farouk said flatly. "She would not accept anything else."

"Do you think she knows where her daughter is?"

"I do not know," Farouk said. "But if she does, she must tell us."

The elevator doors opened and the two of them walked quickly down the corridor until they reached Room 603.

"This is it," Frank said as he knocked lightly.

There was no answer, and so he knocked again.

"She is not sleeping," Farouk said bluntly. Then he tried the door. It opened at his touch, and the two of them walked inside.

The light was on, but the room was empty.

"Do you think she is gone?" Farouk asked.

Frank's eyes shot over to him. "Right out the front door while the woman downstairs was . . ."

Farouk nodded. "Yes."

"So she's out there," Frank said as he walked over to the window, then peered through its slender metal bars, his eyes moving down toward the darkened alleyway. He drew himself back into the room. Everything in it was completely still except for the small blue note he'd brought her a few hours before. It lay faceup on the small bureau, rocking softly in the same breeze that drifted lazily through the curtains. He picked it up immediately.

"It's in another language," he said as he handed it to Farouk.

Farouk glanced at the note, then handed it back. "Yes," he said. "Another language. The Gitano tongue, Romany."

"Do you know what it says?"

Farouk nodded. "Yes," he said. Then he told him. "All things remain. It is not you who shuffles the cards."

Frank took the note from Farouk's hand and stared at the incomprehensible script. "What does it mean?"

"It is the opposite of the Gypsy blessing," Farouk said. "It means that you do not control things anymore, that your destiny has been tossed to the wind."

"What would it mean to the Puri Dai?"

Farouk looked at Frank darkly. "That she has failed to change her daughter's fate, to make her daughter's destiny different from her own."

—26—

They walked quickly out of the center, then headed north, up Eighth Avenue. Farouk moved very rapidly, his enormous frame practically bounding along the cement walkway.

"Where are we going?" Frank asked.

"Back to the old woman," Farouk said. He stopped at the corner of Forty-second Street and glanced to the right, his eyes moving up the neon canyon of porno theaters and burlesque houses. "The Puri Dai could not stay for long on such streets," he said. "She would be too quickly noticed."

"Because of her beauty," Frank said.

Farouk shook his head. "Her dignity," he told him. He glanced to the left, down the darker stretches of the street, along a seedy tunnel of old slum hotels and cheap diners, and then farther west, to the renovated theaters beyond Tenth Avenue. He drew in a long breath. "The Puri Dai would not think of food or shelter." He smiled, as if in terrible and enduring admiration. "She would think only of love . . . and vengeance."

"So where would she go?" Frank asked insistently.

Farouk shook his head. "I do not know," he admitted. "But I know how to discover it." He started moving again, this time even faster, with Frank traveling breathlessly at his side.

They didn't stop until they reached the door of the fortune-teller's storefront. It was entirely dark, but Farouk pounded at the door anyway, slamming his fist into it so hard that the metal grating which covered the adjoining window rattled with the blow.

"Please, madam," he cried, "I must see you."

Finally, a light went on in the back of the building, and Frank could hear footsteps moving softly toward the door.

"It is I, Farouk," Farouk called. "I am in distress. Please, help me, madam." Then, under his breath, "No questions, Frank. No matter what I say here. Yes?"

Puzzled, Frank nodded.

The door inched open, and the woman peered out. "What do you want?" she asked.

"The other woman," Farouk said, "The poor murdered one. She read the tarot, and warned me of swirling waters."

"Yes?"

"And she promised me that I could return to her," Farouk added. "But now, there is only you, and I . . . I am a man of substance, madam . . . you would not regret assisting me."

"Assisting you?"

"To complete my fortune," Farouk explained. "I must know my destiny. I know the hour. I will pay you well."

To Frank's surprise, the door swung open immediately, but began to close again when the old woman spotted him.

Farouk placed his hand against it. "Please, madam. He is a friend.

The woman looked at Frank darkly. "You came before," she said.

"But he is only with me now," Farouk said quickly. "He will not harm you. Please, madam, you must help me."

The woman hesitated an instant longer, then opened the door and allowed the two of them to pass in front of her.

"Take a seat there," she said, as she nodded toward the small metal chair and the little table beside it.

"Yes, thank you," Farouk said. He wrung his hands desperately. "I am sorry to trouble you, but . . ."

"I understand," the woman told him. She took a seat on the other side of the small table. "Give me your hands."

Farouk drew his hands up and laid them down flat on the table.

"Turn them over," the woman commanded.

Farouk did as he was told, and the woman picked up his two large hands and stared at them closely.

"What do you see?" Farouk asked eagerly.

"A moment, please," the woman said. She continued to concentrate on the hands while Frank watched her absently, his arms pressed up against the door which led back into the building, his eyes glancing randomly through the red bead curtain that still hung over it.

"You are a man of great troubles," the fortune-teller said. She lifted her head and closed her eyes. Her voice took on a trancelike monotone. "Great troubles."

Farouk bowed his head slightly. "Yes, yes. What are they?"

"Problems with health," the woman said. One eye fluttered slightly. "Your stomach. Your digestion."

"Oh yes," Farouk groaned. "It is always hurting me."

"And with money," the woman added.

Farouk looked at her worriedly. "Money?"

"You must be careful," the woman told him. "There are those close to you who would . . . who would . . ." She stopped, then lowered her head slightly, staring intently at Farouk's outstretched hands. "Who would betray you," she said finally. "Who would take from you that which is not theirs."

Farouk leaned forward instantly. "Who?" he demanded loudly. "Who would do that?" His eyes narrowed menacingly. "A woman? Is it a woman?"

The Gypsy appeared to think about it, then nodded. "An evil woman. She does not serve you as she should."

"I knew of this," Farouk said suddenly. His eyes shot over to Frank. "You know who she's speaking of, yes?"

Frank shook his head, bewildered.

"Josephina," Farouk said. "She is cheating me." He looked back at the fortune-teller. "That is right, yes? It is Josephina."

Frank gave Farouk a quizzical look. Josephina?

Farouk glanced at him pointedly, instructing him to go along with the tale. Then he returned his attention to the woman. "It must be Josephina," he said.

The fortune-teller said nothing.

"Tall woman," Farouk went on, as if half-crazed with desperation. "Very thin. As they say, a shadow."

The fortune-teller smiled. "That is the one, yes," she said. "A woman full of bad feeling, bitterness. In her, all loyalty is dead."

Farouk looked disturbed. "Loyalty? Is there another man?"

The fortune-teller hesitated again, staring more and more deeply into Farouk's open palms.

"With Gaston," Farouk blurted. "With Gaston, yes?"

The fortune-teller continued to stare at his hand. "I am sorry. It is not clear who is this man."

"It is Gaston," Farouk said firmly. "Believe me. He is the one who has stabbed me in the back." He shook his head. "And after all I have done for him."

"Done for him," the fortune-teller repeated. "Yes, I can see that. You are a generous man. You have done much for him."

"He was like a son to me," Farouk told her. His voice grew deep and mournful. "Like the son that God did not give me." He took out his wallet. "Everything I had, it was also his." He took out a small stack of credit cards. "See all these things," he said.

The fortune-teller's eyes shot open. She stared hungrily at the cards.

"Gaston had all of these, as well," Farouk said bitterly. He swept them from the table in a sudden, violent thrust. "The bastard!" he screamed.

"Do not worry, sir," the fortune-teller said quickly. She dropped to her knees and began to gather up the cards. "Please, you must be careful with such things."

Farouk sunk his face in his hands. "Gaston and Josephina," he moaned. "It is more than I can bear."

"No, no, you will be well," the fortune-teller said as she got back to her feet. She plucked Farouk's wallet from the table and returned the cards he'd swept onto the floor. "Do not despair. All will be well."

"Well?" Farouk groaned. "Never."

The fortune-teller took her seat again, then picked up Farouk's hands and began to stare at them. "See, see there?" she said after a moment.

Farouk looked up. "What? See what?"

"This line here," the fortune-teller said. She touched it lightly, a thin crease near the top of his hand. "That is the dawning of renewal."

"Is it?" Farouk asked wonderingly.

"It is the sign of survival and recovery."

"Yes? Recovery?"

"Those who have it," the fortune-teller assured him, "they will be well in the future."

Farouk looked at her doubtfully.

"You must believe me," the woman said. "About such things, I am never wrong."

Farouk concentrated on the small thin crease. "Recovery?" he whispered. "Survival?"

"The two together," the woman said happily. "You are very fortunate, sir."

A small, hesitant smile fluttered onto Farouk's lips. "That is good, then?"

"Oh, very good," the woman said.

Relief swept into Farouk's face. He took in a deep breath. "Thank you, madam," he said. He stood up and opened his wallet. "Your fee. I do not know what it is. But please, madam, be generous."

The fortune-teller smiled. "It is the same for all," she said sweetly.

"I am happy to pay it," Farouk said.

"One hundred dollars," the woman said.

Farouk did not flinch at the amount. Instantly, he plucked a one-hundred-dollar bill from the wallet and handed it to the woman. "I hope this will be of assistance to yourself and the Puri Dai," he said.

The woman froze, her hand drew back from the bill. "The Puri Dai is in prison," she said coldly.

Farouk shook his head. "Ah, perhaps I can bring you good tidings, madam, as you have brought them to me."

"What are you talking about?"

Farouk pressed the bill toward her. "The Puri Dai is free."

"Free?" the fortune-teller said.

"She has escaped," Farouk said flatly. He inched the bill closer to the fortune-teller, and she finally snapped it from his fingers.

"Escaped?" she said.

"She may return here," Farouk said. "To her family, yes?"

The fortune-teller smiled thinly. "Of course, that is possible."

"Then perhaps you will be so kind as to give her my regards," Farouk said.

The fortune-teller nodded curtly. "Of course."

Farouk nodded toward the bill, which remained clutched in the woman's hand. "And perhaps a sweet, as well. I am sure the Puri Dai has not been treated well."

Again, the fortune-teller smiled. "Yes, a sweet. Of course." She took Farouk's arm and nudged him quickly toward the door. "Good night, then," she said.

"Good night," Farouk said as he stepped out onto the sidewalk. He motioned Frank behind him, then glanced back at the woman. "I wish you well, madam, in all things."

"Thank you."

Farouk leveled his eyes upon her. "And may it always be you who shuffles the cards," he said.

The woman looked at him icily, but said nothing. For a moment her eyes seemed to turn into two brightly shining orbs, then the darkness returned to them and the mask reappeared.

"And you, too, sir," she said gently. Then she closed the door.

"What was that all about?" Frank asked as the two of them made their way up the avenue toward Frank's office.

"If it works," Farouk said, "you will soon know."

"Soon?"

"Yes," Farouk said. He continued on, moving silently up the avenue until he reached the corner of Forty-ninth Street. Then he turned to the right. A pinkish dawn light had begun to break. He stared at it a moment, then turned to Frank. "The day case is beginning," he said. Then he walked hurriedly away.

27

The light was considerably brighter a few hours later when Frank
pulled himself up from the sofa, walked back into the small bathroom and took a quick shower. Outside, he could see the early-
morning pedestrian traffic as it moved east and west along
Forty-ninth Street. The old woman was crumpled up near the bottom of the stairs, her body curled up motionlessly against the brick
wall. A soda can lay on its side near her shoulders. Along the curve
of her back, there was a scattering of crumbs and gnawed chicken
bones, the remains from a red Popeye's Famous Fried Chicken box
that rested near her feet, its open top slapping back and forth in the
breeze from off the river.

As he watched her, he thought of the Puri Dai, trying to imagine
where she might have gone, where she could possibly be sleeping.
It was possible that she'd left the city entirely by now, that she was
already chasing the nomadic Gypsy band that no doubt had her
daughter. If she were still in the city, then it was only because they
were still in it, too.

He glanced up slightly and let the hard morning light settle on his
eyes. They were burning again, but there was nothing he could do
about it but draw them away from the light, back down toward the
shadowy bottom steps where the old woman remained.

He stared at her for a few seconds, then thought of the day case,
and quickly returned to the bathroom, brushed his teeth and show-
ered. His clothes hung in the closet near the window, and one by
one he pulled his shirt and trousers from the metal hangers and put
them on. Before leaving, he took a quick glance at himself, saw his

image in the dusty window, superimposed over the old woman's body, and straightened the loosely fitted knot of his tie.

Once outside, he eased himself up the stairs, carefully stepping over her. Halfway up the stairs, he looked back and noticed that she did not move as she usually did, and as he watched her briefly, he noticed that the single finger he could see jutting out from beneath the long sleeve of her coat was utterly still and very white.

He walked back down the stairs and touched her shoulder gently. There was no response.

He shook her softly. "Ma'am?" he said.

There was still no answer.

He bent somewhat closer to her. "Ma'am?" he repeated, this time a bit more loudly.

He knelt down, pressing his knees against the edge of the bottom step and shook her more forcefully. The body rocked softly, but the old woman did not stir.

Frank drew his lips down close to the pile of smelly clothing. "Mother?" he called softly. "Mother, are you awake?"

No answer.

He could feel a trembling in his hands as he turned her body toward him very slowly, his eyes searching for her face amid the smelly mound of clothes that engulfed her. When he found it, the eyes were staring lifelessly into the morning light and a line of red hung with an odd, affecting beauty, like a child's Christmas ribbon, from the unmoving, silent corner of her mouth.

It was nearly eleven o'clock by the time they finally took her, and Frank was still standing in the small cement square that led from the stairs to his office, his eyes fixed on her body as the two men heaved it onto the stretcher, then laboriously hauled it up the stairs to the waiting EMS ambulance.

"So you didn't know her, is that right?"

Frank pulled his eyes from the stretcher and let them settle back on Tannenbaum again. He shook his head. "No, I didn't know her," he said.

"The autopsy'll tell us if anything happened to her," Tannenbaum said, "but you don't have any reason to be suspicious, do you, Frank?"

"No."

"You didn't hear anything, see anything?"

"No, nothing."

"Was she sleeping here when you got home last night?"

Frank nodded.

"And when was that, do you remember?"

"Early morning."

Tannenbaum smiled. "Like always, right?"

"Like always," Frank said.

Tannenbaum closed his notebook, then shrugged. "Well, we get a lot of this kind of thing these days," he said, "but mostly in the winter. Freezing, that's usually what does it." He glanced up toward the EMS ambulance. A bright midmorning sun was shining silver on its chrome bumpers. "You expect them to make it through the spring."

Frank nodded slowly.

"But sometimes, they don't," Tannenbaum added casually. He looked up toward the ambulance. They were shoving the old woman's body into the back of it. "My guess is, it was her heart. Sometimes they just pop, like a balloon that's been stretched too far." He shook his head as he looked back at Frank. "She looks like she'd been stretched pretty far, doesn't she?"

Frank said nothing.

Tannenbaum looked at him pointedly. "I heard you were the one who found out about that Gypsy, the one who escaped last night."

Frank nodded.

"Funny, you being there and all," Tannenbaum said. "As a matter of fact, why were you there?"

"I had a few things to tell her."

"Really? Like what?"

"Things about the murder."

Tannenbaum's voice took on a tone of warning. "You wouldn't hold anything back on your old friend Tannenbaum, would you, Frank?"

Frank shook his head.

Tannenbaum's eyes narrowed in concentration. "There's a felony warrant out on her now," he said, "so any way you look at it, she's in deep, deep shit."

"I know."

"With only one way out, Frank," Tannenbaum added. "To get her ass right back over to the Women's Center." He shook his head. "There's no way she's not going to do a hell of a lot of time, but if she turns herself in, it might go a little easier on her, you know?"

Frank said nothing.

Tannenbaum continued to stare at him intently. "I'm going to ask you straight out, Frank, and I hope you have sense enough to tell me the truth, because if you don't, I pull your PI license so fast you won't even see it pop out of your pocket."

Frank anticipated the question. "I don't know where she is, Leo," he answered.

For a moment, Tannenbaum seemed to doubt him, then suddenly the doubt dissolved from his face, and his eyes drew back down to the littered area where the old woman's body had just been picked up. "Well, it's over for her now," he said. He closed his notebook and headed up the stairs. When he got to the top of them, he looked back toward Frank. "You know, it's like they say, Frank," he told him. "Life has a way of making you want revenge."

"Yeah," Frank said. And once in a while, he thought, someone ought to get it.

A few minutes later, the ambulance pulled away and Frank found himself entirely alone outside his office. For a while, he thought about walking back in, lying down on the sofa, and simply trying to sleep for at least a few minutes, enough to ease himself back into his steadily ebbing strength. But even as he thought about it, he dismissed the idea, and headed up the stairs instead. He knew that Farouk had been trailing Mrs. Phillips for several hours by then, all during the long morning while he'd waited for the old woman to be picked up, and the interrogations after that. For all that time, Farouk had been working on the day case, and now it was his turn to work on it too.

The offices of Pentatex Laboratories were on East Twenty-eighth Street, and as he walked toward them, shifting incessantly through the crowded midtown traffic, he went over the nightmare jumble of facts he'd collected on the day case, old theories lingering persistently, as if he were afraid to dismiss them from his mind.

He traced her movements again day by day, from the meeting at the Pierre Hotel, to Powers's house in the Village, then on to the next day, the Dakota, the long stroll across Central Park, the small black purse she'd left at the Alice in Wonderland statue.

He shook his head and continued walking, meticulously going over all the details of the case once again. He thought of Devine, then of Business Associates, the small, unlisted business that Mrs. Phillips had called immediately after returning from Connecticut. Why had she called Devine? Was he expecting a drop, or was she supposed to pick one up? He remembered that she'd look strangely distressed after leaving the telephone booth on Madison Avenue.

He thought of Burroughs again, of the limousine that had picked Mrs. Phillips up, then taken her to Trump Tower. He wondered if Burroughs owned an apartment in the Tower, or if he and Mrs. Phillips simply met in the one owned by Devine.

Last, he thought of Mrs. Phillips again, the coldness which had overtaken her, the blank sheet of her past, the changed will she'd been told of, the jewelry she'd pawned, the purse she'd dropped, the meetings at Trump Tower, the ones she never noted in her appointment book.

His mind was still studying the odd logistics of Trump Tower when he finally reached 338 East Twenty-eighth Street. He walked into the building, checked its lighted directory, then took the elevator up to the seventh floor, where Pentatex Laboratories were located.

The outer office looked very clean, and as he entered the glass double doors which led from the corridor into its neat, tiled vestibule, he felt strangely seedy and unkempt, as if his body crawled with millions of small, struggling parasites which the people at Pentatex knew well and worked laboriously to identify.

A woman in a white lab coat sat behind a small white desk, her fingers dancing over the keys of a large phone bank.

"Good morning," she said brightly.

Frank felt as if he should blow the dust off his identification before he gave it to her.

"Private investigator?" the woman asked as she glanced back up at him.

"That's right."

She handed him back the identification. "How can we help you?"

"I'm not sure you can," Frank admitted. "But I'd like to ask somebody a few questions."

"About any particular area?"

"No, just in general."

The woman thought a moment. "Well, I suppose Dr. Kelsey might help you," she said. "He usually handles all our public relations." She smiled cheerfully. "Hold on a minute, and I'll check if he's available."

She called Kelsey's office, explained the situation, then hung up the phone.

"Yes, he can see you now," she said as she stood up. "This way, please."

She led him down a short corridor, then into a large office. "Dr. Kelsey," she said, "this is Mr. Clemons."

The man behind the desk stood up immediately and offered his hand. He was very tall and very slender, with a face that looked as if it had been constructed from parts that didn't quite fit, the nose too large, the eyes too small, a mouth that looked as if it had once belonged to a woman.

"Thanks for seeing me," Frank said as he shook Kelsey's hand.

"Please, sit down," Dr. Kelsey said. He sat down himself, and raked back his thinning brown hair. "How can I help you?" he asked.

"I'm been working on something," Frank told him as he took his seat. "It's the usual kind of thing we do. Routine. But Pentatex came up, and my client needs to know a little about it, so I . . . ."

"Who is your client?" Kelsey asked quickly, before Frank could continue.

"I can't tell you that," Frank said as passively as he could. "He wants everything to be very discreet."

"I see."

"But I do have a few questions," Frank continued, "more or less for background."

"Background on what?"

"On Pentatex Labs," Frank told him.

Dr. Kelsey looked mildly distressed. "I'm surprised that the laboratory has come up in any kind of investigation." He offered a smile. "The things we do here are very common."

"Well, that's what I'm interested in," Frank said.

Kelsey looked puzzled.

"The work you do," Frank explained. "It's mostly for physicians?"

"Almost all our work is done for physicians," Kelsey said cautiously. "And our records are meticulous."

"I'm sure they are," Frank assured him. "I'm just interested in what you do for one particular physician."

Kelsey's face seemed to tighten. "One particular physician?"

"Yes."

Dr. Kelsey looked at Frank hesitantly. "Well, at this point, I'd have to have a name."

"Kevin A. Powers," Frank said.

Kelsey immediately recognized the name. "Dr. Powers is a very valuable customer of ours," he said stiffly. "I hope he's not in any kind of trouble."

Frank said nothing.

Kelsey settled back in his chair. "You have to understand our position, here," he said. "As I said, Dr. Powers is a very good customer. We wouldn't want to do anything that might damage that relationship."

"I understand."

"And there are rules in the medical community, of course," Kelsey added. "I mean, about confidentiality."

"I'm only interested in one patient."

Kelsey looked surprised. "We do a great deal of work for Dr. Powers. He has a very active practice."

Frank took out his notebook. "What sort of work?" he asked.

Kelsey looked at the notebook suspiciously.

"I don't remember things very well," Frank explained. He shrugged casually. "This work that the lab does for Dr. Powers," he went on gently, "what is it, exactly?"

Kelsey hesitated for a moment, then allowed himself to answer. "Well, it's the same that we do for other doctors," he said. "Just the routine laboratory tests that any private medical practice would require."

"What kind of tests?"

"You know, the usual blood and urine tests. Biopsies, things like that."

Frank smiled amiably. "What do you do for Powers?"

"Dr. Powers?" Kelsey repeated. "Well, I suppose you know that he's a gynecologist."

"Yes."

"So that means that in addition to the usual blood work, we do things like pregnancy tests, Pap smears, maybe a few more biopsies than you'd find in other practices."

"So, you'd be doing a lot of things for him?" Frank asked.

"Of course."

Frank wrote it down quickly, then glanced back up. "Where does the work come from?" he asked.

"What do you mean?"

"Whatever he sends you. Whatever it is. Where does it come from?"

"Well, from Dr. Powers's office, of course."

"And he has only one office?"

"One? No, I think he has two."

"There's only one is in the telephone book," Frank said. He flipped back through his notebook. "Here it is, at 485 Fifth Avenue. That's it, isn't it?"

"I suppose."

"But you thought there were two?"

Kelsey shrugged. "For some reason I thought he had a second office."

"Why did you think that?"

"Because some of his lab work comes from somewhere else," Kelsey said. "Not a lot. Very little, as I recall. Perhaps just one or two tests a week."

"Do you remember the address?" Frank asked.

"No."

"Could you look it up?"

"I suppose so," Dr. Kelsey said. He stood up and walked out of the office for a moment, then returned with a large manilla folder. He opened it quickly and began to sort through a large number of papers. "We pick up at doctors' offices once a day, so if there's a change in the route, it goes through our traffic department." He flipped through a few more papers, then stopped and pulled one out. "Here's what I mean," he said as he handed it to Frank.

Frank took the paper and studied it quickly, reading quietly, almost to himself.

"As you can see," Kelsey said, "for every pickup they record the time, date and location."

Frank nodded silently, his eyes continuing to scan the small yellow invoice. It recorded a pickup on April 17, the Monday Mrs. Phillips had gone to Powers's house. "This wasn't picked up at Powers's office," he said.

"No, it wasn't," Kelsey said. "Some place in the Village."

Frank read the address. "One-twenty-four West Twelfth Street." He glanced at the time: 1:22 P.M. He flipped back through his notebook and found the time he'd jotted down as Mrs. Phillips left the office: 1:07 P.M.

"That address," Kelsey said, "is that another office?"

"No," Frank said. He recorded the information on the invoice into his notebook, then handed it back to Kelsey. "What did he send to you that day?" he asked.

Kelsey stared at him hesitantly. "Now, when we get into that sort of information, we have to . . ."

Frank leaned forward, lowering his voice somewhat, as if confiding something important to Kelsey. "We may be dealing with criminal activity," he said darkly.

Kelsey looked alarmed. "Criminal activity?"

"It's possible," Frank said.

"Well, Pentatex couldn't be involved in anything like that."

"Involvement is a funny word," Frank said. "It's not always too clear the way people think about it."

"Yes, that's true," Kelsey said, a little nervously. "We wouldn't want Pentatex's name to come up at all. I mean, in any context, criminal or not."

"No, you wouldn't," Frank said.

"Could you help us with that?" Kelsey said. "I mean, if we were exposed."

"Maybe."

Kelsey glanced back at the invoice, then up at Frank. "And whatever I tell you is . . ."

"Strictly confidential," Frank assured him.

"All right," Kelsey said, after taking in a deep, but shaky breath. "What do you need to know?"

"What did he send you?"

Kelsey glanced at the invoice. "It was a blood sample," he said.

"Was there a name?"

"Yes," Kelsey said. He looked at the invoice again. "Driscoll. Virginia Driscoll."

"And the tests?"

"Well, according to this," Kelsey said, "Dr. Powers only ordered one test on this blood sample." He looked up. "An HIV analysis."

Frank's pen remained motionless on the page. "What's that test for?"

Kelsey closed the folder and let it drop softly onto his desk. "It's only given to determine one thing." His eyes brightened somewhat. "And in this case, it came up negative, so the woman, whoever she is, she doesn't have anything to worry about."

"What's the test for?" Frank asked again.

Kelsey's face grew faintly sorrowful. "AIDS," he said quietly, as if it were a word which should only be whispered.

The pen in Frank's hand leaned slowly backward as he released his grip.

"It's the test for AIDS," Kelsey repeated softly. He shook his head despairingly. "Here at Pentatex, we call it the Death Warrant Analysis."

-28-

Frank left the offices of Pentatex only a few minutes later. Once outside, he drew in a deep breath, then glanced at his watch. It was still almost four hours before he was scheduled to meet Powers, and so he headed back across town to Forty-ninth Street.

From the top of the cement stairs that led to his office, he could see the few scattered chicken bones that were now the only remaining evidence that the old woman had once lived and died at the bottom of the stairs. For a few seconds, he stood in place, his eyes fixed on the thin dark bones. They seemed to press themselves toward him, warning him away, and so he turned back toward the street and headed west, moving silently along the bright sunlit street until he reached the little park on Tenth Avenue where he and Farouk often met in the early evening.

It was almost three in the afternoon, and the park was filled with neighborhood children. They played noisely in the iron swings and and rushed back and forth across the cement basketball courts.

Several yards away, he could see a young girl as she skipped rope by herself in the only part of the park which was more or less deserted. As he watched her, the pace of the swinging rope steadily increased, until, after a time, it seemed to be whirling madly over her, cutting through the air so swiftly that he could hear the hard whirr of its flight as it slashed the air around her.

He leaned forward slightly and rubbed his aching eyes, trying to remove the blur which too often overcame them now, turning his vision into a soft, nearly featureless haze. The slap of the rope drummed relentlessly against the cement floor of the park, and its driving, incessant beat seemed to pierce him sharply. He turned away from it and closed his eyes, rubbing them again, gently at first, then more roughly, his thumbs pressing in against their soft white flesh.

When he opened them again, the rope was no longer whirring loudly, and he could see the little girl as she walked toward him slowly, the red wooden handles of the rope scraping softly over the cement as she drew them along behind her. She had a strange, ghostly look, and he thought of Sarah, his daughter, again, her lost, forsaken eyes, the way she had seemed to dissolve into her death, grow bodiless and void, as if her flesh were peeling from her, leaving nothing but a homeless soul.

Reflexively, he glanced away from the girl, then, just as reflexively, returned to her. She was much closer to him now, and she smiled tentatively as she passed by. He nodded to her gently, his eyes still following her as she made her way out of the park, then began skipping playfully along the sidewalk. For a time, Frank continued to watch her as she sped through the thin pedestrian traffic, gliding past a large woman whose small boy walked beside her, then an old priest who moved shakily along, his hand gripping fiercely at his cane. Toward the end of the block, she darted abruptly to the left as if to avoid someone, and Frank instantly saw the old Gypsy woman who'd told Farouk's fortune the night before.

He stood up, then moved behind a thin stand of trees which rose at the other end of the park. The early spring foliage was quite sparse, and through it, he could watch the old woman as she hurried up Tenth Avenue. She was dressed in a long, flowing skirt which dragged behind her heavily, its hem nearly touching the cement walkway, and her hair was bound up in a bright-red scarf. She walked very determinedly, as if under orders, her eyes staring straight ahead until she reached the liquor store, which stood almost directly across from the park. She went in quickly, and from his position across the avenue, Frank could see her step up to the clerk. She said something to him, and he nodded once, then disappeared into the back of the store.

Frank walked across the street quickly, then eased himself over near the entrance to the store and peered in.

The old woman lingered beside the counter, her head jerking left and right from time to time as if she were being slapped by an invisible hand.

The store clerk returned, his arms wrapped around several tall bottles. He bagged them slowly, inserting small squares of cardboard between the bottles, then handed the bag to the old woman. She paid him in cash, counting out the bills one by one, then turned back toward the door.

Frank stepped away quickly and shrank back into the small cigar store next door. Then he waited, listening for the bell of the liquor store door.

After it had sounded, he eased himself out into the street again, and darted into the liquor store.

The clerk nodded to him as he stepped up to the counter.

"The old woman who was in here just now," he said, "do you know her?"

The clerk shrugged. "She's just a customer."

"What does she buy?"

The clerk didn't answer.

Frank drew a twenty-dollar bill from his pocket, along with his identification.

The man snapped up the bill, his eyes giving the identification only a quick, indifferent glance. "She just starting coming in lately," he said. "I'd say about the last three weeks or so."

"Had you ever seen her before then?"

The clerk shook his head.

"What does she buy?" Frank asked.

"Some weird drink the old owner used to keep around," the clerk said. "We still got about a case and a half left over."

"What's the name?"

"Raki," the man said. He shrugged. "The old owner used to keep specialty items like that. Me, I just stock the usual."

"And she's been buying raki for about three weeks?"

"Yeah."

"About how often?"

"Maybe a bottle every couple of days."

"That's a lot."

"If it was wine, it wouldn't be that much," the clerk said. "I even have heavy stuff going out that often. But liqueurs, shit like that,

that's for sipping, you know? Sweet stuff. Most people don't go through it that fast."

Frank nodded. "Did you ever see anybody with the old woman?"

"No."

"Particularly a man."

The clerk shook his head.

"Did she ever say anything to you?"

"No."

"Nothing at all?"

"Just one word," the clerk said. "No talk. No conversation. She just comes in and she says, 'Raki,' and that's the end of it."

Frank nodded. "Okay," he said. "Thanks." He started for the door.

The clerk glanced at the twenty, as if it carried with it some added obligation. "Today, though, she looked different."

Frank turned back toward him. "Different?"

"Nervouslike," the clerk explained. "Scared."

"She looked scared?"

"Yeah, there was just this funny look in her eyes," the clerk went on. "Like she thought somebody was maybe after her, or something."

"Had she looked that way before?"

The clerk chuckled. "Well, she never did look like a happy-go-lucky type," he said. "But to tell you the truth, today it was different. I noticed it in her eyes, you know. And then, when she was giving me the money, it was like her hand was trembling, you know, like shaking real bad. I mean, enough so's a guy would notice."

Frank smiled at him appreciatively. "Okay, thanks," he said.

"Don't mention it," the clerk told him.

Frank walked back out onto the street and glanced southward, trying to get her in his sight. Far in the distance, barely a small dot in a sea of small dots, he could see the old woman's red scarf bobbing softly like a float in the water.

He glanced at his watch, then started to follow her, shifting quickly through the crowds, edging closer and closer until the old woman reached the storefront and disappeared inside.

Frank held back for a moment. He had already burned his cover with Mrs. Phillips, and it was not a mistake he intended to make again. For a time, he simply waited, then, slowly, he moved toward the window of the storefront. The blue curtain was still in place, but the sign had been taken down. He pressed his back against the window, lining the right side of his body up with the small slit in the blue curtains, then quickly glancing over his shoulder and inside the room.

He could see the old woman as she meticulously drew the bottles out of the bag and placed them carefully in a large canvas bag. There were several small boxes scattered around the room, all of them neatly tied with rope. All the musical instruments had been taken from the walls and were now gathered together in one corner.

Suddenly the old woman's head jerked up, and Frank pulled away from the window. He waited a moment, then cautiously eased himself back and looked in.

The old woman was standing rigidly in place, her eyes staring to her left. For a moment she remained very still, then in a quick, abrupt movement, she stepped back, as if shrinking away from some threatening presence.

Frank glanced toward the floor. He could see a gray shadow as it eased out of his line of sight, then bolted forward suddenly. He looked up and saw a tall, slender man as he leaned forward slightly, his body held just at the edge of Frank's line of sight. He had a black mustache, his head was covered with a bright red handkerchief, almost exactly like the old woman's. He stood very erect, his head lifted haughtily while he spoke to her, pointing here and there, as if giving her a series of very detailed directions. Then he shrank back behind the covering wall and the old woman set to work, gathering up the few items that remained scattered across the floor and placing them carefully in the last empty box.

Frank pulled himself back from the window and tried to think about his next move. He knew that they were leaving, but he didn't know when or how. He stepped over beside the door, away from the small, narrow break in the curtains, and pressed his back against the brick wall. In his mind, he saw the man again, the distant, severe look in his eyes, the hard cut of his jaw. No one had ever looked more entirely in command. In a few minutes, he knew, they could be gone, and once they were out of sight, they would be gone forever. He had to find a means to follow them. He lifted his head slightly and tried to think of a way to cover both the front and back entrances of the storefront. It would be possible only if he were able to get above the building, look down on it, and keep track of them from a kind of watchtower overhead. He glanced across the street, to the long line of squat red tenements that ran along the avenue. Up there, he would be able to see them. He let his eyes move up the ragged face of the building across the way, then up over the top, his eyes widening as he saw her staring down at him, her black eyes fixed on his.

She was standing in full view, as if to display herself, and he moved toward her instantly, his eyes still fixed on hers as he bolted across the street, then up the rickety wooden stairs that led to the roof.

At the top of the stairs, the metal fire door had been locked, so he jerked back and slammed his shoulder into it, breathing heavily now, but slamming forward anyway, first once, then again and again, growing more desperate with each plunge, until the door finally flew up and he went sprawling across the tar-paper surface of the building's roof.

He rolled onto his back, but she was on him instantly, staring down furiously, her knee on his chest. He felt the point of a knife blade at his throat. "I told you that I did not want you," she whispered vehemently.

Frank said nothing. Her face was utterly radiant, her hair beautiful even in disarray, hanging like black seaweed over her broad, brown shoulders.

She pressed the point more firmly against his throat. He could feel a trickle of warm blood as it pierced his skin.

He looked at her longingly, and when she caught the expression in his eyes, Frank could see that hers took on a distant sympathy, as if he could hardly be expected to know what she already knew. Then, suddenly, the sympathy vanished and her face grew very grim.

She felt under his arm, pulled the .45 from his shoulder holster. "There is only one way," she told him determinedly as she raised the pistol high in the air, then brought it crashing down upon him. "To be as dangerous as a man."

29

There was still some light left in the air around him when Frank finally came to. He glanced about slowly, hazily, his mind still trying to orient itself. In his imagination, he could see the ghostly, translucent image of the Puri Dai as she had held herself above him, and in some indecipherably deep corner of himself, he also knew that he yearned for her return.

But she was gone, irretrievably gone, leaving everything in her wake with nothing but a lingering sense of fearful reverence.

He pulled himself into a sitting position, then groggily got to his feet. From the roof, he could see the evening traffic as it made its way toward the Lincoln Tunnel, and beyond it, the flat gray surface of the Hudson. He let his head slump left and right as his eyes stared out over the now deserted roof. Down below, he could see the window of the fortune-teller's shop, but the small neon sign was gone, along with the blue curtain that had once hung over the window and the small table and chair which had rested beyond it. Everything was gone, entirely abandoned.

He took a step, felt his legs regain their force, then headed back down the stairs and onto the street.

Once on the street, the faint light which remained in the air reminded him of the day case, and he realized that he wanted to let it edge out the night case, gently nudge the lost Puri Dai from his mind.

He glanced at his watch. There was still time to make his meeting with Powers, and so he walked swiftly across town.

As he walked, he could feel himself still yearning for the Puri Dai, for the allure of the uncertain, the mysterious and eternal call of those things in life which cannot be pinned down. He saw her kneeling over him again, her knee bearing down upon his chest, her hair hanging toward him like long black ropes, and the vision itself was like something aching softly in his chest, a thin, hairline fracture in his soul.

At the corner of Forty-ninth Street and Sixth Avenue, he turned to the left and headed uptown, moving along the avenue until he reached Fifty-sixth Street. Then he turned right, walking more and more quickly, until he saw the silvery awning of Broadway Lights.

The hostess smiled sweetly as she turned toward him, then instantly looked at him in alarm. "Are you all right, sir?"

"What?"

She pointed toward the left side of his face. "You're bleeding slightly."

Frank touched the side of his head, felt the broken skin and slender trickle of blood. "Oh, no, that's all right," he said. "It was just an accident on the way over."

The hostess didn't seem to believe him, but launched into her usual routine anyway. "Will you be having dinner, then?" she asked.

Frank couldn't imagine it, and for a moment didn't answer. His hand lifted to his throat, and he felt the trickle of blood that now dried there.

"Will you be having dinner?" the woman repeated.

Frank nodded.

"Just yourself this evening?"

"No, I'm waiting for somebody else," Frank told her.

The woman nodded politely. "And is the reservation in your friend's name?"

"Yeah, I guess," Frank said. "Powers."

She recognized the name immediately. "Oh yes, Dr. Powers," she said brightly. "Would you like to wait for him at his table, or at the bar?"

Frank shrugged. "Table's okay."

"Fine," the woman said. "Just follow me, please."

She led him over to a small table at the back of the room. "The restrooms are right over there, if you want to clean up."

Frank smiled. "Thanks."

In the restroom, Frank blotted up the blood, though the cut still looked alarming, and brushed off his clothes. Fortunately, the tussle on the rooftop hadn't done them too much harm.

He returned to the table, glanced at a small ashtray on the table, took out a cigarette and lit it. Then he sat back and let his eyes take in the restaurant's ornate interior. It was large, but cluttered with Broadway memorabilia, old musical instruments, framed original manuscripts of show music from various periods, drawings of famous actors and actresses, and a scattering of costumes, posters, even some famous actor's makeup kit in a glass case by the door. It was the sort of place he'd always heard about, but never seen, the kind that Karen mocked as lowbrow, and he'd simply avoided because the whole atmosphere struck him as contrived, a dream that would never grow legs strong enough to carry it into something real.

But it fit Powers well enough, and when Frank glimpsed him striding toward him from the front section of the restaurant, he was amazed at how much a part of it he seemed. He walked jauntily down the aisle, his white coat now replaced by a bright-red blazer, his head neatly covered with an appropriately graying toupee.

"Well, nice to see you again, Mr. Clemons," he said smartly when he reached Frank's table. "I hope the accommodations are acceptable." He sat down, pulled the napkin into his lap, then looked back up at Frank. "Oh, my goodness," he said suddenly. "What happened to you?"

"Me?" Frank asked.

"That gash on the side of your head," Powers said. "It looks quite nasty."

Reflexively, Frank reached up and touched the wound again. "Oh, yes," he said. He rushed for an explanation. "I had a little fall."

Power leaned toward him, his hand coming near his face. "Want me to have a look?"

Frank pulled back instantly. "No, it's okay," he said. Then he glanced about quickly and tried to change the subject. "Nice place."

"The food's not bad, really," Powers said as he leaned back into his seat. "The only thing you have to worry about is the travel trade."

Frank looked at him quizzically.

"The tourists," Powers explained. "The gawkers from the Great

Plains." He laughed happily. "Anyway, it's nice to see you again."

"You, too," Frank said, trying to keep the edginess from his voice.

The waiter stepped over immediately. "Good evening, Dr. Powers," he said.

"Hello, Jerry," Powers said. "What's the special tonight?"

"We have three."

Powers smiled. "Well, go ahead, then, I have nothing but time, right, Mr. Clemons?"

Frank nodded, then waited as the waiter went through the evening specials.

"I'll have broiled scallops," Powers told him when he'd finished. "And a glass of white wine. The house will do." He looked at Frank. "Decided yet?"

"The rib eye," Frank said. "And a scotch."

The waiter wrote it down, nodded, then vanished behind the kitchen's double doors.

Powers leaned back in his chair and let out a long, slow breath. "Busy day," he said. "At some point I should probably think about a brief vacation."

"Do you have office hours every day?" Frank asked casually, like one businessman talking to another.

"Every single one," Powers replied. "Five days a week, just like everyone else, Monday through Friday, nine to five. And some Saturdays—like today." He smiled gently. "Not that I'm complaining, of course. I live a good life." He looked at Frank pointedly. "Despite the nearly confiscatory tax bill I have to swallow once a year." He frowned. "You might say that once a year I buy the government a new missile silo."

Frank offered him a smile that was small and tentative, but still the best one he could muster. "Do you see all your patients in your office?"

Powers nodded. "Of course, where else would I see them? I don't have a château in the south of France."

"Some people have private patients," Frank said matter-of-factly. "Especially with . . ."

"A Fifth Avenue practice?" Powers asked. "Is that what you mean?"

"That's right."

"Well, I'm not that sort of snob," Powers said. "My patients are all doing quite well, of course." He grinned. "Financially, at least."

Frank let his smile stretch out a bit.

"But, frankly," Powers added, "I don't believe in treating a select few of my patients more luxuriously than others." He shrugged. "Besides, a home is for living, entertaining, enjoying the fruits of one's labor." He laughed. "I mean, really, how would you integrate an examining table or a EKG machine into your overall decor?"

Frank could feel his edginess growing, along with the throbbing in his head. He knew that he could not contain it any longer. The thin, languishing smile dropped dead. "Virginia Driscoll," he said flatly.

Powers's eyes hardened. "What?" He leaned back slightly. "What are you talking about?"

"A woman," Frank said stiffly. "One of your patients."

Power's lower lip drooped to the right. He studied Frank's face silently.

"You see her at your house," Frank told him.

"My house?"

"On Mondays," Frank added. He leaned toward him and let his voice put the squeeze on, even though he wasn't sure what it might squeeze out. "I'm a private investigator," he said. He took out his identification and handed it to Powers.

Powers looked at it a moment, as if checking its authenticity, then returned it to Frank. "And so all this tax consultant thing," he said, "it was just some sort of charade, is that it?" He looked like he couldn't decide whether to be indignant or amused.

"What can you tell me about Virginia Driscoll, Dr. Powers?" Frank asked.

Powers looked at him coolly. "Well, I don't really have to tell you anything, do I? I mean, it's not as if you have a subpoena in your hand, or a warrant for my arrest, or anything official at all."

Frank said nothing.

Powers studied him a moment. He'd evidently decided to be amused. "I must say, Mr. Clemons . . . By the way, is that your real name?"

"Yes."

"Well, I must say, you're quite an actor."

"What can you tell me about Virginia Driscoll?"

Powers laughed. "Excuse the expression, Mr. Clemons, but why don't you go fuck yourself." He started to get up, but Frank grabbed his tie and yanked him down, his chin nearly touching the table. "I've had a bad day," he said. "I'm losing control."

Powers swallowed hard. "For God's sake," he said. "I'm a regular in this place."

Frank gave the tie a quick pull and Powers's chin bounced off the top of the table. "Virginia Driscoll," he said.

"All right, for God's sake," Powers said. "Just let go, will you."

Frank released the tie and Powers straightened himself quickly.

"I don't know very much," he said, then added menacingly, "I suppose you know that you just lost your license as a private investigator in New York State."

Frank leaned toward him threateningly. "A man a lot more powerful than you is interested in Virginia Driscoll," he said. "So I don't give a fuck about you."

Powers looked alarmed. "Who hired you?" he asked with a sudden shakiness.

"Just answer my questions," Frank said coldly. "I followed Virginia Driscoll to your place in the Village on Monday morning. You sent the blood sample out only a few minutes later."

Something registered behind Powers's eyes, but Frank wasn't sure what it was.

"You were at my house?" Powers asked.

"Yes."

Powers eyed Frank closely, a cat watching a mouse. "What do you know already?" he asked seriously.

"That she's a patient," Frank said. "But a special one. One who doesn't come to your office."

Powers suddenly attempted a smile, his tone curiously cooperative. "Normally, I wouldn't talk to you about a patient. You must know that."

Frank said nothing.

"But since you've been engaged by ... whoever it is," Powers said, "presumably Mr. Driscoll. Anyway, since he's gone to that much trouble, I'll give you a few details which might ease his mind." He laughed. "After all, no matter how wealthy Mr. Driscoll is, he shouldn't be spending his money frivolously, now should he?"

Frank said nothing.

"All right," Powers began, "I can tell you this much."

Frank took out his notebook just as the drinks arrived.

Powers took a long sip of his, then returned the glass to the table. "Lovely," he said to the waiter. "Thank you."

Once again the waiter vanished.

Powers looked at Frank. "Here's the situation, Mr. Clemons, and once I've told you, I hope that you can bring whatever assignment you have to a happy conclusion. If you do, I'll forget all about this little encounter we had, and you can continue to work in your chosen field."

Frank kept his pen poised on the open notebook page.

"Mrs. Driscoll is a very discreet woman," Powers said matter-of-factly. "Because of that, she didn't want to come to my office." He smiled. "I assume you've already gathered that?"

"Yes."

Powers drew in a deep breath. "And I also suppose you know that Mr. Driscoll—at least according to his wife—is a good deal older than she is."

Frank watched him expressionlessly.

"Well, it seems that Mr. Driscoll has no heirs," Powers went on casually. "No children at all. And being a man who has accumulated a great deal in life—this again, according to Mrs. Driscoll—he's become concerned about passing it on. I'm sure you can understand that."

Frank said nothing.

"So, biology being destiny, Mr. Driscoll wants a child," Powers continued. "And Mrs. Driscoll, dutiful wife—in case you have any doubts—that she certainly is, she has been trying to provide him with one." He shrugged. "But so far, they have not been blessed."

Frank nodded expressionlessly. "So, why did she come to you?"

"She was interested in determining if she were infertile," Powers said. "To put it bluntly, she wanted to know where the blame was. If it were Mr. Driscoll, then you might say that she was in the clear, as far as heirs were concerned."

"In the clear?"

"That's right," Powers said. "That is to say, she couldn't be blamed." He smiled slyly. "It's a cruel world, Mr. Clemons, and Mrs. Driscoll is not interested in giving her husband a reason to discard her. If she were infertile, he would have a reason."

Frank pretended to write it all down in his notebook. "So she came to you for a fertility test?"

"That's right," Powers said.

"And that's all she wanted?"

"Yes."

"So that was the only test you ordered?"

"Of course," Powers said, a little self-righteously. "I'm not the kind of doctor who orders unnecessary procedures. Mrs. Driscoll wanted a fertility test, and that's all I ordered for her."

"Frank pretended to pursue it. "What were the results?"

"You mean, was she infertile?"

"Yes."

Powers drew back. "Now, Mr. Clemons," he said scoldingly, "that would breach confidentiality, and you know it." He smiled. "But I understand your position. You've been hired to find something out, and you need to come back with some results, right?"

Frank nodded, wondering why Powers seemed to be in such good spirits, why he was being so helpful, why he was lying about the nature of the test. He wanted to bounce his chin off the table again, but held himself back and listened.

"Well, although I wouldn't want to violate the confidential nature of my relationship with Mrs. Driscoll," Powers said, "I suppose I could tell you that if Mr. Driscoll is sound himself, then I would advise him to continue his no doubt pleasurable activities as regards his wife."

Frank faked a smile. "He'll be relieved to know that," he said. He took a sip from his drink, his eyes still watching Powers evenly. "You only saw Mrs. Driscoll once then?"

"Yes."

"How did she happen to come to you?"

"You mean, by way of referral?"

Frank shrugged. "Well, there are lots of doctors in the city, I just wondered how she happened to come to you."

"I have no idea, Mr. Clemons."

"You never saw her before?," Frank asked. "Or had any friends in common, anything like that?"

"No," Powers said flatly. He looked at Frank curiously. "Why are you asking such questions?"

"It's what I get paid for," Frank replied.

"By the hour, I assume?"

"More or less."

"So, I suppose you like to stretch it a bit?"

Frank didn't answer.

Powers chuckled lightly. "Oh, come now, Mr. Clemons, we all swim in the same water."

Frank tried to appear somewhat sheepish, like a little boy who'd been caught with his hand in the cookie jar.

"Ah, you see," Powers said cheerfully, "I've found you out." He laughed again. "But, you don't have to worry, Mr. Clemons, as you have no doubt learned this evening, I take confidences quite seriously."

Frank nodded. "I'll put that in my report," he said.

Powers smiled graciously. "I'm glad to hear it," he said sweetly. Then he hoisted his glass. "Well, as we say in the hallowed halls of medicine, here's to the healing profession."

-30-

The Puri Dai was on Frank's mind again when Farouk came through the door later that evening, but he quickly shook her from his attention and returned again to the day case. "Kevin Powers is full of shit," he said.

Farouk lumbered over to the chair in front of the desk and lowered himself slowly into it. "To stand on the feet too long," he said, "this is a curse for one of my enormity."

"Did you manage to keep track of her?" Frank asked immediately.

Farouk nodded. "Without doubt."

"Where'd she go?"

"In the morning, she pursued her charitable enterprises," Farouk said. "She attended a meeting of the New York Preservation Society until 10:33 A.M. Then she took a cab to the Museum of Modern Art and spoke briefly on the problems of the rain forest." He looked at Frank quizzically. "This appears to be one of her most sincere commitments, yes?"

"Yeah, I guess," Frank said. "Where'd she go after that?" he asked, a bit impatiently.

"To the Hospital for Spinal Injuries," Farouk said. "And after that, she had tea at the Plaza with a group who are interested in preserving something or other."

Frank nodded. "Then what?"

"By then it was 2:07 in the afternoon," Farouk said, "and she returned home."

"And that's it?" Frank asked disappointedly.

Farouk smiled quietly. "No, my friend."

"She left again?"

"At 2:17."

"To Madison Avenue? Another limousine?"

Farouk shook his head. "To Central Park. The place that is called Strawberry Fields."

"Alone?"

"Alone for a time, but not forever."

"She met someone?"

"A man," Farouk told him. "But only for a moment."

"What happened?"

"There is a place, a circular area. A star-burst mosaic, where it is written . . ."

"Imagine," Frank said.

"Yes."

"Near the Dakota, where Devine lives."

Farouk nodded.

"Was it Devine?"

Farouk shook his head. "No, it was not." His eyes drifted down toward Frank's desk.

Frank knew the signal well. "You want a drink?" he asked.

"That would be good, yes," Farouk told him.

Frank brought out the bottle and poured each of them a round.

Farouk lifted his glass. "To the order of things," he said with a wry smile. He took a long drink, then placed the cup on his thigh. "To walk around at such a speed," he said wearily, "this is not made for one who works mostly with his fingers." He took a second sip from the cup. "To the man," he said when he'd finished. "I do not know him. But this much is true, he was not Devine, nor was he the other, he who, as you say, is full of shit, Powers."

"How long were they together?"

"They did not look together at all," Farouk said. "But I recalled the other incident."

"The drop."

"The drop, yes," Farouk said. "And I watched closely to see if such an action might be repeated."

Frank leaned forward slightly. "Was it?"

"Yes," Farouk said.

"A little black bag?"

Farouk shook his head. "I would describe it as a pouch."

"Pouch, bag, whatever," Frank said restlessly. "What did she do, leave it in the bushes or something?"

"As she did before," Farouk told him. "On a bench crowded with other things."

"Where was the man?"

"A small distance away," Farouk said. "He knew his business well, this man. He did not betray himself, and had I not known of the other incident, I too would have followed Mrs. Phillips. But instead, I remained behind to observe the black pouch."

"So the man picked it up," Frank said.

"He did, yes," Farouk said.

Frank took out his notebook. "Can you describe him?"

"Yes," Farouk said. "But there is no need." He drew a small camera from his pocket. "I have captured his likeness," he said with obvious delight. "And in a moment, you shall have it too." He stood up.

Frank looked at him, puzzled. "Where are you going?"

Farouk stared at him quietly, as if coming to some final conclusion about his character. "Come with me," he said finally. "We have much to discover."

Frank stood up. "Where are we going?"

"To the place were I do my work."

"Toby's?"

Farouk laughed and shook his head. "No. I only talk and think in that place." He looked at Frank closely. "I have another place, my true home. Only after much trial do I allow another to enter it."

"I've always wondered where you really went to ground," Frank said. "But where is . . ."

Farouk answered his unspoken question. "It is nearby," he said. "Only a short walk. We will develop the pictures, and then go on to our discoveries." He smiled. "Come now, we have only a little time."

They walked out of the office, turned left and moved slowly westward toward Tenth Avenue. At the corner of the avenue, Frank glanced to the left. In the distance, he could see the dark storefront of the Puri Dai.

"I saw her today," he said, almost to himself.

Farouk looked at him, confused. "But I thought you did not wish to go near Mrs. Phillips again."

"Not Mrs. Phillips," Frank explained. "The Puri Dai."

Farouk's looked at him, surprised. "You found her?"

Frank pointed upward, toward the short brick tenement on the eastern side of the avenue. "There," he said. "She was standing on the roof."

Farouk nodded. "Her place of observation," he said.

"Yeah," Frank said. "I ran up to the roof to try to find her, but she got to me first."

"Got to you?"

Frank shrugged. "I ended up on the ground, and she was on me with some kind of knife, I guess. Anyway, she grabbed my pistol and knocked me out with it."

"And took your gun, yes?" Farouk asked, as if he already knew the answer.

Frank nodded.

"Now she is ready," Farouk said.

Frank looked at him intently. "What's she going to do, Farouk?"

"She is going to get her daughter from those who have taken her," Farouk answered with certainty. "And this is as it should be, do you not think?"

"Yes."

Farouk smiled. "Good," he said. "I am happy that you have not lost the truth of things."

"The problem is the other people," Frank said. "They were packing up before I saw her. And by the time I came to, the whole place was deserted. They were gone."

"They?"

"I saw a man there. He was telling the old woman what to do."

"Of course."

"Do you know who he is?"

"He is the Gypsy Father," Farouk said, "the keeper of the faith, one who insures that it will go on this way forever."

"What way?"

"That the female child will pass on the holy blood."

"The daughter, you mean?"

"Yes."

"Not the Puri Dai?"

Farouk shook his head. "No more, the Puri Dai. She has broken with the *errate,* and if she does as her soul demands, there will be no more women such as she."

Frank saw her again in his mind, standing tall on the rooftop, her skin almost golden in the setting sun that faced her. He had no doubt whatsoever that Farouk was right.

At the corner of Twelfth Avenue, they turned right and walked between the river and the long line of brick buildings which faced it, mostly old warehouses, crumbling with age and and long misuse.

"You have an office down here?" Frank asked unbelievingly.

"It is where I make my life," Farouk answered. He smiled quietly as he continued walking, moving slowly until he swung to the right and went through a small red door.

Frank followed along behind, passing through a narrow corridor, which opened onto a littered courtyard. The courtyard was surrounded on all sides by square brick buildings. It was wild and untended, filled with the accumulated residue of its long neglect. A large ship's anchor leaned against one of the far walls, and along the ground, there were bits of metal, an ancient rust-encrusted sextant, torn sheets of rigging, coils of thick gray rope and, in a single remote corner, a wheelchair turned upside down, its rubberless wheels gray and motionless in the shadowy light.

"It was once a sailor's hospital," Farouk explained as he led Frank across the courtyard. "Sometimes, I would come here, in its last days, and speak with the old ones from the sea. I was young then, a stranger to many things, and here there was much for such a one to learn."

They reached a second door at the other end of the courtyard. It was made of metal and held shut by an enormous chain and lock. Farouk took out a key, unlocked the lock, then pulled the chain through the thick steel loop which held it, and swung open the door.

Inside it was entirely dark until Farouk switched on a light. The ground floor was dusty, and the faintly sweet smell of rotting wood hung heavily in the air.

"Over here," Farouk said. He pointed to a metal staircase to his right and then led Frank up the stairs to the second floor of the building. There was another metal door at the top of the stairs, complete with chain and lock. Farouk repeated his movement down below, then pushed the door open. "Here is the place," he said as he escorted Frank inside.

The air was very dark inside the room, and it turned even darker when Farouk closed the door behind him. Frank turned slowly and saw what looked at first glance like a wall of small lights, some blinking rhythmically, some shining steadily out of the darkness like scores of tiny, motionless eyes.

"This is my workplace," Farouk said. Then he walked to one of the large windows which faced the courtyard and drew open its enormous shade. The dark air brightened instantly, and Frank could see a bank of computers, printers and other indecipherably complex equipment arranged on a large table which stretched almost from one side of the building to the other. Small motors purred softly in the dry, dead air, and to the right, there were long corridors of high metal shelves which reached nearly to the ceiling. They were crammed with hundreds of books and magazines and papers. At the far corner of the room, so far from the window that it remained in deep shadow, Frank could make out a small metal bed which had been neatly made up, a large armchair with a footstool in front of it and, beside the chair, the curved neck of a reading lamp.

"It is all that I require," Farouk said, as if in explanation. He paused a moment, then drew Frank to the right and over to a small room which had been built in one corner of the building. "I will only be a moment," he said as he stepped inside. "You may be here as you are in your own place," he added as he closed the door.

Frank nodded, then strolled across the room to the long lines of gray metal shelves. He headed down one aisle, then another, glancing idly at the books and papers which Farouk had gathered together over the years. Their variety was astonishing. There were books on plants, on chemicals, on all kinds of synthetic materials, and they shared the shelves with other books and magazines on general science.

History came next, and as Frank wandered through what Farouk had saved of man's time on earth he found himself more and more amazed by the scope of his interests. There were books on Oriental, African and European cultures, as well as works of military, civil and legal history. Other books specialized in the history of economic life—usury, revenue, the circulation of money—and next to them were scores of works on both social and natural forms of crisis— books on fires and floods and earthquakes shelved side by side with other books on revolution, insurrection, wars and strikes: a gathering of works which seemed to have been filed under some general category of irrepressible upheaval.

As he continued walking idly among Farouk's books, Frank found himself growing more and more respectful of the kind of knowledge which they contained. There were books on Farouk's many languages, of course, but there were also books on philosophy, religion, mythology, on medicine and pharmacy, sorcery and witchcraft, gardening and etiquette. It was as if Farouk had spent his life searching for that last bit of evidence that would finally break life's dark, unsolvable case and provide him with some ultimate vision of the smoking gun.

"It is finished."

The voice seemed to come from far away, but when Frank glanced back down the long canyon of books and shelves, he saw Farouk standing at the end of it, staring at him solemnly, his arms outstretched as if waiting to embrace him, but with three small photographs held motionlessly in his hands.

"Come," Farouk said as he turned toward the enormous table to his right. "Let us examine."

Frank followed him to the desk, then waited while Farouk arranged the photographs, each turned on its face, as if kept hidden until the best possible moment.

"Now," Farouk said, "observe." He turned over the first picture.

Frank leaned forward and looked at it closely. It showed Mrs. Phillips as she sat near the mosaic tile memorial, her legs primly crossed as she stared out over the park, her head turned in profile.

"Observe the place beside her," Farouk said. Then he pointed to the small black pouch that rested near her right leg. "This will remain after she has departed."

Frank nodded.

"But it will not remain unnoticed for too long a time," Farouk added. "For as always, there is a watcher in the woods." He turned over the next photograph. "He who was waiting."

Frank's eyes squeezed together. In the picture, a man could be seen lightly picking up the pouch. He was very large and dressed in a badly rumpled suit, and although the photograph was in black-and-white, Frank knew that his eyes were blue and that his hair was red. He spoke his name in an astonished whisper: "Sam McBride."

Farouk looked up from the picture. "You know this man?"

Frank nodded silently.

"In what way, may I ask?"

"He works out of Manhattan North," Frank said wonderingly, his eyes still fixed on the picture. "The suicide shift."

Farouk looked at him doubtfully.

"He's just been transferred," Frank explained. "Just over the past week. You wouldn't have met him yet."

Farouk nodded. "I see," he said. "But you are sure?"

Frank looked at the photograph again. "Yes, I'm sure," he said.

Farouk slid the third photograph over the last one. It showed McBride and a second man talking quietly at a table at the rear of a small delicatessen.

"The place was on West Forty-fifth Street," Farouk said. "And the man you recognized, he went there with the pouch."

"And gave it to the second man?" Frank asked.

"Yes," Farouk said.

Frank continued to stare at the picture.

Farouk pointed to the second man. He was middle-aged and balding, with a large paunch which drooped over his belt. "Do you recognize this man as well?" he asked.

Frank shook his head.

"His name is Henry Floyd," Farouk told him. "And he has been around Hell's Kitchen for many years."

Frank looked up instantly. "What's he do?"

Farouk stared at him darkly. "He is for hire," he said. "Once he was a Westie, but since they have been broken up, he is working for himself."

"Doing what?"

"Whatever it is you wish," Farouk said. "For a price, of course."

"You mean anything?"

"He has been known to break a debtor's arm," Farouk said. "He has done things to a rapist who harmed a friend's daughter. This rapist, he will not be doing this particular crime again."

"I see," Frank said.

Farouk shrugged. "And he will kill," he added, almost casually. "If that is what you want."

"Kill?" Frank asked. He thought instantly of Phillips, the changed will, his wife's steadily growing distance. "I've got to call Phillips," he said urgently, then stopped himself. "No, I'd better be sure I know what I'm talking about before I do." He looked at Farouk. Farouk nodded. "I'll have to talk to McBride first." He glanced at his watch. "He doesn't come on until midnight." He looked at Farouk. "That's still a few hours away."

Farouk smiled. "A few hours, yes," he said. "To find the Puri Dai."

-31-

Night had fully fallen by the time Frank and Farouk returned to the street. Frank could feel his edginess building rapidly, but Farouk appeared utterly calm, moving slowly, ponderously, his eyes often drifting over toward the river while he talked.

"Your Mr. Phillips will be all right for the next few hours," he said. "But the Puri Dai—this will happen very soon. Agreed?"

Frank had to admit he was right. It would be irresponsible to go running off to Phillips on such flimsy evidence, at least until they had a chance to talk with McBride. And meanwhile, the Puri Dai was running around somewhere with his gun.

"It is good to know the nature of a person," Farouk said meditatively as he walked. "How they will betray themselves. Sometimes, it is through passion, sometimes through ignorance. These are blameless things, for they are beyond control." He stopped and let his eyes return to Frank. "But greed, that is without the virtue of passion or the helplessness of a natural flaw."

"Greed," Frank repeated. "Are you talking about the Puri Dai?"

"Those who would enslave her."

"The man?"

"And she who serves him."

"The old woman, Maria Jacobe?"

Farouk nodded. "These are two people who do not know themselves," he said. "Who are dead to earth, without being." He shook his head. "These are people who have large spaces in them, and these spaces they fill up with what is ready to their hands, with

271

money, with ritual. These small things they cling to because without them, they would be nothing but emptiness, light as air."

"Where does the Puri Dai fit in?" Frank asked anxiously.

"She is the touch that topples them," Farouk said authoritatively. "The one who has cracked the old design." He smiled again. "But still, in the end, they did it to themselves."

"What?"

"By their greed," Farouk said darkly. He stopped again, this time turning his face to the river. "Do you remember last night when we visited the old woman?"

Frank nodded. "When she read your palm?"

"And I spilled the contents of my wallet onto the floor."

"Yes."

"And the old woman gathered them up?"

"Yes."

"This was part of my design," Farouk said.

"For her to pick up the stuff?"

Farouk nodded. "And in the midst of such confusion, to keep something for herself. In this case, a credit card."

"Did she?"

"She did, yes," Farouk said. "And she gave it to the man as she has always been commanded to do, and with it, this man made a purchase, which I have discovered."

Frank smiled. "On your computer," he said, suddenly recognizing the purpose of all the vast equipment which Farouk had gathered onto the enormous table. "You break computer codes. That's how you get so much information."

Farouk shrugged. "It is a game I play from time to time."

"So you found out what the charges were on the credit card that the old woman stole," Frank continued.

Farouk nodded. "It was used on Fifty-seventh Street," he said. "A place known as Midtown Liquors." His body tightened suddenly, and Frank saw that his own tingling edginess had suddenly swept over Farouk like a wild, electric wind.

Midtown Liquors rested on a corner of Fifty-seventh Street that was not far from what still remained of the old West Side Highway.

It was small and cramped, with tightly packed bottles arranged on wooden shelves that rose to the ceiling.

There was no one behind the counter as the two men entered the store, but a large, round-shouldered man could be seen at the end of the aisle, his body bent forward as he drew bottles of wine from a box and placed them in the cooler at the rear of the store.

Farouk nodded to him as the two of them walked down the aisle.

"What can I do for you?" the man asked as he turned toward them.

Farouk smiled quietly as he pulled out an official-looking ID.

The man glanced at the identification. "Bank investigator?" he asked.

Farouk nodded.

"What are you investigating?"

"Fraud," Farouk answered immediately. "That is to say, the illegal use of a credit card by one who is not entitled to possess it."

The man shrugged. "So?"

"One such card was used in this establishment," Farouk told him.

The man seemed unimpressed. "So?" he repeated.

"We are interested in discovering the identity of this person."

The man said nothing.

"And his whereabouts," Farouk added. "In this, we are also very interested."

The man laughed. "Yeah, I'll bet you are." He snapped the box from the floor and began to break it down. "Well, you get paid for asking questions, but I don't get paid for answering them."

"You will do it out of courtesy," Farouk said evenly. "This has been my experience."

The man leaned forward and laughed again, this time very close to Farouk's face. "Courtesy, is that what you said, fella?"

Farouk faced him expressionlessly. He did not speak.

"Courtesy," the man scoffed. "Where you from, buddy, Mars?"

"Manners are most important in my country," Farouk said solemnly. "We are taught to be careful how we speak."

"Your country?" the man chuckled. He looked at Farouk mockingly. "What are you anyway?"

"We are taught to speak with courtesy to strangers," Farouk went on. "For we do not know the evil or the good that may be in such a person's heart."

The man's face crinkled. "What the fuck are you talking about?"

"And since you do not know a stranger's heart," Farouk continued, his voice now utterly flat, the light in his eyes slowly going out, "we are warned against offending him."

The man stopped laughing. "That sounds like a threat to me."

Farouk said nothing.

The man drew himself to his full height and let the box slip from his fingers. "Why don't you just get your fat ass out of here," he said.

"And we are also taught," Farouk added, "to present ourselves immediately and powerfully to another, so that he will not have time to mistake us for a weaker thing."

The man stepped toward Farouk and placed his large hand on his chest. "Beat it, dickhead."

"So, please, if I may present myself," Farouk said. Then in a lightning turn, he grabbed the man's hand, twisted his arm behind his back and spun him around roughly, so that he could see the cooler just before his face slammed into it.

The bottles inside the cooler rattled loudly as they knocked against each other, but Farouk did not seem to hear them. He pressed the man's face hard against the glass, flattening his nose against it.

"I am Farouk," he said. "I am one who seeks to discover something from you." He pinned the man against the cooler, then drew his head back and slammed it once again into its glass door, "Now, do you know who I am?"

The man groaned.

"Please, you must say my name," Farouk ordered.

"Farrooggg," the man moaned.

Farouk spun him around and slapped him once, almost lightly, with an open hand, in the face. The man's head jerked back against the cooler, then slumped forward into Farouk's open hand.

Farouk lifted the head again and stared into the man's glistening eyes.

"I am looking for one who bought a case of raki with a credit card," he said. "This credit card did not belong to this person, and I wish to discover who he is."

The man stared at Farouk fearfully. "Please," he groaned, "I don't remember every customer."

"A case of raki is not usual," Farouk said. "This you would remember."

The man stared at him pleadingly, but didn't speak.

Farouk gave him a lethal glare. "Do not hesitate," he told him darkly. "I will not be turned aside."

"I don't know his name," the man stammered. "He drives a red car, very fancy, with a white top made out of that velvet-type stuff."

"What kind of car?"

"I don't know," the man told him. "But when he ordered the raki, he was driving it."

"Have you ever seen it parked around here?"

The man nodded brokenly. "Yeah, once or twice."

"Where was this?"

"In front of one of those buildings near the highway," the man said. "You know, on the block."

"North or south?"

The man hesitated. "Who is this guy?" he asked fearfully. "I mean, is he connected?"

Farouk placed his hand around the man's throat and held him tightly against the cooler. "Which building?" he asked.

The man's brief resistance collapsed. "It's just down the block," he whined. "I seen the car in front of it just a few minutes ago. In front of that little dump on the corner. I seen the car parked there."

"Does he live in that building?"

"I guess he does," the man said. "When he bought the raki, that's where he wanted it delivered."

"Did you deliver it?"

"Yeah, the regular guy was out."

"What is the apartment number?"

"It don't remember no number," the man said. "It was just a place at the end of the hall."

"What floor?"

"Third," the man said.

"What did the guy look like?"

The man looked surprised. "You don't know that?"

Farouk's finger tightened around his throat again. "What does he look like?" he repeated.

"He's tall, and he got a black mustache," the man said. "A big thick one that's sort of curled up at the end. And he wears the red thing around his neck, like a handkerchief or something."

Farouk glanced at Frank quizzically.

"That's the man I saw," Frank said.

Farouk released his grip on the man's throat, his eyes glaring at him in a deadly calm. "I am invisible, yes?" he asked.

The man gasped for breath. His hands rose to massage his throat. "I never seen you," he stammered. He swallowed hard. "And I don't want to never see you again."

Farouk nodded, almost politely, then turned and walked out onto the street. Frank followed just behind him, and both of them glanced to the right immediately, their eyes narrowing in on the red car.

"Wait here," Farouk said. "I will return in a moment."

Frank eased himself back against the window of the liquor store and watched as Farouk walked down to the car, passing it casually, with hardly a glance, and then heading on down to the end of the block to where a telephone booth stood at the edge of the curb.

Within only a few minutes he'd returned, ambling slowly up the sidewalk, gawking at the large buildings which stretched up Fifty-seventh Street like a foreigner in the city, overwhelmed by its size and bustle.

"I checked the license number of the car," he said as he joined Frank beside the window. "It is registered in New Jersey under the name of Joseph Fellows."

"Is it stolen?" Frank asked.

Farouk shook his head. "I do not think so. Another call allowed me to discover that Mr. Fellows fits the man you saw, and that he is a man of many complaints."

"Complaints?"

"He has many outstanding warrants on him," Farouk explained. "They are from New Jersey, Connecticut and Massachusetts."

"Nothing from New York?"

"No," Farouk said. "But many from the other places."

"What are the warrants for?"

"Petty matters," Farouk said, as if disappointed. "He is a man of small larcenies. He has done nothing which the local authorities would be interested in pursuing with sufficient speed to save the Puri Dai."

"So it's up to us?"

Farouk nodded.

"How do you want to do it?" Frank asked, meaning the time and the method they would use.

Farouk took the question differently. "With determination," he replied. "And without relent."

—32—

For a little while they lingered in front of the liquor store. Farouk smoked a cigarette while his eyes idly swept up and down the street. He seemed deep in thought, as if considering all the moves it was now possible for the two of them to make.

"Do you think Fellows is in there?" Frank asked after a moment.

"I do not know."

"And the little girl?"

Farouk shrugged. "We will soon discover it," he said confidently. "If he is within the building, he will have to come out. If he is without, we will strike at him before he returns."

Suddenly, something occurred to Frank. "The raki," he said anxiously. "That whole case of raki. It's for the ceremony you talked about. To bathe the little girl."

Farouk nodded.

Frank felt a wave of anger pass over him. "Maybe we shouldn't wait," he said. "Maybe we should go get him now." He stepped away from Farouk. "The little girl may . . ."

Farouk grabbed his arm, interrupting him. "It will not be done here," he said. "It is a celebration. Many will come. It is a festival from ancient days. The little girl has not yet been harmed."

Frank turned westward, to the dilapidated red-brick tenement that rested at the far edge of Fifty-seventh Street, its western corner just beneath the cement canopy of the West Side Highway. "Well, how long do you want to wait?"

"We do not know what we may find inside," Farouk said. "We should try to take him on the street."

"So you just want to stake the place out," Frank said.

"For as long as possible, yes," Farouk said. "But not from here. We must find another place."

"Okay," Frank said. He glanced about, his eyes finally lighting on a small alleyway on the east side of the street. He pointed it out to Farouk. "How about over there?"

Farouk nodded immediately. "Yes, that is good. From there we could observe everything."

They walked to the alley and took up their positions at once, edging themselves into the slender brick corridor, their bodies concealed from the tenement by a single jutting wall.

Farouk took out his cigarette holder, inserted a cigarette and lit it.

Frank kept his eyes on the building, his face pressed up against the corner of the wall while he watched it intently.

"You will never have the Puri Dai," Farouk said after a moment, as if he knew exactly what Frank was thinking.

Frank continued to watch the building. "Do you think she's in there?" he asked softly.

"If she is," Farouk answered bluntly, "then she is already dead."

"She has a gun."

"As all women should have," Farouk said, as if it were an indisputable truth of life that a gun alone would finally be the dark irreducible means of women's deliverance.

"I hope she knows how to use it," Frank said.

Farouk drew in a long, weary breath. "So do I."

Suddenly a light went on at the front of the third-floor landing, held a moment, then went off again. Frank leaned forward, raking his face against the rough cement wall as he peered closely at the now darkened space behind the unshaded windows. He could feel a dull ache in the wound on the side of his head, but it seemed almost a source of pleasure, a physical connection between himself and the Puri Dai, the only one he would ever know. He lifted his fingers to the bruised flesh, explored it gently for a moment, then let his hand drift down again to the empty holster at his side.

"My gun has never been registered," he said.

"Do you wish it to be registered?"

"What do you mean?"

"I can accomplish this," Farouk said. "Long ago I found the key to the Firearms Registry."

Frank looked at him, astonished. "You can register guns?"

Farouk nodded. "To anyone I choose," he said. "Do you wish yours to be registered?"

Frank shook his head. "No. Because if she uses it, it can't be traced back to me."

Farouk smiled knowingly. "You mean through you, to her, yes?" he asked.

Frank didn't answer. He kept his eyes fixed on the unlighted upper windows. "If we find them," he said, "the Puri Dai and her daughter, what do we do?"

"The Puri Dai cannot be released," Farouk said. "She has betrayed the *errate*. She will never be safe from those who will seek vengeance."

"What about her daughter?"

"She is young," Farouk said. "She will grow into another face, another body. One day, she will be released." His face grew very solemn. "But the Puri Dai, she is doomed."

Frank pulled his eyes from the window and looked at Farouk. "I wonder if there was ever a way out for her?" he asked.

"There was only one," Farouk said authoritatively. Then he reached down and opened his coat. The black handle of his pistol peeped out from beneath his arm like the muzzle of a small but fiercely determined animal. "And she has found it," he added. "Blessed be she among women."

It was almost midnight before Frank finally pulled his eyes away from the building again. He could feel the wound she'd given him aching insistently, drawing one wide line of pain from the torn flesh to his weary, throbbing eyes.

"Soon," Farouk said, as if to give him strength.

"Maybe they've already gone."

Farouk shook his head. "I do not think so."

"Why not?"

Farouk lifted his arms helplessly. "Because I am one who lives on faith."

Frank turned back toward the building, once again pressing the side of his face against its rough surface. The front windows of the third-floor landing were still dark, but he could see a faint yellow glow, as if candles were flickering weakly far back in the room.

"He must be in there," Frank said. "Let's just go in and get him."

Farouk pulled himself to his feet, walked over to the edge of the wall and peered up at the windows. "He is not yet there," he said.

Frank looked at him. "How do you know?"

Farouk's eyes were no longer raised, but now stared straight ahead, level with the street. "Because he is there," he said evenly.

Frank immediately turned toward the street. He could see the man ambling slowly down the opposite sidewalk, the large straw hat cocked to the right, its brim shaking slightly in the breeze that swept toward him from the river.

"That is the man, yes?" Farouk asked.

Frank could feel his whole body tightening, as if someone were screwing his loosely fitted bones back into their sockets. "That's him," he said.

Farouk stepped around him, as if to hold him back. "All right, we will act now," he said. "But with care."

The two of them stepped out from behind the concealing wall and headed toward the street. They walked quickly, determinedly, closing in on him. Then, suddenly, the man speeded up, moved rapidly toward the building, then up the stairs and disappeared inside.

Farouk and Frank sprinted after him, bounded up the stairs, then rushed through the small door that divided the littered vestibule from the street itself. They could see the door to the elevator closing slowly down the hall and darted toward it. In the single square of glass that served as the elevator's window, they could see the man's head, his eyes popping and staring; then, in a single, fleeting instant as the elevator began to rise, they glimpsed the Puri Dai beside him, the barrel of her pistol resting evenly in his ear.

"Christ," Frank whispered admiringly. "She's done it."

Farouk glanced left and right, his eyes searching the lobby until they found the door that opened onto the stairs. "There," he said. "Hurry."

They took the stairs two at a time, scrambling hurriedly through its accumulated debris of empty cans, paper wrappers and broken glass.

"All right, wait a moment," Farouk said breathlessly when they reached the top floor. He took out his handkerchief and wiped the sweat from his brow. "Give me just a moment, please," he gasped.

Frank nodded, then stepped in front of him, opened the door slightly and peered out.

Through a slender space of the barely open door he could see the elevator open shakily, its metal door rattling softly as it slid to the left.

Inside, the Puri Dai was standing rigidly beside the frozen figure of the man. She waited until the door was entirely open, then she urged him forward very slowly, the pistol digging into his ear.

Frank glanced quickly at Farouk. "They're going out," he whispered, then turned back toward the hallway.

The man stood rigidly in place, his eyes fixed on the door in front of him, while the Puri Dai felt into the right pocket of his trousers.

Frank looked back at Farouk again. "She's looking for the keys," he whispered desperately. "We have to move." Reflexively, his right hand dropped to his side, his fingers searching frantically through the dead space of his holster until he realized that it was empty. Then he turned to Farouk. "Give me your gun," he said.

Farouk drew himself away. "No, you must wait."

"For what?"

"For me, Frank," Farouk said. "You cannot do this thing alone." He drew in a deep breath, waited another moment to regain his strength. "All right," he said finally. "Now."

Frank opened the door again and felt a kind of relief that the Puri Dai had disappeared into the apartment. "It's too late to get them in the hall," he said.

"It does not matter," Farouk said confidently as he eased himself into the hallway. "Come." He walked to the door, pulled out his pistol and handed it to Frank. "I will go through the door," he said. "And you will follow me with the pistol."

Frank took the gun, pointed it at the ceiling, then pulled himself back against the wall beside the door. "Whenever you're ready," he told him.

Farouk's body seemed to harden into a single massive ball. He aimed his shoulder at the door, then plunged forward.

The door sprang open instantly, and Farouk stumbled into the room, then stopped cold and began to raise his hands as Frank rushed in behind him, his gun bobbing and shifting in the air like a small black nose.

For an instant, he searched the room through the shadowy, faintly yellow light. Then he saw them, poised and frozen just inside the adjoining room. The Puri Dai stood beside the man, the pistol still digging at his ear.

Frank faced her silently, the pistol stretching out toward her like the dark key to their collusion.

The Puri Dai glared at him poisonously. "Leave us," she said.

The man looked at Frank and Farouk with an odd sense of relief, as if they were all old comrades, men who shared some common place in a vast conspiracy. He glanced at the pistol in Frank's hand, then up into his eyes. "Kill her," he said.

The Puri Dai looked as if she thought Frank might obey. Instantly, she drew the gun from the other man's ear and shifted its barrel slightly toward Frank. "Do not move," she said. Then she returned the barrel to the man's head.

"Let him go," Frank told her.

The Puri Dai remained in place. "I have come for my daughter," she said.

"I'll get her for you," Frank assured her.

"It is not for you to do," the Puri Dai said determinedly. She pulled back the cock, turned the pistol back toward Frank and leveled the barrel directly at his eyes. "Leave us," she repeated.

Frank shook his head. "There's a better way."

The Puri Dai's arm stiffened. "Leave us."

They were only a few feet apart, and Frank could see her brown finger as it drew down on the trigger.

"You'll do it, won't you?" he said, almost wonderingly, and with a strange, transcendent urge to praise the will that had transformed her into a woman warrior.

"Leave us," she whispered a final time.

Frank stood in place. He could hear Farouk breathing heavily beside him. For a moment, he wanted to save him from the fury of the Puri Dai, but he realized that he did not want to save himself from that same vengeance, that instead, he wanted to take it, full and without regret, take it for what it finally was, a single shuddering act of age-old retribution.

The Puri Dai's eyes grew cold, and one of them closed slowly as she drew the pistol's small black site down upon her motionless target.

"Magdalena."

It was a woman's voice, and the Puri Dai turned to it immediately.

The old woman stood a few feet behind her, one of her thin brown arms wrapped around a small, dark-eyed girl with long black hair. The other hand held a pearl-handled knife at the girl's throat.

"Let Joseph go," the woman demanded, "or Magdalena will die."

The Puri Dai did not move.

"I will kill you as I killed the other," the old woman said. "You must know your place."

The Puri Dai drew the pistol back to the man's ear. She did not speak, but only stared at the other woman.

"Let him go, Magdalena," the woman said angrily. "It is not for you to decide her place."

The little girl stood rigidly in front of the old woman, her eyes fixed on the Puri Dai.

The old woman stared at the Puri Dai hatefully. "Maria Salome would have helped you," she said, "would have helped you leave your place. And so she died as a lesson to your daughter."

The Puri Dai pressed the barrel of the gun against the man's head. "It was he who commanded you," she said.

"The Gypsy Father always commands," the woman said proudly. "And the Three Marias must obey."

The Puri Dai's eyes drifted toward the little girl, but she said nothing.

"Let him go," the old woman repeated. She pressed the blade against the little girl's throat until a small trick of blood ran in a jagged line down her smooth, brown throat. "Let him go," the old woman said again, "or I will send this child to hell." She pressed the blade downward again, and the little girl winced with pain, her lips parting in a single, softly spoken word: "Mother."

The Puri Dai looked at her in a single agonizing instant, and as she did so, she loosened the grip on her pistol and the man spun around quickly and snapped it from her hand. She did not resist, but only stood, staring at her daughter, while he wheeled to the right and pointed the pistol at Frank and Farouk.

"This is Gypsy business," he said. "You have no place here."

Frank edged the barrel of his pistol over toward him. "You're not going anywhere," he said.

The man smiled sneeringly, then jerked the Puri Dai in front of him and placed the pistol at her head.

Frank felt something in his body empty. "Don't," he said softly. "Don't."

"Gypsy business," the man repeated. He nodded toward the pistol. "Drop it."

Frank didn't move.

The man pressed the barrel of the gun hard against the Puri Dai's head. "Drop it, now!" he screamed.

Frank felt the pistol slip from his hand. It banged loudly against the wooden floor.

"You, fat one," the man said to Farouk. "Kick it over to me."

Farouk obeyed, and the man swept the second pistol from the floor, threw open the chamber and spilled the bullets onto the floor. "I return it to you now," he said snidely as he let it drop from his hand. Then he took a small step forward, pushing the Puri Dai ahead of him, the pistol bearing down in the soft flesh at her temple.

"Let her go," Frank said.

The man motioned Frank and Farouk from his path. "Get out of my way," he said.

The two of them exchanged helpless glances, then did as they were told.

The man smiled haughtily, then stepped through the still open door.

Frank kept his eyes on him. "I will find you," he said.

The man seemed barely to hear him. He nodded toward the old woman and she immediately released the little girl and rushed to his side.

The man smiled. "We only needed the girl to get the Puri Dai," he said. He pressed the gun barrel roughly against her head. "You were right, the girl's blood is spoiled," he said to her. "You violated the *errate*—violated our world. She is useless now. And you have done it. That is why we lured you from prison, to make you think the ceremony would still go on. Because it is your fault that the *errate* has been lost, and now you must pay for it."

The Puri Dai winced slightly, then closed her eyes.

Frank glanced back toward the little girl. She stood toward the back of the room, her eyes staring wildly at her mother.

The Puri Dai opened her eyes briefly, let them settle on her daughter, as if to embrace her, but said nothing.

Frank turned to the man. "Let her go," he said.

The man smiled. "It will be as you wish, my friend," he said coldly. He drew the barrel of the pistol a small distance from the Puri Dai's head and then with an abrupt, demonic jerk, he pulled the trigger.

A burst of blood shot from the side of Puri Dai's head, and as he saw it, Frank felt something at the very center of his life crumble like a great building which had lost its old foundation. He lunged forward with tremendous force, and as he did so, the man stepped back and pushed her body forward into his longing, outstretched arms, then rushed from the room, half-dragging the old woman behind him.

Frank slumped to the floor with the Puri Dai, his arms around her like the lover he would never be.

The child let out a high, keening wail, and Farouk plunged backward and swept her up into his arms.

Frank stared down at the Puri Dai's uplifted face. He could feel her breath on his skin as he cradled her shattered head in his arms. Her eyes were open and staring outward, as if toward some vision that had yet to find its resting place on earth. Her lips moved silently, and he could see that she was trying to speak to him, to tell him something, and he imagined it as a single lost and visionary truth, one which, once uttered, might have saved the world.

It was nearly three in the morning before Tannenbaum had finally finished with him. The Puri Dai had been swept away in a shiny EMS ambulance by then, and Farouk had taken the child with him. Only Frank had remained in the small room on the third floor, his eyes fixed on the blood of the Puri Dai, which still lay, its dark red deepening steadily to black, across the uncarpeted floor while Tannenbaum circled him incessantly, a trail of cigar smoke following his movements like a billowy gray tail.

"So, you don't know who the guy was for sure, right?" Tannenbaum asked wearily.

"Just the name," Frank said. "Joseph Fellows."

"And you figure he was a Gypsy?"

"Yes."

Tannenbaum shook his head. "Well, my guess is, he's long gone by now."

Frank said nothing.

"These people, they off each other once in a while," Tannenbaum added. "And you know how it is, Frank. They live outside our jurisdiction, you might say. They have rules of their own. The only time we'd ever pull out all the stops would be if one of them wasted some big guy, some rich guy or celebrity, something like that."

"He killed a woman," Frank reminded him.

"Sure he did," Tannenbaum said. "And we'll work the case, no doubt about it. I just don't want you to get your hopes up, Frank. You know what I mean, the trail will go cold fast. They won't light

289

a fire downtown on something like this. Not for a Gypsy." He glanced at the blood of the Puri Dai. "Dead or alive."

Frank nodded tiredly, then rubbed his eyes.

"You look beat, Frank," Tannenbaum said. "Why don't you go get some sleep?"

"I still got work," Frank told him. "It's something I want to finish."

"Now? At this hour?"

"Yes."

Tannenbaum looked at him knowingly. "You mean, to get the night case off your mind, right?"

"It's just a quick stop," Frank said. "McBride, you know where he is?"

Tannenbaum looked surprised. "McBride? You want to see McBride?"

"Yeah."

Tannenbaum looked like he'd thought about asking another question, but then decided not to. "He's off tonight."

"Does that mean he's at home?"

Tannenbaum shook his head. "No, he usually stays with his wife."

"Where's she?"

"Over at St. Clare's," Frank said. "She's got a bed over there."

"Okay," Frank said. "Thanks." He turned and headed toward the door.

Tannenbaum's voice turned him around again. "You got to just go on, Frank," he said. "You know what I mean? There's just nothing else to do."

Frank nodded silently. "Yeah," he said, but he was not so sure.

Frank walked slowly down Ninth Avenue, then turned right toward the bleak, unlighted awning of St. Clare's Hospital. The reception desk was almost directly in front of him as he stepped inside the building.

"I know visiting hours are over," Frank said to the woman behind the desk. "But there's someone I need to see."

"I'm afraid you can't see a patient at this hour, sir," the woman told him politely.

"It's not a patient I'm looking for."

"A doctor?" the woman said, before he could tell her.

"A patient's husband," Frank said. "He stays with her at night."

"Who's the patient?"

"Her last name would be McBride," Frank said.

The woman looked over at her computer monitor, tapped out a few letters on the keyboard, then turned back to Frank. "Mrs. McBride is in Room 306," she said. She smiled. "I should have known who you were talking about. Mr. McBride stays here every Saturday night."

"Would he be there now?"

"I really don't know."

"But it would be all right for me to check?"

"Yes, I suppose."

Frank nodded. "Three-oh-six, thanks."

"The stairs are through that door," the woman said.

Frank mounted the stairs slowly, his head still aching with the blow the Puri Dai had struck him, but he resisted the urge to touch the wound itself. Instead, he'd decided simply to wait for it slowly to grow numb.

Room 306 was at the end of a wide corridor. Inside, the room was vacant, except for Mrs. McBride. She lay faceup in a single bed, her eyes closed softly, as if she were asleep. A long plastic tube led from her nostrils to a small, quietly purring oxygen tank. Other tubes ran from her arms to several overhanging bags of liquids. Near the base of the bed, yet another tube drew her urine into yet another bag, and as Frank stepped up to the bed, he saw that it would soon need to be emptied and replaced.

For a time, he simply watched her as she slept, listening silently to her gently gurgling breath. His eyes moved up to the crucifix which hung from the wall, then down to the small shelf beside the bed, and finally along the slender bed rail, which stretched the full length of the bed, from Mrs. McBride's shoulders down to her feet.

At the end of the railing, a medical data board hung from a single aluminum hook. Frank leaned over and glanced at the light-blue cover sheet, his eyes moving down it no farther than the large black letters which gave the patient's name: MARY DRISCOLL McBRIDE.

He drew in a quick breath: DRISCOLL.

He released the board and it swung back to its place, tapping lightly against the railing.

DRISCOLL.

He stood, turned immediately and saw McBride standing massively in the open doorway.

McBride stared at him curiously, his eyes raking across his face like two small green fingers. "Clemons? What are you doing here?"

"I needed to talk to you about something," Frank told him, trying to keep the edginess from his voice.

"That Gypsy case again?" McBride asked, although he already seemed to sense that it was something else.

Frank shook his head. "No, not the Gypsy case." For a terrible instant, he saw the Puri Dai's dark eyes staring at him again, but not from the blood-soaked curve of his arms. Instead, she seemed to watch him from some impossibly distant place, dark and cloud-covered, as if it were still forming from the mists of its own design.

McBride continued to watch him curiously. "Something come up?" he asked warily.

"Let's go outside, Sam," Frank said.

McBride didn't move. "Outside? Why?"

"Someplace where we can talk?" Frank said. He stepped forward and McBride backed into the hallway to let him pass.

"You look like something's on your mind, Frank," McBride said coolly.

Frank faced him squarely. "There is. And I have to talk to you about it right now."

McBride seemed to sense the gravity of the moment. His eyes drew a bead on Frank's face. "All right," he said. "They've got a chapel on this floor. It's just down the hall. Nobody's ever there this time of night."

Frank nodded, then followed McBride's large, hulking frame as it moved slowly down the hallway. His shoulders were hunched and weary, as if he were dragging a heavy weight behind him.

"This'll do," McBride said when he got the chapel. "Private at least."

Frank followed him through the carved wooden door, then to the first wooden pew, where he stopped.

"Right here's okay," McBride said. He sat down in the narrow back pew, then slid over and made a place for Frank.

Frank eased himself into the pew, then stared evenly at McBride. "How long's your wife been here?" he asked.

"Several months now," McBride said.

"Must be expensive."

"It is."

"On a policeman's salary, you'd . . ."

"You didn't come here to talk about my salary, Frank," McBride said. "We're two old southern boys, so let's don't bullshit each other." He leaned back slightly and swung one of his arms over the back of the pew. "What's on your mind?"

Frank drew in a long slow breath. "I was noticing your wife's middle name."

"What about it?"

"Driscoll."

"Yeah."

"Is that her maiden name?"

"That's right."

Frank hesitated a moment longer, trying to find the best way to begin. Finally, he gave up, and went straight to the point.

"I've been tailing this woman who lives over on the East Side."

McBride's eyes stared expressionlessly at Frank. He said nothing.

"Her name is Phillips," Frank added. "She's married to this rich guy over there."

McBride's arm seemed to tighten slightly as the hand crawled up from the back of the pew.

"He's been a little worried about her lately," Frank went on, "because she's been acting sort of strange."

The hand was now lying flat against the top of the pew, the fingers stretched out to their full length.

"So that's why he hired me," Frank said. "To check her out a little, see what's the matter with her."

McBride nodded. "How long you been following her, Frank?" he asked coolly.

"Several days," Frank said.

"Everywhere?"

"From the time she leaves her place to the time she comes home to her husband."

McBride nodded but said nothing.

"She goes by the name of Driscoll sometimes," Frank said. "I was wondering if you might know why."

The fingers of the hand curled into a fist. "She's my sister-in-law," he said. "Any harm in me meeting my sister-in-law?"

Frank shook his head.

"Then what else do you want to know?" McBride asked bluntly.

Frank shrugged gently. "Well, you know how it is, Sam. Things lead to other things. People lead to other people."

McBride's face darkened. "What are you talking about?"

Frank took out the first photograph and handed it to him.

McBride looked at it casually. "That's Virginia in the park," he said. Then he handed it back to Frank. "What am I supposed to say about it?"

"Mrs. Phillips stands to inherit a lot of money, doesn't she?" Frank asked.

"She married a rich man, that's usually how it works."

"And you have a lot of expenses," Frank added.

McBride said nothing.

Frank turned the picture back toward him. "See that little black bag," he said as he pointed to it. "She's going to leave it on the bench."

McBride looked at the photograph silently.

"And you're going to pick it up," Frank added as he took out the second photograph and placed it over the first one. "That's you picking it up, Sam."

McBride nodded. "Yeah, it is." His eyes crawled over to Frank. "Which means you didn't follow Virginia back home."

"No."

"You followed me."

Frank nodded, then pulled out the third photograph. "There's a little deli on West Forty-fifth Street," he said. "It has a few little tables in the back." He handed the picture to McBride. "That's where you took the bag."

McBride didn't bother to look at the picture. "Okay."

Frank returned all the pictures to his jacket pocket. "What are you doing with Henry Floyd, Sam?"

McBride shrugged. "We go back a ways," he said. "There was plenty of Floyds back home."

"You know who he is?"

"Yes."

"You know he's a Westie? One of the last of them?"

McBride nodded.

"You know they have it on the street that they can smoke anybody if the price is right?"

McBride said nothing.

Frank leaned forward and leveled his eyes at McBride. "How much are you paying Henry Floyd to kill Harold Phillips?"

McBride didn't answer.

"You know something, Sam," Frank said. "I've met Mr. Phillips, and he'd not a bad man. He actually loves your sister-in-law. He's actually trying to save her."

"Save her?" McBride snapped with a sudden bitterness. "He's don't even know what she's into."

"What?"

"You think I'm running a hit on Phillips?"

Frank nodded quickly. "That's the way it adds up."

McBride shook his head. "You're way off, Frank, way off, and if I was you, I'd just let it go."

"I can't."

" 'Cause he's your client?"

"That's right."

"What if it was something else?" McBride said. "What if it had nothing to do with Phillips?"

Frank leaned forward slightly. "What are you talking about?"

"Well, justice, I guess," McBride said. "The kind that really puts an end to things."

Frank said nothing. He merely waited.

McBride drew his arm from the back of the pew and let it drift gently into his lap. "When Virginia first come to New York, she had them high hopes, you know, like in the movies. She wanted to be an actress." His eyes rolled upward slightly. "This was maybe six, seven years ago." He shook his head. "She was fresh off the farm. She didn't know nothing about life. But she was a beautiful girl." His mind seemed to return for a moment to an older time. "Like Mary was. Like my wife." He straightened himself slightly and lifted his head. "Anyway, she got connected to this producer or something. Some guy that said he was a producer. But really—this was a few years later—she found out, he was a doctor of some kind."

"Gynecologist," Frank said.

"That's right, a gynecologist," McBride said. "And this guy, he was trying to produce some shows, and that's how she met him."

Frank nodded.

"Well, this other guy was helping him out with the money," McBride went on. "This guy was rich. A real high roller with lots of big-shot friends. He was bankrolling the doctor. But it didn't do no good, according to Virginia, 'cause the show was a flop and every-body went broke on it." He shook his head. "And Virginia didn't have no money, and so the high roller, he come up to her and he said how pretty she was, and she was just a kid in them days, maybe eighteen, and she started working for him, you know, like going around with his friends, showing them the town, stuff like that."

"You mean, an escort service?"

"A special one," McBride said. "Real secret."

"Business Associates."

McBride nodded. "You know about that?"

"Yes."

"You know about the guy?"

"Preston Devine."

McBride looked surprised. "That's right."

"Go on."

"Well, after a while, Devine figured something out," McBride said. "He had a lot of rich business types that liked these young actresses, you know, but this being New York, they were getting scared of them."

"Scared?"

"You know, of getting something," McBride explained. "And I don't mean VD, you know? I mean the one that can kill you—AIDS."

Frank nodded.

"According to Virginia, these guys were really worried about that," McBride said. "It would be a terrible thing for them. I mean, they wanted girls. They wanted them real bad, but times had gotten sort of dangerous, and so they were in the market for something a little different than the usual sort of thing."

"You mean the usual sort of prostitute?"

"That's right," McBride said. "They were getting sort of afraid of that, and that's when Devine figured it all out. He could give them what they wanted, you know, risk-free."

"By testing them," Frank said.

McBride nodded. "And these guys, they were willing to pay a lot of money to get what they wanted, but to get it safe. So what Devine did was, he set up this special service, all the girls guaranteed, you know, to be, what you might say, to be clean." He shrugged. "And Virginia, she was one of them." His voice grew soft and sad. "Don't ask me why. You can blame it on anything. She said she did it once, and after that she couldn't get out, and maybe she just got worn down after a while. You know, by the life."

"Until she met Phillips," Frank said.

"She fell in love with him," McBride said. "They just met at a party. She made up a name for him, Virginia Harris. She made up a job. She made up her whole past. But she couldn't get rid of it."

"But she wanted out?"

"For a long time, she'd wanted that," McBride said. "But after she met Phillips, she got desperate about it. She went to Devine, she begged him."

Frank nodded. "But he wouldn't let her go."

"At first he did," McBride said. " 'Course, she had to pay and it just about broke her. But, at first, he let her go." His lips jerked down into a cruel scar. "But that only lasted awhile, because there was this one customer that didn't want a change. Some fat cat that wanted Virginia back."

"Burroughs."

McBride nodded. "That sounds right," he said. "Anyway, he put the pressure on Devine, and Devine comes back to Virginia. This was maybe six, seven weeks ago, and he told her she had to start up again. He tried to make it sound good, only one client, this Burroughs, but Virginia said no, she was out, and that was it." He shook his head. "But Devine said that just wouldn't do, that she had to come back, and when he kept on after her, threatening her, threatening to tell Phillips, that's when she come to me."

"What did she want you to do?"

"Put the arm on Devine."

"Did you?"

"I did my best," McBride said. "But he looked at me like I was some kind of bug or something, just a little thing he could squash with his foot. He said he had friends in high places, that they'd laugh in my face if I tried to pin something on him, and then, besides, he said, if it come out about him, it'd come out about Virginia too."

"So you decided to kill him," Frank whispered reverently, as if they were the last words of a prayer.

McBride nodded. "She come to me, and I tried what she wanted me to, and it didn't work," he said quietly. "So I said to myself, I said, 'There's one thing I know. I'm Sam McBride, and I don't hurt kids, and I don't rape women.' Now, Frank, that's where it could have stopped. That's where it usually stops. But this time, I took another step. I decided that if I could find a way, I'd fix it so nobody else could do those things either. And I can look you right in the eye and tell you face-to-face that no matter what happens, I'll stand by what I did."

Frank nodded.

"But I couldn't do it myself," McBride added. "I knew old Henry Floyd from way back when, and I knew that he could handle business like this." He shook his head. "Hell, Frank, old Henry's killed men a hundred times better than Preston Devine with a little-bitty pistol."

Frank thought a moment, his eyes moving away from McBride, up toward the front of the chapel where a large plaster statue of the Holy Mother stood in silent dignity above a spray of roses. She looked strangely weak and defenseless, terribly unarmed. Then he thought of the Puri Dai, the pistol in her hand, the vengeance that should have been hers but never would be, and suddenly, he saw it all in a strange and intricate pattern of lost power and unnatural restraints, of that fallen dignity which had to be regained in a world that respected nothing, but paid very close attention to a gun.

He drew out a pistol and lifted it toward McBride.

McBride stared at him silently. He did not move to take the pistol. "What's on your mind, Frank?"

"Use this," Frank told him flatly.

McBride watched him warily. "Whose is it?"

"That doesn't matter," Frank said. "But by tomorrow morning it'll be registered under the name of Joseph Fellows at a New Jersey address. He'll be on the run by then because he killed another woman tonight. The problem is, she was a Gypsy, a nobody, and they won't really go after him for it." He pressed the gun toward him gently. "But if he's connected to Preston Devine's murder, then they won't stop until they find him."

"He may have an alibi for Devine."

"He probably will, but it won't matter, because once they've got him for that, they'll have him for the other murder, too."

McBride smiled quietly, then drew the pistol from Frank's grasp. "All right," he said.

"And one other thing," Frank said.

"What's that?"

"Virginia Phillips should do it herself."

"She wouldn't know how."

"Then she needs to learn," Frank said firmly.

McBride looked at him intently, his eyes studying each weary line of his face. Then, suddenly, he seemed to grasp the whole desperate design, and the two of them stared at each other silently in a few seconds of wild collusion.

"So it's going to be woman's work," McBride said as he tucked the pistol in his pocket.

Frank nodded. "Woman's work," he said. "The way it should have always been."

Frank walked home slowly. His eyes were aching again, along with the Puri Dai's unmistakable wound, but he didn't move to soothe either one with the rough touch of his hands.

At Forty-seventh Street, he turned east and took his seat at the back of Smith's Bar. The old crowd was motionless and silent, and for a moment, he felt as if all the world's hunched legions had died during the long pull of the night, and that he was left now with nothing but a memory of what they had meant to him, both the ones who'd sat it out, filing down their days until there was nothing left but grayish dust, and those who'd drunk it down to the last drop, then turned their glasses over and slipped away.

It was dawn by the time he left, and as he walked uptown, then turned west and headed down Forty-ninth Street, the air around him was like a fine pink mist.

The pink deepened into red inside his office, and for a moment, as he took his seat behind his desk, he felt as if he'd finally settled into some smoldering backroom where the coals glowed eternally, despite the season, and where he would never feel again, neither ice nor fire, but simply the old featureless warmth that meant nothing at all except that blood still flowed through his thin, rubbery veins.

He closed his eyes, saw the Puri Dai, opened them, and to his vast surprise, saw her daughter standing before him, Farouk's massive hand resting firmly on her shoulder.

"I have brought her to you," Farouk said.

Frank pulled himself forward in his chair, his tired, aching eyes fixed on the wild young black ones of the little girl.

"I have prepared all the necessary papers, as well," Farouk added.

She was dressed in a white blouse, bare at the shoulders, and a dark-red skirt that stretched almost to the floor. Her skin was very brown, but with a somewhat greenish hue, and her black hair fell over her shoulders in the wild tangle she'd inherited from her mother.

"You do not have to keep her," Farouk said.

Frank glanced up at him only long enough to catch the quiet radiance of his smile. Then his eyes settled upon the little girl, the black eyes, the long brown neck, and he felt the still rising breath of her dead mother, heard once again the wail that he'd first heard in Atlanta, the one that had risen above that sacrificial ground he had fled so many years before.

Farouk watched him softly. "I only ask that she stay with you until you can find—if you ever can find, my friend—one who would be a better father."

Frank felt a sudden, inexplicable tremor move through him like the steadily building waves of a nearly lost resolve.

"Will you keep her, then?" Farouk asked quietly.

She took a small, graceful step toward him, and as he rose to meet her, Frank realized that it was this, and not some mythical case, which all that he'd done wrong now prepared him to do right.

"Yes," he said.